*Further Chronicles
of Avonlea*

BY L. M. MONTGOMERY

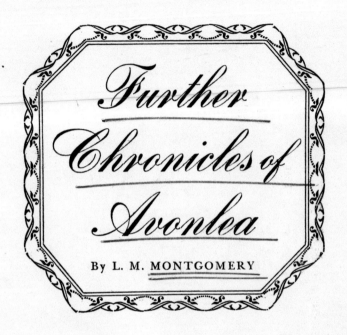

Further Chronicles of Avonlea

By L. M. MONTGOMERY

Grosset & Dunlap

PUBLISHERS

NEW YORK

INTRODUCTION

It is no exaggeration to say that what Long-
fellow did for Acadia, Miss Montgomery has done
for Prince Edward Island. More than a mil-
lion readers, young people as well as their parents
and uncles and aunts, possess in the picture-galler-
ies of their memories the exquisite landscapes of
Avonlea, limned with as poetic a pencil as Long-
fellow wielded when he told the ever-moving story
of Grand Pré.

Only genius of the first water has the ability to
conjure up such a character as Anne Shirley, the
heroine of Miss Montgomery's first novel, "Anne
of Green Gables," and to surround her with people
so distinctive, so real, so true to psychology. Anne
is as lovable a child as lives in all fiction. Natasha
in Count Tolstoï's great novel, "War and Peace,"
dances into our ken, with something of the same
buoyancy and naturalness; but into what a commonplace young woman she develops! Anne,
whether as the gay little orphan in her conquest of
the master and mistress of Green Gables, or as the
maturing and self-forgetful maiden of Avonlea,

keeps up to concert-pitch in her charm and her winsomeness. There is nothing in her to disappoint hope or imagination.

Part of the power of Miss Montgomery — and the largest part — is due to her skill in compounding humor and pathos. The humor is honest and golden; it never wearies the reader; the pathos is never sentimentalized, never degenerates into bathos, is never morbid. This combination holds throughout all her works, longer or shorter, and is particularly manifest in the present collection of fifteen short stories, which, together with those in the first volume of the Chronicles of Avonlea, present a series of piquant and fascinating pictures of life in Prince Edward Island.

The humor is shown not only in the presentation of quaint and unique characters, but also in the words which fall from their mouths. Aunt Cynthia "always gave you the impression of a full-rigged ship coming gallantly on before a favorable wind;" no further description is needed — only one such personage could be found in Avonlea. You would recognize her at sight. Ismay Meade's disposition is summed up when we are told that she is "good at having presentiments — after things happen." What cleverer embodiment of innate obstinacy than in Isabella Spencer — "a wisp of a woman who looked as if a breath would sway her but was so set in her ways that a tornado would hardly have caused her to swerve an inch from her chosen path;" or than in Mrs. Eben Andrews (in "Sara's Way") who "looked like a woman whose opinions were always very decided and warranted to wear!"

This gift of characterization in a few words is lavished also on material objects, as, for instance; what more is needed to describe the forlornness of the home from which Anne was rescued than the statement that even the trees around it "looked like orphans"?

The poetic touch, too, never fails in the right place and is never too frequently introduced in her descriptions. They throw a glamor over that Northern land which otherwise you might imagine as rather cold and barren. What charming Springs they must have there! One sees all the fruit-trees clad in bridal garments of pink and white; and what a translucent sky smiles down on the ponds and the reaches of bay and cove!

"In the east, clouds tinged with gold and crimson announced the early rising sun."

"She was slender as a reed and had the grace of a young doe. Her hair was dark and fluffy and framed her lovely face like a luminous halo, and her eyes were as blue as a cloudless sky on a perfect June day."

Sentiment with a humorous touch to it prevails in the first two stories of the present book. The one relates the disappearance of a valuable white Persian cat with a blue spot in its tail. "Fatima" is like the apple of her eye to the rich old aunt who leaves her with two nieces, with a stern injunction not to let her out of the house. Of course both Sue and Ismay detest cats; Ismay hates them, Sue loathes them; but Aunt Cynthia's favor is worth preserving. You become as much interested in Fatima's fate as if she were your own pet, and the climax is no less unexpected than it is natural, especially when it is made also the last act of a pretty comedy of love.

Miss Montgomery delights in depicting the romantic episodes hidden in the hearts of elderly spinsters as, for instance, in the case of Charlotte Holmes, whose maid Nancy would have sent for the doctor and subjected her to a porous plaster while waiting for him, had she known that up stairs there was a note-book full of original poems. Rather than bear the stigma of never having had a love-affair, this sentimental lady invents one to tell her mocking young friends. The dramatic and unexpected dénouement is delightful fun.

Another note-book reveals a deeper romance in the case of Miss Emily; this is related by Anne of Green Gables, who once or twice flashes across the scene, though for the most part her friends and neighbors at White Sands or Newbridge or Grafton as well as at Avonlea are the persons involved.

In one story, the last, " Tannis of the Flats," the secret of Elinor Blair's spinsterhood is revealed

in an episode which carries the reader from Avonlea to Saskatchewan and shows the unselfish devotion of a half-breed Indian girl. The story is
both poignant and dramatic. Its one touch of
humor is where Jerome Carey curses his fate in
being compelled to live in that desolate land in
" the picturesque language permissible in the far
Northwest."

Self-sacrifice, as the real basis of happiness, is a
favorite theme in Miss Montgomery's fiction. It
is raised to the nth power in the story entitled " In
Her Selfless Mood," where an ugly, misshapen girl
devotes her life and renounces marriage for the
sake of looking after her weak and selfish half-
brother. The same spirit is found in " Only a
Common Fellow," who is haloed with a certain
splendor by renouncing the girl he was to marry
in favor of his old rival, supposed to have been
killed in France, but happily delivered from that
tragic fate.

Miss Montgomery loves to introduce a little child
or a baby as a solvent of old feuds or domestic
quarrels. In " The Dream Child," a foundling boy,
drifting in through a storm in a dory, saves a
heart-broken mother from insanity. In " Jane's
Baby," a baby-cousin brings reconciliation between
the two sisters, Rosetta and Carlotta, who had
not spoken for twenty years because " the slack-
twisted " Jacob married the younger of the two.

Happiness generally lights up the end of her

stories, however tragic they may set out to be. In
" The Son of His Mother," Thyra is a stern woman, as " immovable as a stone image." She had
only one son, whom she worshipped; " she never
wanted a daughter, but she pitied and despised all
sonless women." She demanded absolute obedience from Chester — not only obedience, but also
utter affection, and she hated his dog because the
boy loved him: " She could not share her love
even with a dumb brute." When Chester falls in
love, she is relentless toward the beautiful young
girl and forces Chester to give her up. But a
terrible sorrow brings the old woman and the
young girl into sympathy, and unspeakable joy is
born of the trial.

Happiness also comes to " The Brother who
Failed." The Monroes had all been successful in
the eyes of the world except Robert: one is a millionaire, another a college president, another a
famous singer. Robert overhears the old aunt,
Isabel, call him a total failure, but, at the family
dinner, one after another stands up and tells how
Robert's quiet influence and unselfish aid had
started them in their brilliant careers, and the old
aunt, wiping the tears from her eyes, exclaims:
" I guess there's a kind of failure that's the best
success."

In one story there is an element of the super-
natural, when Hester, the hard older sister, comes
between Margaret and her lover and, dying, makes

her promise never to become Hugh Blair's wife, but she comes back and unites them. In this, Margaret, just like the delightful Anne, lives up to the dictum that "nothing matters in all God's universe except love." The story of the revival at Avonlea has also a good moral.

There is something in these continued Chronicles of Avonlea, like the delicate art which has made "Cranford" a classic: the characters are so homely and homelike and yet tinged with beautiful romance! You feel that you are made familiar with a real town and its real inhabitants; you learn to love them and sympathize with them. Further Chronicles of Avonlea is a book to read; and to know.

NATHAN HASKELL DOLE.

CONTENTS

CONTENTS

I

AUNT CYNTHIA'S PERSIAN CAT

MAX always blesses the animal when it is referred to; and I don't deny that things have worked together for good after all. But when I think of the anguish of mind which Ismay and I underwent on account of that abominable cat, it is not a blessing that arises uppermost in my thoughts.

I never was fond of cats, although I admit they are well enough in their place, and I can worry along comfortably with a nice, matronly old tabby who can take care of herself and be of some use in the world. As for Ismay, she hates cats and always did.

But Aunt Cynthia, who adored them, never could bring herself to understand that any one could possibly dislike them. She firmly believed that Ismay and I really liked cats deep down in our hearts, but that, owing to some perverse twist in our moral natures, we would not own up to it, but willfully persisted in declaring we didn't.

Of all cats I loathed that white Persian cat of Aunt Cynthia's.   And, indeed, as we always suspected and finally proved, Aunt herself looked upon the creature with more pride than affection.   She would have taken ten times the comfort in a good, common puss that she did in that spoiled beauty.   But a Persian cat with a recorded pedigree and a market value of one hundred dollars tickled Aunt Cynthia's pride of possession to such an extent that she deluded herself into believing that the animal was really the apple of her eye.

It had been presented to her when a kitten by a missionary nephew who had brought it all the way home from Persia ; and for the next three years Aunt Cynthia's household existed to wait on that cat, hand and foot.   It was snow-white, with a bluish-gray spot on the tip of its tail ; and it was blue-eyed and deaf and delicate.   Aunt Cynthia was always worrying lest it should take cold and die.   Ismay and I used to wish that it would — we were so tired of hearing about it and its whims.   But we did not say so to Aunt Cynthia.   She would probably never have spoken to us again and there was no wisdom in offending Aunt Cynthia.   When you have an unencumbered aunt, with a fat bank account, it is just as well to keep on good terms with her, if you can.

Besides, we really liked Aunt Cynthia very much — at times. Aunt Cynthia was one of those rather exasperating people who nag at and find fault with you until you think you are justified in hating them, and who then turn round and do something so really nice and kind for you that you feel as if you were compelled to love them dutifully instead.

So we listened meekly when she discoursed on Fatima — the cat's name was Fatima — and, if it was wicked of us to wish for the latter's decease, we were well punished for it later on.

One day, in November, Aunt Cynthia came sailing out to Spencervale. She really came in a phaeton, drawn by a fat gray pony, but somehow Aunt Cynthia always gave you the impression of a full rigged ship coming gallantly on before a favorable wind.

That was a Jonah day for us all through. Everything had gone wrong. Ismay had spilled grease on her velvet coat, and the fit of the new blouse I was making was hopelessly askew, and the kitchen stove smoked and the bread was sour. Moreover, Huldah Jane Keyson, our tried and trusty old family nurse and cook and general " boss," had what she called the " realagy " in her shoulder; and, though Huldah Jane is as good an old creature as ever lived, when she has the " realagy " other people who are in the house want to get out of it and, if they can't, feel about as comfortable as St. Lawrence on his gridiron.

And on the top of this came Aunt Cynthia's call and request.

" Dear me," said Aunt Cynthia, sniffing, " don't I smell smoke? You girls must manage your range very badly. Mine never smokes. But it is no more than one might expect when two girls try to keep house without a man about the place."

" We get along very well without a man about the place," I said loftily. Max hadn't been in for four whole days and, though nobody wanted to see him particularly, I couldn't help wondering why. " Men are nuisances."

" I dare say you would like to pretend you think so," said Aunt Cynthia, aggravatingly. " But no woman ever does really think so, you know. I imagine that pretty Anne Shirley, who is visiting Ella Kimball, doesn't. I saw her and Dr. Irving out walking this afternoon, looking very well satisfied with themselves. If you dilly-dally much longer, Sue, you will let Max slip through your fingers yet."

That was a tactful thing to say to *me*, who had refused Max Irving so often that I had lost count. I was furious, and so I smiled most sweetly on my maddening aunt.

" Dear Aunt, how amusing of you," I said, smoothly. " You talk as if I wanted Max."

" So you do," said Aunt Cynthia.

"If so, why should I have refused him time and again?" I asked, smilingly. Right well Aunt Cynthia knew I had. Max always told her.

"Goodness alone knows why," said Aunt Cynthia, "but you may do it once too often and find yourself taken at your word. There is something very fascinating about this Anne Shirley."

"Indeed there is," I assented. "She has the loveliest eyes I ever saw. She would be just the wife for Max, and I hope he will marry her."

"Humph," said Aunt Cynthia. "Well, I won't entice you into telling any more fibs. And I didn't drive out here to-day in all this wind to talk sense into you concerning Max. I'm going to Halifax for two months and I want you to take charge of Fatima for me, while I am away."

"Fatima!" I exclaimed.

"Yes. I don't dare to trust her with the servants. Mind you always warm her milk before you give it to her, and don't on any account let her run out of doors."

I looked at Ismay and Ismay looked at me. We knew we were in for it. To refuse would mortally offend Aunt Cynthia. Besides, if I betrayed any unwillingness, Aunt Cynthia would be sure to put it down to grumpiness over what she had said about Max, and rub it in for years. But I ventured to ask, " What if anything happens to her while you are away? "

" It is to prevent that, I'm leaving her with you," said Aunt Cynthia. " You simply must not let anything happen to her. It will do you good to have a little responsibility. And you will have a chance to find out what an adorable creature Fatima really is. Well, that is all settled. I'll send Fatima out tomorrow."

" You can take care of that horrid Fatima beast yourself," said Ismay, when the door closed behind Aunt Cynthia. " I won't touch her with a yardstick. You had no business to say we'd take her."

" Did I say we would take her? " I demanded, crossly. " Aunt Cynthia took our consent for granted. And you know, as well as I do, we couldn't have refused. So what is the use of being grouchy? "

" If anything happens to her Aunt Cynthia will hold us responsible," said Ismay darkly.

" Do you think Anne Shirley is really engaged to Gilbert Blythe? " I asked curiously.

" I've heard that she was," said Ismay, absently. " Does she eat anything but milk? Will it do to give her mice? "

" Oh, I guess so. But do you think Max has really fallen in love with her? "

" I dare say.   What a relief it will be for you if he has."

" Oh, of course," I said, frostily.   " Anne Shirley or Anne Anybody Else, is perfectly welcome to Max if she wants him.   *I* certainly do not.   Ismay Meade, if that stove doesn't stop smoking I shall fly into bits.   This is a detestable day.   I hate that creature ! "

" Oh, you shouldn't talk like that, when you don't even know her," protested Ismay.   " Every one says Anne Shirley is lovely —"

" I was talking about Fatima," I cried in a rage.

" Oh ! " said Ismay.

Ismay is stupid at times.   I thought the way she said " Oh " was inexcusably stupid.

Fatima arrived the next day.   Max brought her out in a covered basket, lined with padded crimson satin.   Max likes cats and Aunt Cynthia.   He explained how we were to treat Fatima and when Ismay had gone out of the room — Ismay always went out of the room when she knew I particularly wanted her to remain — he proposed to me again.   Of course I said no, as usual, but I was rather pleased. Max had been proposing to me about every two months for two years.   Sometimes, as in this case, he went three months, and then I always wondered why.   I concluded that he could not be really interested in Anne Shirley, and I was relieved.   I didn't want to marry Max but it was pleasant and convenient to have him around, and we would miss him dreadfully if any other girl snapped him up. He was so useful and always willing to do anything for us — nail a shingle on the roof, drive us to town, put down carpets — in short, a very present help in all our troubles.

So I just beamed on him when I said no. Max began counting on his fingers. When he got as far as eight he shook his head and began over again.

"What is it?" I asked.

"I'm trying to count up how many times I have proposed to you," he said. "But I can't remember whether I asked you to marry me that day we dug up the garden or not. If I did it makes —"

"No, you didn't," I interrupted.

"Well, that makes it eleven," said Max reflectively. "Pretty near the limit, isn't it? My manly pride will not allow me to propose to the same girl more than twelve times. So the next time will be the last, Sue darling."

"Oh," I said, a trifle flatly. I forgot to resent his calling me darling. I wondered if things wouldn't be rather dull when Max gave up proposing to me. It was the only excitement I had. But of course it would be best — and he couldn't go on at it forever, so, by the way of gracefully dismissing the subject, I asked him what Miss Shirley was like.

"Very sweet girl," said Max. "You know I always admired those gray-eyed girls with that splendid Titian hair."

I am dark, with brown eyes. Just then I detested Max. I got up and said I was going to get some milk for Fatima.

I found Ismay in a rage in the kitchen. She had been up in the garret, and a mouse had run across her foot. Mice always get on Ismay's nerves.

"We need a cat badly enough," she fumed, "but not a useless, pampered thing, like Fatima. That garret is literally swarming with mice. You'll not catch me going up there again."

Fatima did not prove such a nuisance as we had feared. Huldah Jane liked her, and Ismay, in spite of her declaration that she would have nothing to do with her, looked after her comfort scrupulously. She even used to get up in the middle of the night and go out to see if Fatima was warm. Max came in every day and, being around, gave us good advice.

Then one day, about three weeks after Aunt Cynthia's departure, Fatima disappeared — just simply disappeared as if she had been dissolved into thin air. We left her one afternoon, curled up asleep in her basket by the fire, under Huldah Jane's eye, while we went out to make a call.   When we came home Fatima was gone.

Huldah Jane wept and was as one whom the gods had made mad.   She vowed that she had never let Fatima out of her sight the whole time, save once for three minutes when she ran up to the garret for some summer savory.   When she came back the kitchen door had blown open and Fatima had vanished.

Ismay and I were frantic.   We ran about the garden and through the out-houses, and the woods behind the house, like wild creatures, calling Fatima, but in vain.   Then Ismay sat down on the front doorsteps and cried.

" She has got out and she'll catch her death of cold and Aunt Cynthia will never forgive us."

" I'm going for Max," I declared.   So I did, through the spruce woods and over the field as fast as my feet could carry me, thanking my stars that there was a Max to go to in such a predicament.

Max came over and we had another search, but without result.   Days passed, but we did not find Fatima.   I would certainly have gone crazy had it not been for Max.   He was worth his weight in gold during the awful week that followed.   We did not dare advertise, lest Aunt Cynthia should see it; but we inquired far and wide for a white Persian cat with a blue spot on its tail, and offered a reward for it; but nobody had seen it, although people kept coming to the house, night and day, with every kind of a cat in baskets, wanting to know if it was the one we had lost.

"We shall never see Fatima again," I said hopelessly to Max and Ismay one afternoon.   I had just turned away an old woman with a big, yellow tommy which she insisted must be ours —" cause it kem to our place, mem, a-yowling fearful, mem, and it don't belong to nobody not down Grafton way, mem."

"I'm afraid you won't," said Max.   "She must have perished from exposure long ere this."

"Aunt Cynthia will never forgive us," said Ismay, dismally.   "I had a presentiment of trouble the moment that cat came to this house."

We had never heard of this presentiment before, but Ismay is good at having presentiments — after things happen.

"What shall we do?" I demanded, helplessly. "Max, can't you find some way out of this scrape for us?"

"Advertise in the Charlottetown papers for a white Persian cat," suggested Max.   "Some one may have one for sale.   If so, you must buy it, and palm it off on your good Aunt as Fatima.   She's very short-sighted, so it will be quite possible."

"But Fatima has a blue spot on her tail," I said.

"You must advertise for a cat with a blue spot on its tail," said Max.

"It will cost a pretty penny," said Ismay dolefully. "Fatima was valued at one hundred dollars."

"We must take the money we have been saving for our new furs," I said, sorrowfully. "There is no other way out of it. It will cost us a good deal more if we lose Aunt Cynthia's favor. She is quite capable of believing that we have made away with Fatima deliberately and with malice aforethought."

So we advertised. Max went to town and had the notice inserted in the most important daily. We asked any one who had a white Persian cat, with a blue spot on the tip of its tail, to dispose of, to communicate with M. I., care of the *Enterprise*.

We really did not have much hope that anything would come of it, so we were surprised and delighted over the letter Max brought home from town four days later. It was a type-written screed from Halifax stating that the writer had for sale a white Persian cat answering to our description. The price was a hundred and ten dollars and, if M. I. cared to go to Halifax and inspect the animal, it would be found at 110 Hollis Street, by inquiring for "Persian."

"Temper your joy, my friends," said Ismay, gloomily. "The cat may not suit. The blue spot may be too big or too small or not in the right place.

I consistently refuse to believe that any good thing can come out of this deplorable affair."

Just at this moment there was a knock at the door and I hurried out. The postmaster's boy was there with a telegram. I tore it open, glanced at it, and dashed back into the room.

"What is it now?" cried Ismay, beholding my face.

I held out the telegram. It was from Aunt Cynthia. She had wired us to send Fatima to Halifax by express immediately.

For the first time Max did not seem ready to rush into the breach with a suggestion. It was I who spoke first.

"Max," I said, imploringly, "you'll see us through this, won't you? Neither Ismay nor I can rush off to Halifax at once. You must go to-morrow morning. Go right to 110 Hollis Street and ask for 'Persian.' If the cat looks enough like Fatima, buy it and take it to Aunt Cynthia. If it doesn't — but it must! You'll go, won't you?"

"That depends," said Max.

I stared at him. This was so unlike Max.

"You are sending me on a nasty errand," he said, coolly. "How do I know that Aunt Cynthia will be deceived after all, even if she be short-sighted. Buying a cat in a poke is a huge risk. And if she should see through the scheme I shall be in a pretty mess."

"Oh, Max," I said, on the verge of tears.

"Of course," said Max, looking meditatively into the fire, "if I were really one of the family, or had any reasonable prospect of being so, I would not mind so much. It would be all in the day's work then. But as it is —"

Ismay got up and went out of the room.

"Oh, Max, please," I said.

"Will you marry me, Sue?" demanded Max sternly. "If you will agree, I'll go to Halifax and beard the lion in his den unflinchingly. If necessary, I will take a black street cat to Aunt Cynthia, and swear that it is Fatima. I'll get you out of the scrape, if I have to prove that you never had Fatima, that she is safe in your possession at the present time, and that there never was such an animal as Fatima anyhow. I'll do anything, say anything — but it must be for my future wife."

"Will nothing else content you?" I said helplessly.

"Nothing."

I thought hard. Of course Max was acting abominably — but — but — he was really a dear fellow — and this was the twelfth time — and there was Anne Shirley! I knew in my secret soul that life would be a dreadfully dismal thing if Max were not around somewhere.   Besides, I would have married him long ago had not Aunt Cynthia thrown us so pointedly at each other's heads ever since he came to Spencervale.

"Very well," I said crossly.

Max left for Halifax in the morning.   Next day we got a wire saying it was all right.   The evening of the following day he was back in Spencervale. Ismay and I put him in a chair and glared at him impatiently.

Max began to laugh and laughed until he turned blue.

"I am glad it is so amusing," said Ismay severely. "If Sue and I could see the joke it might be more so."

"Dear little girls, have patience with me," implored Max.   "If you knew what it cost me to keep a straight face in Halifax you would forgive me for breaking out now."

"We forgive you — but for pity's sake tell us all about it," I cried.

"Well, as soon as I arrived in Halifax I hurried to 110 Hollis Street, but — see here!   Didn't you tell me your Aunt's address was 10 Pleasant Street?"

"So it is."

"'T isn't.   You look at the address on a telegram next time you get one.   She went a week ago to visit another friend who lives at 110 Hollis."

" Max!"

" It's a fact.   I rang the bell, and was just going to ask the maid for ' Persian ' when your Aunt Cynthia herself came through the hall and pounced on me.

" ' Max,' she said, ' have you brought Fatima? '

" ' No,' I answered, trying to adjust my wits to this new development as she towed me into the library.   ' No, I — I — just came to Halifax on a little matter of business.'

" ' Dear me,' said Aunt Cynthia, crossly, ' I don't know what those girls mean.   I wired them to send Fatima at once.   And she has not come yet and I am expecting a call every minute from some one who wants to buy her.'

" ' Oh!' I murmured, mining deeper every minute.

" ' Yes,' went on your aunt, ' there is an advertisement in the Charlotteville *Enterprise* for a Persian cat, and I answered it.   Fatima is really quite a charge, you know — and so apt to die and be a dead loss '— did your aunt mean a pun, girls? —' and so, although I am considerably attached to her, I have decided to part with her.'

" By this time I had got my second wind, and I promptly decided that a judicious mixture of the truth was the thing required.

" ' Well, of all the curious coincidences,' I exclaimed. ' Why, Miss Ridley, it was I who advertised for a Persian cat — on Sue's behalf. She and Ismay have decided that they want a cat like Fatima for themselves.'

" You should have seen how she beamed. She said she knew you always really liked cats, only you would never own up to it. We clinched the dicker then and there. I passed her over your hundred and ten dollars — she took the money without turning a hair — and now you are the joint owners of Fatima. Good luck to your bargain! "

" Mean old thing," sniffed Ismay. She meant Aunt Cynthia, and, remembering our shabby furs, I didn't disagree with her.

" But there is no Fatima," I said, dubiously. " How shall we account for her when Aunt Cynthia comes home? "

" Well, your aunt isn't coming home for a month yet. When she comes you will have to tell her that the cat — is lost — but you needn't say *when* it happened. As for the rest, Fatima is your property now, so Aunt Cynthia can't grumble. But she will have a poorer opinion than ever of your fitness to run a house alone."

When Max left I went to the window to watch him down the path. He was really a handsome fellow, and I was proud of him. At the gate he turned to wave me good-by, and, as he did, he glanced upward. Even at that distance I saw the look of amazement on his face. Then he came bolting back.

"Ismay, the house is on fire!" I shrieked, as I flew to the door.

"Sue," cried Max, "I saw Fatima, or her ghost, at the garret window a moment ago!"

"Nonsense!" I cried. But Ismay was already half way up the stairs and we followed. Straight to the garret we rushed. There sat Fatima, sleek and complacent, sunning herself in the window.

Max laughed until the rafters rang.

"She can't have been up here all this time," I protested, half tearfully. "We would have heard her meowing."

"But you didn't," said Max.

"She would have died of the cold," declared Ismay.

"But she hasn't," said Max.

"Or starved," I cried.

"The place is alive with mice," said Max. "No, girls, there is no doubt the cat has been here the whole fortnight. She must have followed Huldah Jane up here, unobserved, that day. It's a wonder you didn't hear her crying — if she did cry. But perhaps she didn't, and, of course, you sleep downstairs. To think you never thought of looking here for her!"

"It has cost us over a hundred dollars," said Ismay, with a malevolent glance at the sleek Fatima.

"It has cost me more than that," I said, as I turned to the stairway.

Max held me back for an instant, while Ismay and Fatima pattered down.

"Do you think it has cost too much, Sue?" he whispered.

I looked at him sideways. He was really a dear, and he fairly radiated niceness.

"No-o-o," I said, "but when we are married you will have to take care of Fatima, *I* won't."

"Dear Fatima," said Max gratefully.

II

THE MATERIALIZING OF CECIL

It had never worried me in the least that I wasn't married, although everybody in Avonlea pitied old maids; but it *did* worry me, and I frankly confess it, that I had never had a chance to be. Even Nancy, my old nurse and servant, knew that, and pitied me for it. Nancy is an old maid herself, but she has had two proposals. She did not accept either of them because one was a widower with seven children, and the other a very shiftless, good-for-nothing fellow; but, if anybody twitted Nancy on her single condition, she could point triumphantly to those two as evidence that " she could an she would." If I had not lived all my life in Avonlea I might have had the benefit of the doubt; but I had, and everybody knew everything about me — or thought they did.

I had really often wondered why nobody had ever fallen in love with me. I was not at all homely; indeed, years ago, George Adoniram Maybrick had written a poem addressed to me, in which he praised my beauty quite extravagantly; that didn't mean anything because George Adoniram wrote poetry to all the good-looking girls and never went with anybody but Flora King, who was cross-eyed and red-haired, but it proves that it was not my appearance that put me out of the running.   Neither was it the fact that I wrote poetry myself — although not of George Adoniram's kind — because nobody ever knew that. When I felt it coming on I shut myself up in my room and wrote it out in a little blank book I kept locked up.   It is nearly full now, because I have been writing poetry all my life.   It is the only thing I have ever been able to keep a secret from Nancy. Nancy, in any case, has not a very high opinion of my ability to take care of myself; but I tremble to imagine what she would think if she ever found out about that little book.   I am convinced she would send for the doctor post-haste and insist on mustard plasters while waiting for him.

Nevertheless, I kept on at it, and what with my flowers and my cats and my magazines and my little book, I was really very happy and contented.   But it *did* sting that Adella Gilbert, across the road, who has a drunken husband, should pity " poor Charlotte " because nobody had ever wanted her.   Poor Charlotte indeed!   If I had thrown myself at a man's head the way Adella Gilbert did at — but there, there, I must refrain from such thoughts.   I must not be uncharitable.

The Sewing Circle met at Mary Gillespie's on my fortieth birthday. I have given up talking about my birthdays, although that little scheme is not much good in Avonlea where everybody knows your age — or if they make a mistake it is never on the side of youth. But Nancy, who grew accustomed to celebrating my birthdays when I was a little girl, never gets over the habit, and I don't try to cure her, because, after all, it's nice to have some one make a fuss over you. She brought me up my breakfast before I got up out of bed — a concession to my laziness that Nancy would scorn to make on any other day of the year. She had cooked everything I like best, and had decorated the tray with roses from the garden and ferns from the woods behind the house. I enjoyed every bit of that breakfast, and then I got up and dressed, putting on my second best muslin gown. I would have put on my really best if I had not had the fear of Nancy before my eyes; but I knew she would never condone *that,* even on a birthday. I watered my flowers and fed my cats, and then I locked myself up and wrote a poem on June. I had given up writing birthday odes after I was thirty.

In the afternoon I went to the Sewing Circle. When I was ready for it I looked in my glass and wondered if I could really be forty. I was quite sure I didn't look it. My hair was brown and wavy, my cheeks were pink, and the lines could hardly be seen at all, though possibly that was because of the dim light. I always have my mirror hung in the darkest corner of my room. Nancy cannot imagine why. I know the lines are there, of course; but when they don't show very plain I forget that they are there.

We had a large Sewing Circle, young and old alike attending. I really cannot say I ever enjoyed the meetings — at least not up to that time — although I went religiously because I thought it my duty to go. The married women talked so much of their husbands and children, and of course I had to be quiet on those topics; and the young girls talked in corner groups about their beaux, and stopped it when I joined them, as if they felt sure that an old maid who had never had a beau couldn't understand at all. As for the other old maids, they talked gossip about every one, and I did not like that either. I knew the minute my back was turned they would fasten into me and hint that I used hair-dye and declare it was perfectly ridiculous for a woman of *fifty* to wear a pink muslin dress with lace-trimmed frills.

There was a full attendance that day, for we were getting ready for a sale of fancy work in aid of parsonage repairs. The young girls were merrier and noisier than usual. Wilhelmina Mercer was there, and she kept them going. The Mercers were quite new to Avonlea, having come here only two months previously.

I was sitting by the window and Wilhelmina Mercer, Maggie Henderson, Susette Cross and Georgie Hall were in a little group just before me. I wasn't listening to their chatter at all, but presently Georgie exclaimed teasingly:

" Miss Charlotte is laughing at us. I suppose she thinks we are awfully silly to be talking about beaux."

The truth was that I was simply smiling over some very pretty thoughts that had come to me about the roses which were climbing over Mary Gillespie's sill. I meant to inscribe them in the little blank book when I went home. Georgie's speech brought me back to harsh realities with a jolt. It hurt me, as such speeches always did.

" Didn't you ever have a beau, Miss Holmes? " said Wilhelmina laughingly.

Just as it happened, a silence had fallen over the room for a moment, and everybody in it heard Wilhelmina's question.

I really do not know what got into me and possessed me. I have never been able to account for what I said and did, because I am naturally a truthful person and hate all deceit. It seemed to me that I simply could not say " No " to Wilhelmina before that whole roomful of women. It was *too* humiliating. I suppose all the prickles and stings and slurs I had endured for fifteen years on account of never having had a lover had what the new doctor calls " a cumulative effect " and came to a head then and there.

" Yes, I had one once, my dear," I said calmly.

For once in my life I made a sensation. Every woman in that room stopped sewing and stared at me. Most of them, I saw, didn't believe me, but Wilhelmina did. Her pretty face lighted up with interest.

" Oh, won't you tell us about him, Miss Holmes? " she coaxed, " and why you didn't marry him? "

" That is right, Miss Mercer," said Josephine Cameron, with a nasty little laugh. " Make her tell. We're all interested. It's news to us that Charlotte ever had a beau."

If Josephine had not said that, I might not have gone on. But she did say it, and, moreover, I caught Mary Gillespie and Adella Gilbert exchanging significant smiles. That settled it, and made me quite reckless. " In for a penny, in for a pound," thought I, and I said with a pensive smile:

" Nobody here knew anything about him, and it was all long, long ago."

" What was his name? " asked Wilhelmina.

" Cecil Fenwick," I answered promptly. Cecil

had always been my favorite name for a man; it figured quite frequently in the blank book. As for the Fenwick part of it, I had a bit of newspaper in my hand, measuring a hem, with "Try Fenwick's Porous Plasters" printed across it, and I simply joined the two in sudden and irrevocable matrimony.

"Where did you meet him?" asked Georgie.

I hastily reviewed my past. There was only one place to locate Cecil Fenwick. The only time I had ever been far enough away from Avonlea in my life was when I was eighteen and had gone to visit an aunt in New Brunswick.

"In Blakely, New Brunswick," I said, almost believing that I had when I saw how they all took it in unsuspectingly. "I was just eighteen and he was twenty-three."

"What did he look like?" Susette   wanted to know.

"Oh, he was very handsome." I proceeded glibly to sketch my ideal. To tell the dreadful truth, I was enjoying myself; I could see respect dawning in those girls' eyes, and I knew that I had forever thrown off my reproach. Henceforth I should be a woman with a romantic past, faithful to the one love of her life — a very, very different thing from an old maid who had never had a lover.

"He was tall and dark, with lovely, curly black hair and brilliant, piercing eyes. He had a splendid chin, and a fine nose, and the most fascinating smile!"

"What was he?" asked Maggie.

"A young lawyer," I said, my choice of profession decided by an enlarged crayon portrait of Mary Gillespie's deceased brother on an easel before me. He had been a lawyer.

"Why didn't you marry him?" demanded Susette.

"We quarreled," I answered sadly. "A terribly bitter quarrel. Oh, we were both so young and so foolish. It was my fault. I vexed Cecil by flirting with another man"— wasn't I coming on!—"and he was jealous and angry. He went out West and never came back. I have never seen him since, and I do not even know if he is alive. But — but — I could never care for any other man."

"Oh, how interesting!" sighed Wilhelmina. "I do so love sad love stories. But perhaps he will come back some day yet, Miss Holmes."

"Oh, no, never now," I said, shaking my head. "He has forgotten all about me, I dare say. Or if he hasn't, he has never forgiven me."

Mary Gillespie's Susan Jane announced tea at this moment, and I was thankful, for my imagination was giving out, and I didn't know what question those girls would ask next. But I felt already a change in the mental atmosphere surrounding me, and all through supper I was thrilled with a secret exultation. Repentant? Ashamed? Not a bit of it! I'd have done the same thing over again, and all I felt sorry for was that I hadn't done it long ago.

When I got home that night Nancy looked at me wonderingly and said:

" You look like a girl, to-night, Miss Charlotte."

" I feel like one," I said laughing; and I ran to my room and did what I had never done before — wrote a second poem in the same day. I had to have some outlet for my feelings. I called it " In Summer Days of Long Ago," and I worked Mary Gillespie's roses and Cecil Fenwick's eyes into it, and made it so sad and reminiscent and minor-musicky that I felt perfectly happy.

For the next two months all went well and merrily. Nobody ever said anything more to me about Cecil Fenwick, but the girls all chattered freely to me of their little love affairs, and I became a sort of general confidant for them. It just warmed up the cockles of my heart, and I began to enjoy the Sewing Circle famously. I got a lot of pretty new dresses and the dearest hat, and I went everywhere I was asked and had a good time.

But there is one thing you can be perfectly sure of. If you do wrong you are going to be punished for it sometime, somehow and somewhere. My punishment was delayed for two months, and then it de-scended on my head and I was crushed to the very dust.

Another new family besides the Mercers had come to Avonlea in the spring — the Maxwells. There were just Mr. and Mrs. Maxwell; they were a middle-aged couple and very well off. Mr. Maxwell had bought the lumber mills, and they lived up at the old Spencer place which had always been " the " place of Avonlea. They lived quietly, and Mrs. Maxwell hardly ever went anywhere because she was delicate. She was out when I called and I was out when she returned my call, so that I had never met her.

It was the Sewing Circle day again — at Sarah Gardiner's this time. I was late; everybody else was there when I arrived, and the minute I entered the room I knew something had happened, although I couldn't imagine what. Everybody looked at me in the strangest way. Of course, Wilhelmina Mercer was the first to set her tongue going.

" Oh, Miss Holmes, have you seen him yet? " she exclaimed.

" Seen whom? " I said non-excitedly, getting out my thimble and patterns.

" Why, Cecil Fenwick. He's here — in Avonlea — visiting his sister, Mrs. Maxwell."

I suppose I did what they expected me to do. I dropped everything I held, and Josephine Cameron said afterwards that Charlotte Holmes would never be paler when she was in her coffin.   If they had just known why I turned so pale!

"It's impossible!" I said blankly.

"It's really true," said Wilhelmina, delighted at this development, as she supposed it, of my romance. "I was up to see Mrs. Maxwell last night, and I met him."

"It — can't be — the same — Cecil Fenwick," I said faintly, because I had to say something.

"Oh, yes, it is. He belongs in Blakely, New Brunswick, and he's a lawyer, and he's been out West twenty-two years.   He's oh! so handsome, and just as you described him, except that his hair is quite gray.   He has never married — I asked Mrs. Maxwell — so you see he has never forgotten you, Miss Holmes.   And, oh, I believe everything is going to come out all right."

I couldn't exactly share her cheerful belief. Everything seemed to me to be coming out most horribly wrong.   I was so mixed up I didn't know what to do or say.   I felt as if I were in a bad dream — it *must* be a dream — there couldn't really be a Cecil Fenwick!   My feelings were simply indescribable.   Fortunately every one put my agitation down to quite a different cause, and they very kindly left me alone to recover myself.   I shall never forget that awful afternoon.   Right after tea I excused myself and went home as fast as I could go.   There

I shut myself up in my room, but *not* to write poetry in my blank book. No, indeed! I felt in no poetical mood.

I tried to look the facts squarely in the face. There was a Cecil Fenwick, extraordinary as the coincidence was, and he was here in Avonlea. All my friends — and foes — believed that he was the estranged lover of my youth. If he stayed long in Avonlea, one of two things was bound to happen. He would hear the story I had told about him and deny it, and I would be held up to shame and derision for the rest of my natural life; or else he would simply go away in ignorance, and everybody would suppose he had forgotten me and would pity me maddeningly. The latter possibility was bad enough, but it wasn't to be compared to the former; and oh, how I prayed — yes, I *did* pray about it — that he would go right away. But Providence had other views for me.

Cecil Fenwick didn't go away. He stayed right on in Avonlea, and the Maxwells blossomed out socially in his honor and tried to give him a good time. Mrs. Maxwell gave a party for him. I got a card — but you may be very sure I didn't go, although Nancy thought I was crazy not to. Then every one else gave parties in honor of Mr. Fenwick and I was invited and never went. Wilhelmina Mercer came and pleaded and scolded and told me

if I avoided Mr. Fenwick like that he would think
I still cherished bitterness against him, and he
wouldn't make any advances towards a reconciliation. Wilhelmina means well, but she hasn't a great
deal of sense.

Cecil Fenwick seemed to be a great favorite with
everybody, young and old. He was very rich, too,
and Wilhelmina declared that half the girls were
after him.

" If it wasn't for you, Miss Holmes, I believe I'd
have a try for him myself, in spite of his gray hair
and quick temper — for Mrs. Maxwell says he has
a pretty quick temper, but it's all over in a minute,"
said Wilhelmina, half in jest and wholly in
earnest.

As for me, I gave up going out at all, even to
church. I fretted and pined and lost my appetite
and never wrote a line in my blank book. Nancy
was half frantic and insisted on dosing me with her
favorite patent pills. I took them meekly, because
it is a waste of time and energy to oppose Nancy, but,
of course, they didn't do me any good. My trouble
was too deep-seated for pills to cure. If ever a
woman was punished for telling a lie I was that
woman. I stopped my subscription to the *Weekly
Advocate* because it still carried that wretched porous plaster advertisement, and I couldn't bear to see
it. If it hadn't been for that I would never have

thought of Fenwick for a name, and all this trouble would have been averted.

One evening, when I was moping in my room, Nancy came up.

"There's a gentleman in the parlor asking for you, Miss Charlotte."

My heart just gave one horrible bounce.

"What — sort of a gentleman, Nancy?" I faltered.

"I think it's that Fenwick man that there's been such a time about," said Nancy, who didn't know anything about my imaginary escapades, "and he looks to be mad clean through about something, for such a scowl I never seen."

"Tell him I'll be down directly, Nancy," I said quite calmly.

As soon as Nancy had clumped downstairs again I put on my lace fichu and put two hankies in my belt, for I thought I'd probably need more than one. Then I hunted up an old *Advocate* for proof, and down I went to the parlor. I know exactly how a criminal feels going to execution, and I've been opposed to capital punishment ever since.

I opened the parlor door and went in, carefully closing it behind me, for Nancy has a deplorable habit of listening in the hall. Then my legs gave out completely, and I couldn't have walked another step to save my life. I just stood there, my hand on the knob, trembling like a leaf.

A man was standing by the south window looking out; he wheeled around as I went in, and, as Nancy said, he had a scowl on and looked angry clear through. He was very handsome, and his gray hair gave him such a distinguished look. I recalled this afterward, but just at the moment you may be quite sure I wasn't thinking about it at all.

Then all at once a strange thing happened. The scowl went right off his face and the anger out of his eyes. He looked astonished, and then foolish. I saw the color creeping up into his cheeks. As for me, I still stood there staring at him, not able to say a single word.

" Miss Holmes, I presume. " he said at last, in a deep, thrilling voice. " I — I — oh, confound it! I have called — I heard some foolish stories and I came here in a rage. I've been a fool — I know now they weren't true. Just excuse me and I'll go away and kick myself."

" No," I said, finding my voice with a gasp, " you mustn't go until you've heard the truth. It's dreadful enough, but not as dreadful as you might otherwise think. Those — those stories — I have a confession to make. I did tell them, but I didn't know there was such a person as Cecil Fenwick in existence."

He looked puzzled, as well he might. Then he smiled, took my hand and led me away from the door — to the knob of which I was still holding with all my might — to the sofa.

" Let's sit down and talk it over ' comfy,' " he said.

1408444

I just confessed the whole shameful business. It was terribly humiliating, but it served me right. I told him how people were always twitting me for never having had a beau, and how I had told them I had; and then I showed him the porous plaster advertisement.

He heard me right through without a word, and then he threw back his big, curly, gray head and laughed.

" This clears up a great many mysterious hints I've been receiving ever since I came to Avonlea," he said, " and finally a Mrs. Gilbert came to my sister this afternoon with a long farrago of nonsense about the love affair I had once had with some Charlotte Holmes here. She declared you had told her about it yourself. I confess I flamed up. I'm a peppery chap, and I thought — I thought — oh, confound it, it might as well out: I thought you were some lank old maid who was amusing herself telling ridiculous stories about me. When you came into the room I knew that, whoever was to blame, you were not."

"But I was," I said ruefully. "It wasn't right of me to tell such a story — and it was very silly, too. But who would ever have supposed that there could be a real Cecil Fenwick who had lived in Blakely? I never heard of such a coincidence."

"It's more than a coincidence," said Mr. Fenwick decidedly. "It's predestination; that is what it is. And now let's forget it and talk of something else."

We talked of something else — or at least Mr. Fenwick did, for I was too ashamed to say much — so long that Nancy got restive and clumped through the hall every five minutes; but Mr. Fenwick never took the hint. When he finally went away he asked if he might come again.

"It's time we made up that old quarrel, you know," he said, laughing.

And I, an old maid of forty, caught myself blushing like a girl. But I felt like a girl, for it was such a relief to have that explanation all over. I couldn't even feel angry with Adella Gilbert. She was always a mischief maker, and when a woman is born that way she is more to be pitied than blamed. I wrote a poem in the blank book before I went to sleep; I hadn't written anything for a month, and it was lovely to be at it once more.

Mr. Fenwick did come again — the very next evening, but one. And he came so often after that that even Nancy got resigned to him. One day I had to tell her something. I shrank from doing it, for I feared it would make her feel badly.

"Oh, I've been expecting to hear it," she said grimly. "I felt the minute that man came into the house he brought trouble with him. Well, Miss Charlotte, I wish you happiness. I don't know how the climate of California will agree with me, but I suppose I'll have to put up with it."

"But, Nancy," I said, "I can't expect you to go away out there with me. It's too much to ask of you."

"And where else would I be going?" demanded Nancy in genuine astonishment. "How under the canopy could you keep house without me? I'm not going to trust you to the mercies of a yellow Chinee with a pig-tail. Where you go I go, Miss Charlotte, and there's an end of it."

I was very glad, for I hated to think of parting with Nancy even to go with Cecil. As for the blank book, I haven't told my husband about it yet, but I mean to some day. And I've subscribed for the *Weekly Advocate* again.

III

" WE must invite your Aunt Jane, of course," said Mrs. Spencer.

Rachel made a protesting movement with her large, white, shapely hands — hands which were so different from the thin, dark, twisted ones folded on the table opposite her. The difference was not caused by hard work or the lack of it; Rachel had worked hard all her life. It was a difference inherent in temperament. The Spencers, no matter what they did, or how hard they labored, all had plump, smooth, white hands, with firm, supple fingers; the Chiswicks, even those who toiled not, neither did they spin, had hard, knotted, twisted ones. Moreover the contrast went deeper than externals, and twined itself with the innermost fibers of life, and thought, and action.

" I don't see why we must invite Aunt Jane," said Rachel, with as much impatience as her soft, throaty voice could express. " Aunt Jane doesn't like me, and I don't like Aunt Jane."

" I'm sure I don't see why you don't like her," said Mrs. Spencer. " It's ungrateful of you. She has always been very kind to you."

" She has always been very kind with one hand,"
smiled Rachel. " I remember the first time I ever
saw Aunt Jane. I was six years old. She held out
to me a small velvet pincushion with beads on it.
And then, because I did not, in my shyness, thank her
quite as promptly as I should have done, she rapped
my head with her bethimbled finger to ' teach me
better manners.' It hurt horribly — I've always
had a tender head. And that has been Aunt Jane's
way ever since. When I grew too big for the thimble treatment she used her tongue instead — and
that hurt worse. And you know, mother, how she
used to talk about my engagement. She is able to
spoil the whole atmosphere if she happens to come in
a bad humor. I don't want her."

" She must be invited. People would talk so if
she wasn't."

" I don't see why they should. She's only my
great-aunt by marriage. I wouldn't mind in the
least if people did talk. They'll talk anyway — you
know that, mother."

" Oh, we must have her," said Mrs. Spencer, with
the indifferent finality that marked all her words and
decisions — a finality against which it was seldom
of any avail to struggle. People, who knew, rarely
attempted it; strangers occasionally did, misled by
the deceit of appearances.

Isabella Spencer was a wisp of a woman, with a

pale, pretty face, uncertainly-colored, long-lashed, grayish eyes, and great masses of dull, soft, silky, brown hair. She had delicate aquiline features and a small, babyish, red mouth. She looked as if a breath would sway her. The truth was that a tornado would hardly have caused her to swerve an inch from her chosen path.

For a moment Rachel looked rebellious; then she yielded, as she generally did in all differences of opinion with her mother. It was not worth while to quarrel over the comparatively unimportant matter of Aunt Jane's invitation. A quarrel might be inevitable later on; Rachel wanted to save all her resources for that. She gave her shoulders a shrug, and wrote Aunt Jane's name down on the wedding list in her large, somewhat untidy handwriting — a handwriting which always seemed to irritate her mother. Rachel never could understand this irritation. She could never guess that it was because her writing looked so much like that in a certain packet of faded letters which Mrs. Spencer kept at the bottom of an old horsehair trunk in her bedroom. They were postmarked from seaports all over the world. Mrs. Spencer never read them or looked at them; but she remembered every dash and curve of the handwriting.

Isabella Spencer had overcome many things in her life by the sheer force and persistency of her will. But she could not get the better of heredity. Rachel was her father's daughter at all points, and Isabella Spencer escaped hating her for it only by loving her the more fiercely because of it. Even so, there were many times when she had to avert her eyes from Rachel's face because of the pang of the more subtle remembrances; and never, since her child was born, could Isabella Spencer bear to gaze on that child's face in sleep.

Rachel was to be married to Frank Bell in a fortnight's time. Mrs. Spencer was pleased with the match. She was very fond of Frank, and his farm was so near to her own that she would not lose Rachel altogether. Rachel fondly believed that her mother would not lose her at all; but Isabella Spencer, wiser by olden experience, knew what her daughter's marriage must mean to her, and steeled her heart to bear it with what fortitude she might.

They were in the sitting-room, deciding on the wedding guests and other details. The September sunshine was coming in through the waving boughs of the apple tree that grew close up to the low window. The glints wavered over Rachel's face, which was as pale as a lily, with only a tinge of color in her cheeks. She wore her sleek, golden hair in a quaint arch around it. Her forehead was very broad and white. She was fresh and young and hopeful. The mother's heart contracted in a spasm

of pain as she looked at her. How like the girl was
to — to — to the Spencers! Those easy, curving
outlines, those large, mirthful blue eyes, that finely
molded chin! Isabella Spencer shut her lips firmly,
and crushed down some unbidden, unwelcome memories.

"There will be about sixty guests, all told," she
said, as if she were thinking of nothing else. "We
must move the furniture all out of this room and set
the supper-table here. The dining-room is too small.
We must borrow Mrs. Bell's forks and spoons.
She offered to lend them. I'd never have been willing to ask her. The damask table cloths with the
ribbon pattern must be bleached to-morrow. Nobody else in Avonlea has such tablecloths. And
we'll put the little dining-room table on the hall
landing, upstairs, for the presents."

Rachel was not thinking about the presents, or the
housewifely details of the wedding. Her breath
was coming quicker, and the faint blush on her
smooth cheeks had deepened to crimson. She knew
that a critical moment was approaching. With a
steady hand she wrote the last name on her list and
drew a line under it.

"Well, have you finished?" asked her mother
impatiently. "Hand it here and let me look over
it to make sure that you haven't left anybody out
that should be in."

Rachel passed the paper across the table in silence. The room seemed to her to have grown very still. She could hear the flies buzzing on the panes, the soft purr of the wind about the low eaves and through the apple boughs, the jerky beating of her own heart. She felt frightened and nervous, but resolute.

Mrs. Spencer glanced down the list, murmuring the names aloud and nodding approval at each. But when she came to the last name, she did not utter it. She cast a black glance at Rachel, and a spark leaped up in the depths of her pale eyes. On her face were anger, amazement, incredulity, the last predominating.

The final name on the list of wedding guests was the name of David Spencer. David Spencer lived alone in a little cottage down at the Cove. He was a combination of sailor and fisherman. He was also Isabella Spencer's husband and Rachel's father.

"Rachel Spencer, have you taken leave of your senses? What do you mean by such nonsense as this?"

"I simply mean that I am going to invite my father to my wedding," answered Rachel quietly.

"Not in my house," cried Mrs. Spencer, her lips as white as if her fiery tone had scathed them.

Rachel leaned forward, folded her large, capable hands deliberately on the table, and gazed unflinch-

ingly into her mother's bitter face. Her fright and
nervousness were gone. Now that the conflict was
actually on she found herself rather enjoying it.
She wondered a little at herself, and thought that
she must be wicked. She was not given to self-
analysis, or she might have concluded that it was the
sudden assertion of her own personality, so long
dominated by her mother's, which she was finding so
agreeable.

"Then there will be no wedding, mother," she
said. "Frank and I will simply go to the manse,
be married, and go home. If I cannot invite my
father to see me married, no one else shall be invited."

Her lips narrowed tightly. For the first time in
her life Isabella Spencer saw a reflection of herself
looking back at her from her daughter's face — a
strange, indefinable resemblance that was more of
soul and spirit than of flesh and blood. In spite of
her anger her heart thrilled to it. As never before,
she realized that this girl was her own and her husband's child, a living bond between them wherein
their conflicting natures mingled and were reconciled. She realized too, that Rachel, so long sweetly
meek and obedient, meant to have her own way in
this case — and would have it.

"I must say that I can't see why you are so set
on having your father see you married," she said

with a bitter sneer. "*He* has never remembered that he is your father. He cares nothing about you — never did care."

Rachel took no notice of this taunt. It had no power to hurt her, its venom being neutralized by a secret knowledge of her own in which her mother had no share.

"Either I shall invite my father to my wedding, or I shall not have a wedding," she repeated steadily, adopting her mother's own effective tactics of repetition undistracted by argument.

"Invite him then," snapped Mrs. Spencer, with the ungraceful anger of a woman, long accustomed to having her own way, compelled for once to yield. "It'll do neither good nor harm. He won't come anyway."

Rachel made no response. Now that the battle was over, and the victory won, she found herself tremulously on the verge of tears. She rose quickly and went upstairs to her own room, a dim little place shadowed by the white birches growing thickly outside — a virginal room, where everything bespoke the maiden. She lay down on the blue and white patchwork quilt on her little bed, and cried softly and bitterly.

Her heart, at this crisis in her life, yearned for her father, who was almost a stranger to her. She knew that her mother had probably spoken the truth

when she said that he would not come.   Rachel felt
that her marriage vows would be lacking in some
indefinable sacredness if her father were not by to
hear them spoken.

Twenty-five years before this, David Spencer and
Isabella Chiswick had been married.   Spiteful people
said there could be no doubt that Isabella had married David for love, since he had neither lands nor
money to tempt her into a match of bargain and
sale.   David was a handsome fellow, with the blood
of a seafaring race in his veins.

He had been a sailor, like his father and grand-
father before him; but, when he married Isabella, she
induced him to give up the sea and settle down with
her on a snug farm her father had left her.   Isabella
liked farming, and loved her fertile acres and opu-
lent orchards.   She abhorred the sea and all that per-
tained to it, less from any dread of its dangers than
from an inbred conviction that sailors were " low "
in the social scale — a species of necessary vaga-
bonds.   In her eyes there was a taint of disgrace
in such a calling.   David must be transformed
into a respectable, home-abiding tiller of broad
lands.

For five years all went well enough.   If, at times,
David's longing for the sea troubled him, he stifled
it, and listened not to its luring voice.   He and Isabella were very happy; the only drawback to their

happiness lay in the regretted fact that they were childless.

Then, in the sixth year, came a crisis and a change. Captain Barrett, an old crony of David's, wanted him to go with him on a voyage as mate. At the suggestion all David's long-repressed craving for the wide blue wastes of the ocean, and the wind whistling through the spars with the salt foam in its breath, broke forth with a passion all the more intense for that very repression. He must go on that voyage with James Barrett — he *must!* That over, he would be contented again; but go he must. His soul struggled within him like a fettered thing.

Isabella opposed the scheme vehemently and unwisely, with mordant sarcasm and unjust reproaches. The latent obstinacy of David's character came to the support of his longing — a longing which Isabella, with five generations of land-loving ancestry behind her, could not understand at all.

He was determined to go, and he told Isabella so.

"I'm sick of plowing and milking cows," he said hotly.

"You mean that you are sick of a respectable life," sneered Isabella.

"Perhaps," said David, with a contemptuous shrug of his shoulders. "Anyway, I'm going."

"If you go on this voyage, David Spencer, you need never come back here," said Isabella resolutely.

David had gone; he did not believe that she meant it. Isabella believed that he did not care whether she meant it or not. David Spencer left behind him a woman, calm outwardly, inwardly a seething volcano of anger, wounded pride, and thwarted will.

He found precisely the same woman when he came home, tanned, joyous, tamed for a while of his *wanderlust,* ready, with something of real affection, to go back to the farm fields and the stock-yard.

Isabella met him at the door, smileless, cold-eyed, set-lipped.

" What do you want here? " she said, in the tone she was accustomed to use to tramps and Syrian peddlers.

" Want! " David's surprise left him at a loss for words. " Want! Why, I — I — want my wife. I've come home."

" This is not your home. I'm no wife of yours. You made your choice when you went away," Isabella had replied. Then she had gone in, shut the door, and locked it in his face.

David had stood there for a few minutes like a man stunned. Then he had turned and walked away up the lane under the birches. He said nothing — then or at any other time. From that day no reference to his wife or her concerns ever crossed his lips.

He went directly to the harbor, and shipped with

Captain Barrett for another voyage. When he came back from that in a month's time, he bought a small house and had it hauled to the "Cove," a lonely inlet from which no other human habitation was visible. Between his sea voyages he lived there the life of a recluse; fishing and playing his violin were his only employments. He went nowhere and encouraged no visitors.

Isabella Spencer also had adopted the tactics of silence. When the scandalized Chiswicks, Aunt Jane at their head, tried to patch up the matter with argument and entreaty, Isabella met them stonily, seeming not to hear what they said, and making no response. She worsted them totally. As Aunt Jane said in disgust, "What can you do with a woman who won't even *talk?*"

Five months after David Spencer had been turned from his wife's door, Rachel was born. Perhaps, if David had come to them then, with due penitence and humility, Isabella's heart, softened by the pain and joy of her long and ardently desired motherhood might have cast out the rankling venom of resentment that had poisoned it and taken him back into it. But David had not come; he gave no sign of knowing or caring that his once longed-for child had been born.

When Isabella was able to be about again, her pale face was harder than ever; and, had there been about her any one discerning enough to notice it, there was a subtle change in her bearing and manner. A certain nervous expectancy, a fluttering restlessness was gone. Isabella had ceased to hope secretly that her husband would yet come back. She had in her secret soul thought he would; and she had meant to forgive him when she had humbled him sufficiently, and when he had abased himself as she considered he should. But now she knew that he did not mean to sue for her forgiveness; and the hate that sprang out of her old love was a rank and speedy and persistent growth.

Rachel, from her earliest recollection, had been vaguely conscious of a difference between her own life and the lives of her playmates. For a long time it puzzled her childish brain. Finally, she reasoned it out that the difference consisted in the fact that they had fathers and she, Rachel Spencer, had none — not even one in the graveyard, as Carrie Bell and Lilian Boulter had. Why was this? Rachel went straight to her mother, put one little dimpled hand on Isabella Spencer's knee, looked up with great searching blue eyes, and said gravely,

" Mother, why haven't I got a father like the other little girls? "

Isabella Spencer laid aside her work, took the seven year old child on her lap, and told her the whole story in a few direct and bitter words that imprinted themselves indelibly on Rachel's remembrance. She understood clearly and hopelessly that she could never have a father — that, in this respect, she must always be unlike other people.

"Your father cares nothing for you," said Isabella Spencer in conclusion. "He never did care. You must never speak of him to anybody again."

Rachel slipped silently from her mother's knee and ran out to the Springtime garden with a full heart. There she cried passionately over her mother's last words. It seemed to her a terrible thing that her father should not love her, and a cruel thing that she must never talk of him.

Oddly enough, Rachel's sympathies were all with her father, in as far as she could understand the old quarrel. She did not dream of disobeying her mother and she did not disobey her. Never again did the child speak of her father; but Isabella had not forbidden her to think of him, and thenceforth Rachel thought of him very constantly — so constantly that, in some strange way, he seemed to become an unguessed-of part of her inner life — the unseen, ever-present companion in all her experiences.

She was an imaginative child, and in fancy she made the acquaintance of her father. She had never seen him, but he was more real to her than most of the people she had seen. He played and talked with her as her mother never did; he walked with her in the orchard and field and garden; he sat by her pillow in the twilight; to him she whispered secrets she told to none other.

Once her mother asked her impatiently why she talked so much to herself.

" I am not talking to myself.   I am talking to a very dear friend of mine," Rachel answered gravely.

" Silly child," laughed her mother, half tolerantly, half disapprovingly.

Two years later something wonderful had happened to Rachel. One summer afternoon she had gone to the harbor with several of her little playmates. Such a jaunt was a rare treat to the child, for Isabella Spencer seldom allowed her to go from home with anybody but herself. And Isabella was not an entertaining companion. Rachel never particularly enjoyed an outing with her mother.

The children wandered far along the shore; at last they came to a place Rachel had never seen before. It was a shallow cove where the waters purred on the yellow sands. Beyond it, the deep-blue, restless sea was flashing and sparkling in the sunlight. Outside, the wind was gusty and strong; here, it was temperate and calm. A white boat was hauled up on the skids, and there was a queer little house close down to the sands, like a big shell tossed up by the waves.

Rachel looked on it all with secret delight; she, too, loved the lonely places of sea and shore, as her father had done.   She wanted to linger awhile in this dear spot and revel in it.

"I'm tired, girls," she announced.   "I'm going to stay here and rest for a spell.   I don't want to go to Gull Point.   You go on yourselves; I'll wait for you here."

"All alone?" said Carrie Bell, wonderingly.

"I'm not so afraid of being alone as some people are," said Rachel, with dignity.

The other girls went on, leaving Rachel sitting on the skids, in the shadow of the big white boat.   She sat there for a time dreaming happily, with her blue eyes on the far, pearly horizon, and her golden head leaning against the boat.

Suddenly she heard a step behind her.   When she turned her head a man was standing beside her, looking down at her with big, merry, blue eyes.   Rachel was quite sure that she had never seen him before; yet those eyes seemed to her to have a strangely familiar look.   She liked him.   She felt no shyness nor timidity, such as usually afflicted her in the presence of strangers.

He was a tall, stout man, dressed in a rough fishing suit, and wearing an oilskin cap on his head. His hair was very thick and curly and fair; his cheeks were tanned and red; his teeth, when he smiled, were very even and white. Rachel thought he must be quite old, because there was a good deal of gray mixed with his fair hair.

"Are you watching for the mermaids?" he said.

Rachel nodded gravely. From any one else she would have scrupulously hidden such a thought.

"Yes, I am," she said. "Mother says there is no such thing as a mermaid, but I like to think there is. Have you ever seen one?"

The big man sat down on a bleached log of driftwood and smiled at her.

"No, I'm sorry to say that I haven't. But I have seen many other very wonderful things. I might tell you about some of them, if you would come over here and sit by me."

Rachel went unhesitatingly. When she reached him he pulled her down on his knee, and she liked it.

"What a nice little craft you are," he said. "Do you suppose, now, that you could give me a kiss?"

As a rule Rachel hated kissing. She could seldom be prevailed upon to kiss even her uncles — who knew it and liked to tease her for kisses until they aggravated her so terribly that she told them she couldn't bear men. But now she promptly put her arms about this strange man's neck and gave him a hearty smack.

"I like you," she said frankly.

She felt his arms tighten suddenly about her.

The blue eyes looking into hers grew misty and very tender. Then, all at once, Rachel knew who he was. He was her father. She did not say anything, but she laid her curly head down on his shoulder and felt a great happiness, as of one who had come into some longed-for haven.

If David Spencer realized that she understood he said nothing. Instead, he began to tell her fascinating stories of far lands he had visited, and strange things he had seen. Rachel listened entranced, as if she were hearkening to a fairy tale. Yes, he was just as she had dreamed him. She had always been sure he could tell beautiful stories.

" Come up to the house and I'll show you some pretty things," he said finally.

Then followed a wonderful hour. The little low-ceilinged room, with its square window, into which he took her, was filled with the flotsam and jetsam of his roving life — things beautiful and odd and strange beyond all telling. The things that pleased Rachel most were two huge shells on the chimney piece — pale pink shells with big crimson and purple spots.

" Oh, I didn't know there could be such pretty things in the world," she exclaimed.

" If you would like," began the big man; then he paused for a moment. " I'll show you something prettier still."

Rachel felt vaguely that he meant to say something else when he began; but she forgot to wonder what it was when she saw what he brought out of a little corner cupboard. It was a teapot of some fine, glistening purple ware, coiled over by golden dragons with gilded claws and scales. The lid looked like a beautiful golden flower and the handle was a coil of a dragon's tail. Rachel sat and looked at it rapt-eyed.

" That's the only thing of any value I have in the world — now," he said.

Rachel knew there was something very sad in his eyes and voice. She longed to kiss him again and comfort him. But suddenly he began to laugh, and then he rummaged out some goodies for her to eat, sweetmeats more delicious than she had ever imag-ined. While she nibbled them he took down an old violin and played music that made her want to dance and sing. Rachel was perfectly happy. She wished she might stay forever in that low, dim room with all its treasures.

" I see your little friends coming around the point," he said, finally. " I suppose you must go. Put the rest of the goodies in your pocket."

He took her up in his arms and held her tightly against his breast for a single moment. She felt him kissing her hair.

"There, run along, little girl. Good-by," he said gently.

"Why don't you ask me to come and see you again?" cried Rachel, half in tears. "I'm coming *anyhow.*"

"If you can come, *come,*" he said. "If you don't come, I shall know it is because you can't — and that is much to know. I'm very, very, *very* glad, little woman, that you have come once."

Rachel was sitting demurely on the skids when her companions came back. They had not seen her leaving the house, and she said not a word to them of her experiences. She only smiled mysteriously when they asked her if she had been lonesome.

That night, for the first time, she mentioned her father's name in her prayers. She never forgot to do so afterwards. She always said "bless mother — and father," with an instinctive pause between the two names — a pause which indicated new realization of the tragedy which had sundered them. And the tone in which she said "father" was softer and more tender than the one which voiced "mother."

Rachel never visited the Cove again. Isabella Spencer discovered that the children had been there, and, although she knew nothing of Rachel's interview with her father, she told the child that she must never again go to that part of the shore.

Rachel shed many a bitter tear in secret over this

command; but she obeyed it. Thenceforth there
had been no communication between her and her
father, save the unworded messages of soul to soul
across whatever may divide them.

David Spencer's invitation to his daughter's wedding was sent with the others, and the remaining
days of Rachel's maidenhood slipped away in a whirl
of preparation and excitement in which her mother
reveled, but which was distasteful to the girl.

The wedding day came at last, breaking softly and
fairly over the great sea in a sheen of silver and
pearl and rose, a September day, as mild and beautiful as June.

The ceremony was to be performed at eight o'clock
in the evening. At seven Rachel stood in her room,
fully dressed and alone. She had no bridesmaid,
and she had asked her cousins to leave her to herself
in this last solemn hour of girlhood. She looked
very fair and sweet in the sunset-light that showered
through the birches. Her wedding gown was a fine,
sheer organdie, simply and daintily made. In the
loose waves of her bright hair she wore her bridegroom's flowers, roses as white as a virgin's dream.
She was very happy; but her happiness was faintly
threaded with the sorrow inseparable from all
change.

Presently her mother came in, carrying a small
basket.

"Here is something for you, Rachel. One of the boys from the harbor brought it up. He was bound to give it into your own hands — said that was his orders. I just took it and sent him to the right-about — told him I'd give it to you at once, and that that was all that was necessary."

She spoke coldly. She knew quite well who had sent the basket, and she resented it; but her resentment was not quite strong enough to overcome her curiosity. She stood silently by while Rachel unpacked the basket.

Rachel's hands trembled as she took off the cover. Two huge pink-spotted shells came first. How well she remembered them! Beneath them, carefully wrapped up in a square of foreign-looking, strangely scented silk, was the dragon teapot. She held it in her hands and gazed at it with tears gathering thickly in her eyes.

"Your father sent that," said Isabella Spencer with an odd sound in her voice. "I remember it well. It was among the things I packed up and sent after him. His father had brought it home from China fifty years ago, and he prized it beyond anything. They used to say it was worth a lot of money."

"Mother, please leave me alone for a little while," said Rachel, imploringly. She had caught sight of a little note at the bottom of the basket, and she felt that she could not read it under her mother's eyes.

Mrs. Spencer went out with unaccustomed acqui-escence, and Rachel went quickly to the window, where she read her letter by the fading gleams of twilight.   It was very brief, and the writing was that of a man who holds a pen but seldom.

" My dear little girl," it ran, " I'm sorry I can't go to your wedding.   It was like you to ask me — for I know it was your doing.   I wish I could see you married, but I can't go to the house I was turned out of.   I hope you will be very happy.   I am send-ing you the shells and teapot you liked so much. Do you remember that day we had such a good time? I would liked to have seen you again before you were married, but it can't be.

> " Your loving father,
> " DAVID SPENCER."

Rachel resolutely blinked away the tears that filled her eyes.   A fierce desire for her father sprang up in her heart — an insistent hunger that would not be denied.   She *must* see her father; she *must* have his blessing on her new life.   A sudden determina-tion took possession of her whole being — a deter-mination that swept aside all conventionalities and objections as if they had not been.

It was now almost dark.   The guests would not be coming for half an hour yet.   It was only fifteen minutes' walk over the hill to the Cove.   Hastily Rachel shrouded herself in her new raincoat, and drew a dark, protecting hood over her gay head. She opened her door and slipped noiselessly downstairs. Mrs. Spencer and her assistants were all busy in the back part of the house. In a moment Rachel was out in the dewy garden. She would go straight over the fields. Nobody would see her.

It was quite dark when she reached the Cove. In the crystal cup of the sky over her the stars were blinking. The sound of rippling waves, lapping on the shore, broke the stillness. A soft little wind was crooning about the eaves of the little gray house where David Spencer was sitting, alone in the twilight, his violin on his knee. He had been trying to play, but could not. His heart yearned after his daughter — yes, and after a long-estranged bride of his youth. His love of the sea was sated forever; his love for wife and child still cried for its own under all his old anger and stubbornness.

The door opened suddenly and the very Rachel of whom he was dreaming came suddenly in, flinging off her wraps and standing forth in her young beauty and bridal adornments, a splendid creature, almost lighting up the gloom with her radiance.

"Father," she cried, brokenly, and her father's eager arms closed around her.

Back in the house she had left, the guests were coming to the wedding. There were jests and laughter and friendly greeting. The bridegroom came, too, a slim, dark-eyed lad who tiptoed bashfully upstairs to the spare room, from which he presently emerged to confront Mrs. Spencer on the landing.

"I want to see Rachel before we go down," he said, blushing.

Mrs. Spencer deposited a wedding present of linen on the table which was already laden with gifts, opened the door of Rachel's room, and called her. There was no reply; the room was dark and still. In sudden alarm, Isabella Spencer snatched the lamp from the hall table and held it up. The little white room was empty. No blushing, white-clad bride tenanted it. But David Spencer's letter was lying on the stand. She caught it up and read it.

"Rachel is gone," she gasped. A flash of intuition had revealed to her where and why the girl had gone.

"Gone!" echoed Frank, his face blanching. His pallid dismay recalled Mrs. Spencer to herself. She gave a bitter, ugly little laugh.

"Oh, you needn't look so scared, Frank. She hasn't run away from you. Hush; come in here — shut the door. Nobody must know of this. Nice gossip it would make! That little fool has gone to the Cove to see her — her father. I know she has. It's just like what she would do. He sent her those presents — look — and this letter. Read it. She has gone to coax him to come and see her married. She was crazy about it. And the minister is here and it is half-past seven. She'll ruin her dress and shoes in the dust and dew. And what if some one has seen her! Was there ever such a little fool?"

Frank's presence of mind had returned to him. He knew all about Rachel and her father. She had told him everything.

" I'll go after her," he said gently. " Get me my hat and coat. I'll slip down the back stairs and over to the Cove."

" You must get out of the pantry window, then," said Mrs. Spencer firmly, mingling comedy and tragedy after her characteristic fashion. " The kitchen is full of women. I won't have this known and talked about if it can possibly be helped."

The bridegroom, wise beyond his years in the knowledge that it was well to yield to women in little things, crawled obediently out of the pantry window and darted through the birch wood. Mrs. Spencer had stood quakingly on guard until he had disappeared.

So Rachel had gone to her father! Like had broken the fetters of years and fled to like.

" It isn't much use fighting against nature, I guess," she thought grimly. " I'm beat. He must have thought something of her, after all, when he sent her that teapot and letter. And what does he mean about the ' day they had such a good time '? Well, it just means that she's been to see him before, sometime, I suppose, and kept me in ignorance of it all."

Mrs. Spencer shut down the pantry window with a vicious thud.

" If only she'll come quietly back with Frank in time to prevent gossip I'll forgive her," she said, as she turned to the kitchen.

Rachel was sitting on her father's knee, with both her white arms around his neck, when Frank came in. She sprang up, her face flushed and appealing, her eyes bright and dewy with tears. Frank thought he had never seen her look so lovely.

" Oh, Frank, is it very late? Oh, are you angry? " she exclaimed timidly.

" No, no, dear. Of course I'm not angry. But don't you think you'd better come back now? It's nearly eight and everybody is waiting."

" I've been trying to coax father to come up and see me married," said Rachel. " Help me, Frank."

" You'd better come, sir," said Frank heartily, " I'd like it as much as Rachel would."

David Spencer shook his head stubbornly.

" No, I can't go to that house. I was locked out of it. Never mind me. I've had my happiness in this half hour with my little girl. I'd like to see her married, but it isn't to be."

"Yes, it is to be — it shall be," said Rachel resolutely. "You *shall* see me married. Frank, I'm going to be married here in my father's house! That is the right place for a girl to be married. Go back and tell the guests so, and bring them all down."

Frank looked rather dismayed. David Spencer said deprecatingly: "Little girl, don't you think it would be —"

"I'm going to have my own way in this," said Rachel, with a sort of tender finality. "Go, Frank. I'll obey you all my life after, but you must do this for me. Try to understand," she added beseechingly.

"Oh, I understand," Frank reassured her. "Besides, I think you are right. But I was thinking of your mother. She won't come."

"Then you tell her that if she doesn't come I shan't be married at all," said Rachel. She was betraying unsuspected ability to manage people. She knew that ultimatum would urge Frank to his best endeavors.

Frank, much to Mrs. Spencer's dismay, marched boldly in at the front door upon his return. She pounced on him and whisked him out of sight into the supper room.

"Where's Rachel? What made you come that way? Everybody saw you!"

"It makes no difference. They will all have to know, anyway. Rachel says she is going to be married from her father's house, or not at all. I've come back to tell you so."

Isabella's face turned crimson.

"Rachel has gone crazy. I wash my hands of this affair. Do as you please. Take the guests — the supper, too, if you can carry it."

"We'll all come back here for supper," said Frank, ignoring the sarcasm. "Come, Mrs. Spencer, let's make the best of it."

"Do you suppose that *I* am going to David Spencer's house?" said Isabella Spencer violently.

"Oh you *must* come, Mrs. Spencer," cried poor Frank desperately. He began to fear that he would lose his bride past all finding in this maze of triple stubbornness. "Rachel says she won't be married at all if you don't go, too. Think what a talk it will make. You know she will keep her word."

Isabella Spencer knew it. Amid all the conflict of anger and revolt in her soul was a strong desire not to make a worse scandal than must of necessity be made. The desire subdued and tamed her, as nothing else could have done.

"I will go, since I have to," she said icily.

" What can't be cured must be endured. Go and tell them."

Five minutes later the sixty wedding guests were all walking over the fields to the Cove, with the minister and the bridegroom in the front of the procession. They were too amazed even to talk about the strange happening. Isabella Spencer walked behind, fiercely alone.

They all crowded into the little room of the house at the Cove, and a solemn hush fell over it, broken only by the purr of the sea-wind around it and the croon of the waves on the shore. David Spencer gave his daughter away; but, when the ceremony was concluded, Isabella was the first to take the girl in her arms. She clasped her and kissed her, with tears streaming down her pale face, all her nature melted in a mother's tenderness.

" Rachel, Rachel! My child, I hope and pray that you may be happy," she said brokenly.

In the surge of the suddenly merry crowd of well-wishers around the bride and groom, Isabella was pushed back into a shadowy corner behind a heap of sails and ropes. Looking up, she found herself crushed against David Spencer. For the first time in twenty years the eyes of husband and wife met. A strange thrill shot to Isabella's heart; she felt herself trembling.

" Isabella." It was David's voice in her ear —

a voice full of tenderness and pleading — the voice
of the young wooer of her girlhood —" Is it too late
to ask you to forgive me? I've been a stubborn fool
— but there hasn't been an hour in all these years
that I haven't thought about you and our baby and
longed for you."

Isabella Spencer had hated this man; yet her hate
had been but a parasite growth on a nobler stem,
with no abiding roots of its own. It withered under
his words, and lo, there was the old love, fair and
strong and beautiful as ever.

" Oh — David — I — was — all — to — blame,"
she murmured brokenly.

Further words were lost on her husband's lips.

When the hubbub of handshaking and congratula-
tions had subsided, Isabella Spencer stepped out before the company. She looked almost girlish and
bridal herself, with her flushed cheeks and bright
eyes.

" Let's go back now and have supper, and be
sensible," she said crisply. " Rachel, your father
is coming, too. He is coming to *stay* "— with a defiant glance around the circle. " Come, everybody."

They went back with laughter and raillery over the
quiet autumn fields, faintly silvered now by the moon
that was rising over the hills. The young bride and
groom lagged behind; they were very happy, but
they were not so happy, after all, as the old bride

and groom who walked swiftly in front. Isabella's hand was in her husband's and sometimes she could not see the moonlit hills for a mist of glorified tears.

"David," she whispered, as he helped her over the fence, "how can you ever forgive me?"

"There's nothing to forgive," he said. "We're only just married. Who ever heard of a bridegroom talking of forgiveness? Everything is beginning over new for us, my girl."

IV

JANE'S BABY

Miss Rosetta Ellis, with her front hair in curl-papers, and her back hair bound with a checked apron, was out in her breezy side yard under the firs, shaking her parlor rugs, when Mr. Nathan Patterson drove in. Miss Rosetta had seen him coming down the long red hill, but she had not supposed he would be calling at that time of the morning. So she had not run. Miss Rosetta always ran if anybody called and her front hair was in curl-papers; and, though the errand of the said caller might be life or death, he or she had to wait until Miss Rosetta had taken her hair out. Everybody in Avonlea knew this, because everybody in Avonlea knew everything about everybody else.

But Mr. Patterson had wheeled into the lane so quickly and unexpectedly that Miss Rosetta had had no time to run; so, twitching off the checked apron, she stood her ground as calmly as might be under the disagreeable consciousness of curl-papers.

"Good morning, Miss Ellis," said Mr. Patterson, so somberly that Miss Rosetta instantly felt that he was the bearer of bad news. Usually Mr. Patter-

70

son's face was as broad and beaming as a harvest moon. Now his expression was very melancholy and his voice positively sepulchral.

"Good morning," returned Miss Rosetta, crisply and cheerfully. She, at any rate, would not go into eclipse until she knew the reason therefor. "It is a fine day."

"A very fine day," assented Mr. Patterson, solemnly. "I have just come from the Wheeler place, Miss Ellis, and I regret to say —"

"Charlotte is sick!" cried Miss Rosetta, rapidly. "Charlotte has got another spell with her heart! I knew it! I've been expecting to hear it! Any woman that drives about the country as much as she does is liable to heart disease at any moment. *I* never go outside of my gate but I meet her gadding off somewhere. Goodness knows who looks after her place. I shouldn't like to trust as much to a hired man as she does. Well, it is very kind of you, Mr. Patterson, to put yourself out to the extent of calling in to tell me that Charlotte is sick, but I don't really see why you should take so much trouble — I really don't. It doesn't matter to me whether Charlotte is sick or whether she isn't. *You* know that perfectly well, Mr. Patterson, if anybody does. When Charlotte went and got married, on the sly, to that good-for-nothing Jacob Wheeler —"

"Mrs. Wheeler is quite well," interrupted Mr.

Patterson desperately. "Quite well. Nothing at all the matter with her, in fact. I only —"

"Then what do you mean by coming here and telling me she wasn't, and frightening me half to death?" demanded Miss Rosetta, indignantly. "My own heart isn't very strong — it runs in our family — and my doctor warned me to avoid all shocks and excitement. I don't want to be excited, Mr. Patterson. I won't be excited, not even if Charlotte has another spell. It's perfectly useless for you to try to excite me, Mr. Patterson."

"Bless the woman, I'm not trying to excite anybody!" declared Mr. Patterson in exasperation. "I merely called to tell you —"

"To tell me *what?*" said Miss Rosetta. "How much longer do you mean to keep me in suspense, Mr. Patterson. No doubt you have abundance of spare time, but — I — have *not*."

"— that your sister, Mrs. Wheeler, has had a letter from a cousin of yours, and she's in Charlottetown. Mrs. Roberts, I think her name is —"

"Jane Roberts," broke in Miss Rosetta. "Jane Ellis she was, before she was married. What was she writing to Charlotte about? Not that I want to know, of course. I'm not interested in Charlotte's correspondence, goodness knows. But if Jane had anything in particular to write about she should have written to *me*. I am the oldest. Charlotte had no business to get a letter from Jane Roberts without consulting me. It's just like her underhanded ways. She got married the same way. Never said a word to me about it, but just sneaked off with that unprincipled Jacob Wheeler —"

"Mrs. Roberts is very ill. I understand," persisted Mr. Patterson, nobly resolved to do what he had come to do, "dying, in fact, and —"

"Jane ill! Jane dying!" exclaimed Miss Rosetta. "Why, she was the healthiest girl I ever knew! But then I've never seen her, nor heard from her, since she got married fifteen years ago. I dare say her husband was a brute and neglected her, and she's pined away by slow degrees. I've no faith in husbands. Look at Charlotte! Everybody knows how Jacob Wheeler used her. To be sure, she deserved it, but —"

"Mrs. Roberts' husband is dead," said Mr. Patterson. "Died about two months ago, I understand, and she has a little baby six months old, and she thought perhaps Mrs. Wheeler would take it for old times' sake —"

"Did Charlotte ask you to call and tell me this?" demanded Miss Rosetta eagerly.

"No; she just told me what was in the letter. She didn't mention you; but I thought, perhaps, you ought to be told —"

"I knew it," said Miss Rosetta in a tone of bitter

assurance. " I could have told you so. Charlotte wouldn't even let me know that Jane was ill. Charlotte would be afraid I would want to get the baby, seeing that Jane and I were such intimate friends long ago. And who has a better right to it than me, I should like to know? Ain't I the oldest? And haven't I had experience in bringing up babies? Charlotte needn't think she is going to run the affairs of our family just because she happened to get married. Jacob Wheeler —"

" I must be going," said Mr. Patterson, gathering up his reins thankfully.

" I am much obliged to you for coming to tell me about Jane," said Miss Rosetta, " even though you have wasted a lot of precious time getting it out. If it hadn't been for you I suppose I should never have known it at all. As it is, I shall start for town just as soon as I can get ready."

" You'll have to hurry if you want to get ahead of Mrs. Wheeler," advised Mr. Patterson. " She's packing her trunk and going on the morning train."

" I'll pack a valise and go on the afternoon train," retorted Miss Rosetta triumphantly. " I'll show Charlotte she isn't running the Ellis affairs. She married out of them into the Wheelers. She can attend to them. Jacob Wheeler was the most —"

But Mr. Patterson had driven away. He felt that he had done his duty in the face of fearful odds, and he did not want to hear anything more about Jacob Wheeler.

Rosetta Ellis and Charlotte Wheeler had not exchanged a word for ten years. Before that time they had been devoted to each other, living together in the little Ellis cottage on the White Sands road, as they had done ever since their parents' death. The trouble began when Jacob Wheeler had commenced to pay attention to Charlotte, the younger and prettier of two women who had both ceased to be either very young or very pretty. Rosetta had been bitterly opposed to the match from the first. She vowed she had no use for Jacob Wheeler. There were not lacking malicious people to hint that this was because the aforesaid Jacob Wheeler had selected the wrong sister upon whom to bestow his affections. Be that as it might, Miss Rosetta certainly continued to render the course of Jacob Wheeler's true love exceedingly rough and tumultuous. The end of it was that Charlotte had gone quietly away one morning and married Jacob Wheeler without Miss Rosetta's knowing anything about it. Miss Rosetta had never forgiven her for it, and Charlotte had never forgiven the things Rosetta had said to her when she and Jacob returned to the Ellis cottage. Since then the sisters had been avowed and open foes, the only difference being that Miss Rosetta aired her grievances publicly, in season and out of season, while Charlotte was never heard to mention Rosetta's name. Even the death of Jacob Wheeler, five years after the marriage, had not healed the breach.

Miss Rosetta took out her curl-papers, packed her valise, and caught the late afternoon train for Charlottetown, as she had threatened. All the way there she sat rigidly upright in her seat and held imaginary dialogues with Charlotte in her mind, running something like this on her part: —

" No, Charlotte Wheeler, you are not going to have Jane's baby, and you're very much mistaken if you think so. Oh, all right — we'll see! You don't know anything about babies, even if you are married. I do. Didn't I take William Ellis's baby, when his wife died? Tell me that, Charlotte Wheeler! And didn't the little thing thrive with me, and grow strong and healthy? Yes, even you have to admit that it did, Charlotte Wheeler. And yet you have the presumption to think that you ought to have Jane's baby! Yes, it is presumption, Charlotte Wheeler. And when William Ellis got married again, and took the baby, didn't the child cling to me and cry as if I was its real mother? You know it did, Charlotte Wheeler. I'm going to get and keep Jane's baby in spite of you, Charlotte Wheeler, and I'd like to see you try to prevent me — you that went and got married and never so much as let your own sister know of it! If I had got married in such a fashion, Charlotte Wheeler, I'd be ashamed to look anybody in the face for the rest of my natural life!"

Miss Rosetta was so interested in thus laying down the law to Charlotte, and in planning out the future life of Jane's baby, that she didn't find the journey to Charlottetown so long or tedious as might have been expected, considering her haste. She soon found her way to the house where her cousin lived. There, to her dismay and real sorrow, she learned that Mrs. Roberts had died at four o'clock that afternoon.

"She seemed dreadful anxious to live until she heard from some of her folks out in Avonlea," said the woman who gave Miss Rosetta the information. "She had written to them about her little girl. She was my sister-in-law, and she lived with me ever since her husband died. I've done my best for her; but I've a big family of my own and I can't see how I'm to keep the child. Poor Jane looked and longed for some one to come from Avonlea, but she couldn't hold out. A patient, suffering creature she was!"

"I'm her cousin," said Miss Rosetta, wiping her eyes, "and I have come for the baby. I'll take it home with me after the funeral; and, if you please, Mrs. Gordon, let me see it right away, so it can get accustomed to me. Poor Jane! I wish I could have got here in time to see her, she and I were such friends long ago. We were far more intimate and confidential than ever her and Charlotte was. Charlotte knows that, too!"

The vim with which Miss Rosetta snapped this out rather amazed Mrs. Gordon, who couldn't understand it at all. But she took Miss Rosetta upstairs to the room where the baby was sleeping.

"Oh, the little darling," cried Miss Rosetta, all her old maidishness and oddity falling away from her like a garment, and all her innate and denied motherhood shining out in her face like a transforming illumination. "Oh, the sweet, dear, pretty little thing!"

The baby was a darling—a six-months' old beauty with little golden ringlets curling and glistening all over its tiny head. As Miss Rosetta hung over it, it opened its eyes and then held out its tiny hands to her with a gurgle of confidence.

"Oh, you sweetest!" said Miss Rosetta rapturously, gathering it up in her arms. "You belong to me, darling — never, never, to that under-handed Charlotte! What is its name, Mrs. Gordon?"

"It wasn't named," said Mrs. Gordon. "Guess you'll have to name it yourself, Miss Ellis."

"Camilla Jane," said Miss Rosetta without a moment's hesitation. "Jane after its mother, of course; and I have always thought Camilla the prettiest name in the world. Charlotte would be sure to give it some perfectly heathenish name. I wouldn't put it past her calling the poor innocent Mehitable."

Miss Rosetta decided to stay in Charlottetown until after the funeral. That night she lay with the baby on her arm, listening with joy to its soft little breathing. She did not sleep or wish to sleep. Her waking thoughts were preferable to any fancies of slumberland. Moreover, she gave a spice to them by occasionally snapping some vicious sentences out loud at Charlotte.

Miss Rosetta fully expected Charlotte along on the following morning and girded herself for the fray; but no Charlotte appeared. Night came; no Charlotte. Another morning and no Charlotte. Miss Rosetta was hopelessly puzzled. What had happened? Dear, dear, had Charlotte taken a bad heart spell, on hearing that she, Rosetta, had stolen a march on her to Charlottetown? It was quite likely. You never knew what to expect of a woman who had married Jacob Wheeler!

The truth was, that the very evening Miss Rosetta had left Avonlea Mrs. Jacob Wheeler's hired man had broken his leg and had had to be conveyed to his distant home on a feather bed in an express wagon. Mrs. Wheeler could not leave home until she had obtained another hired man. Consequently it was the evening after the funeral when Mrs. Wheeler whisked up the steps of the Gordon house and met Miss Rosetta coming out with a big white bundle in her arms.

The eyes of the two women met defiantly. Miss Rosetta's face wore an air of triumph, chastened by a remembrance of the funeral that afternoon. Mrs. Wheeler's face, except for eyes, was as expressionless as it usually was. Unlike the tall, fair, fat Miss Rosetta, Mrs. Wheeler was small and dark and thin, with an eager, careworn face.

" How is Jane? " she said abruptly, breaking the silence of ten years in saying it.

" Jane is dead and buried, poor thing," said Miss Rosetta calmly. " I am taking her baby, little Camilla Jane, home with me."

" The baby belongs to me," cried Mrs. Wheeler passionately. " Jane wrote to me about her. Jane meant that I should have her. I've come for her."

" You'll go back without her, then," said Miss Rosetta, serene in the possession that is nine points of the law. " The child is mine, and she is going to stay mine. You can make up your mind to that, Charlotte Wheeler. A woman who eloped to get married isn't fit to be trusted with a baby, anyhow. Jacob Wheeler —"

But Mrs. Wheeler had rushed past into the house. Miss Rosetta composedly stepped into the cab and drove to the station. She fairly bridled with triumph; and underneath the triumph ran a queer undercurrent of satisfaction over the fact that Charlotte had spoken to her at last. Miss Rosetta would not look at this satisfaction, or give it a name, but it was there.

Miss Rosetta arrived safely back in Avonlea with Camilla Jane and within ten hours everybody in the settlement knew the whole story, and every woman who could stand on her feet had been up to the Ellis cottage to see the baby. Mrs. Wheeler arrived home twenty-four hours later, and silently betook herself to her farm. When her Avonlea neighbors sympathized with her in her disappointment, she said nothing, but looked all the more darkly determined. Also, a week later, Mr. William J. Blair, the Carmody storekeeper, had an odd tale to tell. Mrs. Wheeler had come to the store and bought a lot of fine flannel and muslin and valenciennes. Now, what in the name of time, did Mrs. Wheeler want with such stuff? Mr. William J. Blair couldn't make head or tail of it, and it worried him. Mr. Blair was so accustomed to know what everybody bought anything for that such a mystery quite upset him.

Miss Rosetta had exulted in the possession of little Camilla Jane for a month, and had been so happy that she had almost given up inveighing against Charlotte. Her conversation, instead of tending always to Jacob Wheeler now ran Camilla Janeward; and this, folks thought, was an improvement.

One afternoon, Miss Rosetta, leaving Camilla Jane snugly sleeping in her cradle in the kitchen, had slipped down to the bottom of the garden to pick her currants. The house was hidden from her sight by the copse of cherry trees, but she had left the kitchen window open, so that she could hear the baby if it awakened and cried. Miss Rosetta sang happily as she picked her currants. For the first time since Charlotte had married Jacob Wheeler Miss Rosetta felt really happy — so happy that there was no room in her heart for bitterness. In fancy she looked forward to the coming years, and saw Camilla Jane growing up into girlhood, fair and lovable.

" She'll be a beauty," reflected Miss Rosetta complacently. " Jane was a handsome girl. She shall always be dressed as nice as I can manage it, and I'll get her an organ, and have her take painting and music lessons. Parties, too! I'll give her a real coming-out party when she's eighteen and the very prettiest dress that's to be had. Dear me, I can hardly wait for her to grow up, though she's sweet enough now to make one wish she could stay a baby forever."

When Miss Rosetta returned to the kitchen, her eyes fell on an empty cradle. Camilla Jane was gone!

Miss Rosetta promptly screamed. She understood at a glance what had happened. Six months' old babies do not get out of their cradles and disappear through closed doors without any assistance.

"Charlotte has been here," gasped Miss Rosetta. "Charlotte has stolen Camilla Jane! I might have expected it. I might have known when I heard that story about her buying muslin and flannel. It's just like Charlotte to do such an underhand trick. But I'll go after her! I'll show her! She'll find out she has got Rosetta Ellis to deal with and no Wheeler!"

Like a frantic creature and wholly forgetting that her hair was in curl-papers, Miss Rosetta hurried up the hill and down the shore road to the Wheeler Farm — a place she had never visited in her life before.

There was an off-shore wind which rippled the surface of the bay. Fleecy, drifting puffs of clouds cast fleeting shadows upon the blue water, darkening its color here and there.

The little gray house, so close to the purring waves that in storms their spray splashed over its very doorstep, seemed deserted. Miss Rosetta pounded lustily on the front door. This producing no result, she marched around to the back door and knocked. No answer. Miss Rosetta tried the door. It was locked.

"Guilty conscience," sniffed Miss Rosetta. "Well, I shall stay here until I see that perfidious Charlotte, if I have to camp in the yard all night."

Miss Rosetta was quite capable of doing this, but she was spared the necessity; walking boldly up to the kitchen window, and peering through it, she felt her heart swell with anger as she beheld Charlotte sitting calmly by the table with Camilla Jane on her knee. Beside her was a befrilled and bemuslined cradle, and on a chair lay the garments in which Miss Rosetta had dressed the baby. It was clad in an entirely new outfit, and seemed quite at home with its new possessor. It was laughing and cooing, and making little dabs at her with its dimpled hands.

"Charlotte Wheeler," cried Miss Rosetta, rapping sharply on the window-pane. "I've come for that child! Bring her out to me at once — at once, I say! How dare you come to my house and steal a baby? You're no better than a common burglar. Give me Camilla Jane, I say!"

Charlotte came over to the window with the baby in her arms and triumph glittering in her eyes.

"There is no such child as Camilla Jane here," she said. "This is Barbara Jane. She belongs to me."

With that Mrs. Wheeler pulled down the shade.

Miss Rosetta had to go home. There was nothing else for her to do. On her way she met Mr. Patterson and told him in full the story of her wrongs. It was all over Avonlea by night, and created quite a sensation. Avonlea had not had such a toothsome bit of gossip for a long time.

Mrs. Wheeler exulted in the possession of Barbara Jane for six weeks, during which Miss Rosetta broke her heart with loneliness and longing, and meditated futile plots for the recovery of the baby. It was hopeless to think of stealing it back or she would have tried to. The hired man at the Wheeler place reported that Mrs. Wheeler never left it night or day for a single moment. She even carried it with her when she went to milk the cows.

" But my turn will come," said Miss Rosetta grimly. " Camilla Jane is mine, and if she was called Barbara for a century it wouldn't alter that fact. Barbara, indeed! Why not have called her Methusaleh and have done with it? "

One afternoon in October, when Miss Rosetta was picking her apples and thinking drearily about lost Camilla Jane, a woman came running breathlessly down the hill and into the yard. Miss Rosetta gave an exclamation of amazement, and dropped her basket of apples. Of all incredible things! The woman was Charlotte — Charlotte who had never set foot on the grounds of the Ellis cottage since her marriage ten years ago, Charlotte, bare-headed, wild-eyed, distraught, wringing her hands and sobbing.

Miss Rosetta flew to meet her.

"You've scalded Camilla Jane to death!" she exclaimed. "I always knew you would — always expected it!"

"Oh, for heaven's sake, come quick, Rosetta!" gasped Charlotte. "Barbara Jane is in convulsions and I don't know what to do. The hired man has gone for the doctor. You were the nearest, so I came to you. Jenny White was there when they came on, so I left her and ran. Oh, Rosetta, come, come, if you have a spark of humanity in you! You know what to do for convulsions — you saved the Ellis baby when it had them. Oh, come and save Barbara Jane!"

"You mean Camilla Jane, I presume?" said Miss Rosetta firmly, in spite of her agitation.

For a second Charlotte Wheeler hesitated. Then she said passionately: "Yes, yes, Camilla Jane — any name you like! Only come."

Miss Rosetta went, and not a moment too soon, either. The doctor lived eight miles away and the baby was very bad. The two women and Jenny White worked over her for hours. It was not until dark, when the baby was sleeping soundly and the doctor had gone, after telling Miss Rosetta that she had saved the child's life, that a realization of the situation came home to them.

"Well," said Miss Rosetta, dropping into an armchair with a long sigh of weariness, "I guess you'll admit now, Charlotte Wheeler, that you are hardly a fit person to have charge of a baby, even if you had to go and steal it from me. I should think your conscience would reproach you — that is, if any woman who would marry Jacob Wheeler in such an underhanded fashion has a —"

"I — I wanted the baby," sobbed Charlotte, tremulously. "I was so lonely here. I didn't think it was any harm to take her, because Jane gave her to me in her letter. But you have saved her life, Rosetta, and you — you can have her back, although it will break my heart to give her up. But, oh, Rosetta, won't you let me come and see her sometimes? I love her so I can't bear to give her up entirely."

"Charlotte," said Miss Rosetta firmly, "the most sensible thing for you to do is just to come back with the baby. You are worried to death trying to run this farm with the debt Jacob Wheeler left on it for you. Sell it, and come home with me. And we'll both have the baby then."

"Oh, Rosetta, I'd love to," faltered Charlotte. "I've — I've wanted to be good friends with you again so much. But I thought you were so hard and bitter you'd never make up."

"Maybe I've talked too much," conceded Miss Rosetta, "but you ought to know me well enough to know I didn't mean a word of it. It was your never saying anything, no matter what I said, that riled me up so bad. Let bygones be bygones, and come home, Charlotte."

"I will," said Charlotte resolutely, wiping away her tears. "I'm sick of living here and putting up with hired men. I'll be real glad to go home, Rosetta, and that's the truth. I've had a hard enough time. I s'pose you'll say I deserved it; but I was fond of Jacob, and —"

"Of course, of course. Why shouldn't you be?" said Miss Rosetta briskly. "I'm sure Jacob Wheeler was a good enough soul, if he was a little slack-twisted. I'd like to hear anybody say a word against him in my presence. Look at that blessed child, Charlotte. Isn't she the sweetest thing? I'm desperate glad you are coming back home, Charlotte. I've never been able to put up a decent mess of mustard pickles since you went away, and you were always such a hand with them! We'll be real snug and cozy again — you and me and little Camilla Barbara Jane."

V

THE DREAM-CHILD

A MAN's heart — aye, and a woman's, too — should be light in the spring. The spirit of resurrection is abroad, calling the life of the world out of its wintry grave, knocking with radiant fingers at the gates of its tomb. It stirs in human hearts, and makes them glad with the old primal gladness they felt in childhood. It quickens human souls, and brings them, if so they will, so close to God that they may clasp hands with Him. It is a time of wonder and renewed life, and a great outward and inward rapture, as of a young angel softly clapping his hands for creation's joy. At least, so it should be; and so it always had been with me until the spring when the dream-child first came into our lives.

That year I hated the spring — I, who had always loved it so. As boy I had loved it, and as man. All the happiness that had ever been mine, and it was much, had come to blossom in the spring. time. It was in the spring that Josephine and I had first loved each other, or, at least, had first come into the full knowledge that we loved. I think that we must have loved each other all our lives, and that each succeeding spring was a word in the revelation of that love, not to be understood until, in the fullness of time, the whole sentence was written out in that most beautiful of all beautiful springs.

How beautiful it was! And how beautiful she was! I suppose every lover thinks that of his lass; otherwise he is a poor sort of lover. But it was not only my eyes of love that made my dear so appealing and lovely.

She was slender as a reed and had the grace of a young doe. Her hair was dark and fluffy and framed her lovely face like a luminous halo, and her eyes were as blue as a cloudless sky on a perfect June day. She had long, black lashes and a tiny red mouth that trembled when she was glad or sad, or when she spoke of her love for me. And at such a time there was naught for me to do but kiss her.

The next spring we were married, and I brought her home to my gray old homestead on the gray old harbor shore. A lonely place for a young bride, said Avonlea people. Nay, it was not so. She was happy here, even in my absences. She loved the great, restless harbor and the vast, misty sea beyond; she loved the tides, keeping their world-old tryst with the shore, and the gulls, and the croon of the waves, and the call of the winds in the fir woods at noon and even; she loved the moonrises and the sunsets, and the clear, calm nights when the stars seemed to have fallen into the water and to be a little dizzy from such a fall.   She loved these things, even as I did.   No, she was never lonely here then.

The third spring came, and our boy was born. We thought we had been happy before; now we knew that we had only dreamed a pleasant dream of happiness, and had awakened to this exquisite reality. We had thought our love for each other was a thing perfect and complete.   But as I gazed upon my wife's face, pale and drawn from the pain and anguish she had endured, and looked into her deeply dark blue eyes, dewy with tears, yet reflecting the glow and happiness of motherhood, I realized that only now, with the birth of our son, had we come into love's ordained fulfillment.   And I thrilled to the joy and pride of parenthood.

"All my thoughts are poetry since baby came," my wife said once, rapturously.

Our boy lived for twenty months. He was a sturdy, toddling rogue, so full of life and laughter and mischief that, when he died, one day, after the illness of an hour, it seemed a most absurd thing that he should be dead — a thing I could have laughed at, until belief forced itself into my soul like a burning, searing iron.

I think I grieved over my little son's death as deeply and sincerely as ever man did, or could.   But the heart of the father is not as the heart of the mother.   Time brought no healing to Josephine; she fretted and pined; her cheeks lost their pretty oval, and her red mouth grew pale and drooping.

I hoped that spring might work its miracle upon her.   When the buds swelled, and the old earth grew green in the sun, and the gulls came back to the gray harbor, whose very grayness grew golden and mellow, I thought I should see her smile again. But, when the spring came, came the dream-child, and the fear that was to be my companion, at bed and board, from sunsetting to sunsetting.

One night I wakened from sleep, realizing in the moment of awakening that I was alone.   I listened to hear whether my wife were moving about the house.   I heard nothing but the little splash of waves on the shore below and the low moan of the distant ocean.

I rose and searched the house.   She was not in it.   I did not know where to seek her; but, at a venture, I started along the shore.

It was pale, fainting moonlight.   The harbor looked like a phantom harbor, and the night was as still and cold and calm as the face of a dead man. At last I saw my wife coming to me along the shore. When I saw her, I knew what I had feared and how great my fear had been.

As she drew near, I saw that she had been crying;

her face was stained with tears, and her dark hair hung loose over her shoulders in little, glossy ringlets like a child's. She seemed to be very tired, and at intervals she wrung her small hands together.

She showed no surprise when she met me, but only held out her hands to me as if glad to see me.

"I followed him — but I could not overtake him," she said with a sob. "I did my best — I hurried so; but he was always a little way ahead. And then I lost him — and so I came back. But I did my best — indeed I did. And oh, I am so tired!"

"Josie, dearest, what do you mean, and where have you been?" I said, drawing her close to me. "Why did you go out so — alone in the night?"

She looked at me wonderingly.

"How could I help it, David? He called me. I had to go."

"*Who* called you?"

"The child," she answered in a whisper. "Our child, David — our pretty boy. I awakened in the darkness and heard him calling to me down on the shore. Such a sad, little wailing cry, David, as if he were cold and lonely and wanted his mother. I hurried out to him, but I could not find him. I could only hear the call, and I followed it on and on, far down the shore. Oh, I tried so hard to overtake it, but I could not. Once I saw a little white hand beckoning to me far ahead in the moonlight. But still I could not go fast enough. And then the cry ceased, and I was there all alone on that terrible, cold, gray shore. I was so tired and I came home. But I wish I could have found him. Perhaps he does not know that I tried to. Perhaps he thinks his mother never listened to his call. Oh, I would not have him think that."

"You have had a bad dream, dear," I said. I tried to say it naturally; but it is hard for a man to speak naturally when he feels a mortal dread striking into his very vitals with its deadly chill.

"It was no dream," she answered reproachfully. "I tell you I heard him calling me — me, his mother. What could I do but go to him? You cannot understand — you are only his father. It was not you who gave him birth. It was not you who paid the price of his dear life in pain. He would not call to you — he wanted his mother."

I got her back to the house and to her bed, whither she went obediently enough, and soon fell into the sleep of exhaustion. But there was no more sleep for me that night. I kept a grim vigil with dread.

When I had married Josephine, one of those officious relatives that are apt to buzz about a man's marriage told me that her grandmother had been insane all the latter part of her life. She had grieved over the death of a favorite child until she lost her mind, and, as the first indication of it, she had sought by nights a white dream-child which always called her, so she said, and led her afar with a little, pale, beckoning hand.

I had smiled at the story then. What had that grim old bygone to do with springtime and love and Josephine? But it came back to me now, hand in hand with my fear. Was this fate coming on my dear wife? It was too horrible for belief. She was so young, so fair, so sweet, this girl-wife of mine. It had been only a bad dream, with a frightened, bewildered waking. So I tried to comfort myself.

When she awakened in the morning she did not speak of what had happened and I did not dare to. She seemed more cheerful that day than she had been, and went about her household duties briskly and skillfully. My fear lifted. I was sure now that she had only dreamed. And I was confirmed in my hopeful belief when two nights had passed away uneventfully.

Then, on the third night, the dream-child called to her again. I wakened from a troubled doze to find her dressing herself with feverish haste.

" He is calling me," she cried. " Oh, don't you hear him? Can't you hear him? Listen — listen — the little, lonely cry! Yes, yes, my precious, mother is coming. Wait for me. Mother is coming to her pretty boy! "

I caught her hand and let her lead me where she would. Hand in hand we followed the dream-child down the harbor shore in that ghostly, clouded moonlight. Ever, she said, the little cry sounded before her. She entreated the dream-child to wait for her; she cried and implored and uttered tender mother-talk. But, at last, she ceased to hear the cry; and then, weeping, wearied, she let me lead her home again.

What a horror brooded over that spring — that so beautiful spring! The time had come of lazy days, sunny blue skies, of the soft patter of sudden showers welcomed by the yet-to-be weeded soil; of daffodils and iris and violets; of orchards transformed into pink and white fairylands; of the murmuring of babbling brooks and the sweet song of birds. Yes, the delicious joys of spring were abroad in the land. Almost every night of this wonderful time the dream-child called his mother, and we roved the gray shore in quest of him.

In the day she was herself; but, when the night fell, she was restless and uneasy until she heard the call. Then follow it she would, even through storm and darkness. It was then, she said, that the cry sounded loudest and nearest, as if her pretty boy were frightened by the tempest. What wild, terrible rovings we had, she straining forward, eager to overtake the dream-child; I, sick at heart, following, guiding, protecting, as best I could; then afterwards leading her gently home, heart-broken because she could not reach the child.

I bore my burden in secret, determining that gossip should not busy itself with my wife's condition so long as I could keep it from becoming known. We had no near relatives — none with any right to share any trouble — and so I carried on alone, for grief is ever proud.

I thought, however, that I should have medical advice, and I took our old doctor into my confidence. He looked grave when he heard my story. I did not like his expression nor his few guarded remarks. He said he thought human aid would avail little; she might come all right in time; humor her, as far as possible, watch over her, protect her. He needed not to tell me *that*.

The spring went out and summer came in — and the horror deepened and darkened. I knew that suspicions were being whispered from lip to lip. We had been seen on our nightly quests. Men and women began to look at us pityingly when we went abroad.

One day, on a dull, drowsy afternoon, the dream-child called. I knew then that the end was near; the end had been near in the old grandmother's case sixty years before when the dream-child called in the day. The doctor looked graver than ever when

I told him, and said that the time had come when I must have help in my task. I could not watch by day and night. Unless I had assistance I would break down.

I did not think that I should. Love is stronger than that. And on one thing I was determined — they should never take my wife from me. No restraint sterner than a husband's loving hand should ever be put upon her, my pretty, piteous darling.

I never spoke of the dream-child to her. The doctor advised against it. It would, he said, only serve to deepen the delusion. When he hinted at an asylum I gave him a look that would have been a fierce word for another man. He never spoke of it again.

One night in August there was a dull, murky sunset after a dead, breathless day of heat, with not a wind stirring. The sea was not blue as a sea should be, but pink — all pink — a ghastly, staring, painted pink. I lingered on the harbor shore below the house until dark. The evening bells were ringing faintly and mournfully in a church across the harbor. Behind me, in the kitchen, I heard my wife singing. Sometimes now her spirits were fitfully high, and then she would sing the old songs of her girlhood. But even in her singing was something strange. as if a wailing, unearthly cry rang through it. Nothing about her was sadder than that strange singing.

When I went back to the house the rain was beginning to fall; but there was no wind or sound in the air — only that dismal stillness, as if the world were holding its breath in expectation of a calamity.

Josie was standing by the window, looking out and listening. I tried to induce her to go to bed, but she only shook her head.

"I might fall asleep and not hear him when he called," she said. "I am always afraid to sleep, now, for fear he should call and his mother fail to hear him."

Knowing it was of no use to entreat, I sat down by the table and tried to read. Three hours passed on. When the clock struck midnight she started up, with the wild light in her sunken blue eyes.

"He is calling," she cried, "calling out there in the storm. Yes, yes, sweet, I am coming!"

She opened the door and fled down the path to the shore. I snatched a lantern from the wall, lighted it, and followed. It was the blackest night I was ever out in, dark with the very darkness of death. The rain fell thickly and heavily. I overtook Josie, caught her hand, and stumbled along in her wake, for she went with the speed and recklessness of a distraught woman. We moved in the little flitting circle of light shed by the lantern. All around us and above us was a horrible, voiceless darkness, held, as it were, at bay by the friendly light.

"If I could only overtake him once," moaned Josie. "If I could just kiss him once, and hold him close against my aching heart. This pain, that never leaves me, would leave me then. Oh, my pretty boy, wait for mother! I am coming to you. Listen, David; he cries — he cries so pitifully; listen! Can't you hear it?"

I *did* hear it! Clear and distinct, out of the deadly still darkness before us, came a faint, wailing cry. What was it? Was I, too, going mad, or *was* there something out there — something that cried and moaned — longing for human love, yet ever retreating from human footsteps? I am not a superstitious man; but my nerve had been shaken by my long trial, and I was weaker than I thought. Terror took possession of me — terror unnameable. I trembled in every limb; clammy perspiration oozed from my forehead; I was possessed by a wild impulse to turn and flee — anywhere, away from that unearthly cry. But Josephine's cold hand gripped mine firmly, and led me on. That strange cry still rang in my ears. But it did not recede; it sounded clearer and stronger; it was a wail, but a loud, insistent wail; it was nearer — nearer; it was in the darkness just beyond us.

Then we came to it; a little dory had been beached

on the pebbles and left there by the receding tide. There was a child in it — a boy, of perhaps two years old, who crouched in the bottom of the dory in water to his waist, his big, blue eyes wild and wide with terror, his face white and tear-stained. He wailed again when he saw us, and held out his little hands.

My horror fell away from me like a discarded garment. *This* child was living. How he had come there, whence and why, I did not know and, in my state of mind, did not question. It was no cry of parted spirit I had heard — that was enough for me.

"Oh, the poor darling!" cried my wife.

She stooped over the dory and lifted the baby in her arms. His long, fair curls fell on her shoulder; she laid her face against his and wrapped her shawl around him.

"Let me carry him, dear," I said. "He is very wet, and too heavy for you."

"No, no, I must carry him. My arms have been so empty — they are full now. Oh, David, the pain at my heart has gone. He has come to me to take the place of my own. God has sent him to me out of the sea. He is wet and cold and tired. Hush, sweet one, we will go home."

Silently I followed her home. The wind was rising, coming in sudden, angry gusts; the storm was at hand, but we reached shelter before it broke.

Just as I shut our door behind us it smote the house with the roar of a baffled beast. I thanked God that we were not out in it, following the dream-child.

"You are very wet, Josie," I said. "Go and put on dry clothes at once."

"The child must be looked to first," she said firmly. "See how chilled and exhausted he is, the pretty dear. Light a fire quickly, David, while I get dry things for him."

I let her have her way. She brought out the clothes our own child had worn and dressed the waif in them, rubbing his chilled limbs, brushing his wet hair, laughing over him, mothering him. She seemed like her old self.

For my own part, I was bewildered. All the questions I had not asked before came crowding to my mind now. Whose child was this? Whence had he come? What was the meaning of it all?

He was a pretty baby, fair and plump and rosy. When he was dried and fed, he fell asleep in Josie's arms. She hung over him in a passion of delight. It was with difficulty I persuaded her to leave him long enough to change her wet clothes. She never asked whose he might be or from where he might have come. He had been sent to her from the sea; the dream-child had led her to him; that was what she believed, and I dared not throw any doubt on that belief. She slept that night with the baby on her arm, and in her sleep her face was the face of a girl in her youth, untroubled and unworn.

I expected that the morrow would bring some one seeking the baby. I had come to the conclusion that he must belong to the "Cove" across the harbor, where the fishing hamlet was; and all day, while Josie laughed and played with him, I waited and listened for the footsteps of those who would come seeking him. But they did not come. Day after day passed, and still they did not come.

I was in a maze of perplexity. What should I do? I shrank from the thought of the boy being taken away from us. Since we had found him the dream-child never had called. My wife seemed to have turned back from the dark borderland, where her feet had strayed, to walk again with me in our own homely paths. Day and night she was her old, bright self, happy and serene in the new motherhood that had come to her. The only thing strange in her was her calm acceptance of the event. She never wondered who or whose the child might be — never seemed to fear that he would be taken from her; and she gave him our dream-child's name.

At last, when a full week had passed, I went, in my bewilderment, to our old doctor.

"A most extraordinary thing," he said thoughtfully. "The child, as you say, must belong to the Spruce Cove people. Yet it is an almost unbelievable thing that there has been no search or inquiry after him. Probably there is some simple explanation of the mystery, however. I advise you to go over to the Cove and inquire. When you find the parents or guardians of the child, ask them to allow you to keep it for a time. It may prove your wife's salvation. I have known such cases. Evidently on that night the crisis of her mental disorder was reached. A little thing might have sufficed to turn her feet either way — back to reason and sanity, or into deeper darkness. It is my belief that the former has occurred, and that, if she is left in undisturbed possession of this child for a time, she will recover completely."

I drove around the harbor that day with a lighter heart than I had hoped ever to possess again. When I reached Spruce Cove the first person I met was old Abel Blair. I asked him if any child were missing from the Cove or along shore. He looked at me in surprise, shook his head, and said he had not heard of any. I told him as much of the tale as was necessary, leaving him to think that my wife and I had found the dory and its small passenger during an ordinary walk along the shore.

" A green dory!" he exclaimed. " Ben Forbes' old green dory has been missing for a week, but it was so rotten and leaky he didn't bother looking for it. But this child, sir — it beats me. What might he be like?"

I described the child as closely as possible.

"That fits little Harry Martin to a hair," said old Abel, perplexedly, "but, sir, it can't be. Or, if it is, there's been foul work somewhere. James Martin's wife died last winter, sir, and he died the next month. They left a baby and not much else. There weren't nobody to take the child but Jim's half-sister, Maggie Fleming. She lived here at the Cove, and, I'm sorry to say, sir, she hadn't too good a name. She didn't want to be bothered with the baby, and folks say she neglected him scandalous. Well, last spring she begun talking of going away to the States. She said a friend of hers had got her a good place in Boston, and she was going to go and take little Harry. We supposed it was all right. Last Saturday she went, sir. She was going to walk to the station, and the last seen of her she was trudging along the road, carrying the baby. It hasn't been thought of since. But, sir, d'ye suppose she set that innocent child adrift in that old leaky dory to send him to his death? I knew Maggie was no better than she should be, but I can't believe she was as bad as that."

"You must come over with me and see if you can identify the child," I said. "If he is Harry Martin I shall keep him. My wife has been very lonely since our baby died, and she has taken a fancy to this little chap."

When we reached my home old Abel recognized the child as Harry Martin.

He is with us still. His baby hands led my dear wife back to health and happiness. Other children have come to us, she loves them all dearly; but the boy who bears her dead son's name is to her — aye, and to me — as dear as if she had given him birth. He came from the sea, and at his coming the ghostly dream-child fled, nevermore to lure my wife away from me with its exciting cry. Therefore I look upon him and love him as my first-born.

VI

THE BROTHER WHO FAILED

THE Monroe family were holding a Christmas re-union at the old Prince Edward Island homestead at White Sands. It was the first time they had all been together under one roof since the death of their mother, thirty years before. The idea of this Christmas reunion had originated with Edith Monroe the preceding spring, during her tedious convalescence from a bad attack of pneumonia among strangers in an American city, where she had not been able to fill her concert engagements, and had more spare time in which to feel the tug of old ties and the homesick longing for her own people than she had had for years. As a result, when she recovered, she wrote to her second brother, James Monroe, who lived on the homestead; and the consequence was this gathering of the Monroes under the old roof-tree. Ralph Monroe for once laid aside the cares of his railroads, and the deceitfulness of his millions, in Toronto and took the long-promised, long-deferred trip to the homeland. Malcolm Monroe journeyed from the far western university of which he was president. Edith came, flushed with the triumph of her latest and most successful concert tour. Mrs. Woodburn, who had been Margaret Monroe, came from the Nova Scotia town where she lived a busy, happy life as the wife of a rising young lawyer. James, prosperous and hearty, greeted them warmly at the old homestead whose fertile acres had well repaid his skillful management.

They were a merry party, casting aside their cares and years, and harking back to joyous boyhood and girlhood once more. James had a family of rosy lads and lasses; Margaret brought her two blue-eyed little girls; Ralph's dark, clever-looking son accompanied him, and Malcolm brought his, a young man with a resolute face, in which there was less of boyishness than in his father's, and the eye of a keen, perhaps a hard bargainer. The two cousins were the same age to a day, and it was a family joke among the Monroes that the stork must have mixed the babies, since Ralph's son was like Malcolm in face and brain, while Malcolm's boy was a second edition of his Uncle Ralph.

To crown all, Aunt Isabel came, too — a talkative, clever, shrewd old lady, as young at eighty-five as she had been at thirty, thinking the Monroe stock the best in the world, and beamingly proud of her nephews and nieces, who had gone out from this humble, little farm to destinies of such brilliance and influence in the world beyond.

I have forgotten Robert.   Robert Monroe was apt to be forgotten.   Although he was the oldest of the family, White Sands people, in naming over the various members of the Monroe family, would add, " and Robert," in a tone of surprise over the remembrance of his existence.

He lived on a poor, sandy little farm down by the shore, but he had come up to James' place on the evening when the guests arrived; they had all greeted him warmly and joyously, and then did not think about him again in their laughter and conversation. Robert sat back in a corner and listened with a smile, but he never spoke.   Afterwards he had slipped noiselessly away and gone home, and nobody noticed his going.   They were all gayly busy recalling what had happened in the old times and telling what had happened in the new.

Edith recounted the successes of her concert tours; Malcolm expatiated proudly on his plans for developing his beloved college; Ralph described the country through which his new railroad ran, and the difficulties he had had to overcome in connection with it.   James, aside, discussed his orchard and his crops with Margaret, who had not been long enough away from the farm to lose touch with its interests. Aunt Isabel knitted and smiled complacently on all, talking now with one, now with the other, secretly quite proud of herself that she, an old woman of eighty-five, who had seldom been out of White Sands in her life, could discuss high finance with Ralph, and higher education with Malcolm, and hold her own with James in an argument on drainage.

The White Sands school teacher, an arch-eyed, red-mouthed bit of a girl — a Bell from Avonlea — who boarded with the James Monroes, amused herself with the boys. All were enjoying themselves hugely, so it is not to be wondered at that they did not miss Robert, who had gone home early because his old housekeeper was nervous if left alone at night.

He came again the next afternoon. From James, in the barnyard, he learned that Malcolm and Ralph had driven to the harbor, that Margaret and Mrs. James had gone to call on friends in Avonlea, and that Edith was walking somewhere in the woods on the hill. There was nobody in the house except Aunt Isabel and the teacher.

" You'd better wait and stay the evening," said James indifferently. " They'll all be back soon."

Robert went across the yard and sat down on the rustic bench in the angle of the front porch. It was a fine December evening, as mild as autumn; there had been no snow, and the long fields, sloping down from the homestead, were brown and mellow. A quiet hush, holding something of magic in it, rested like an unseen mantle on the dark forest, brooding field and the once flowering, fertile valley. The earth was like a tired old man patiently awaiting his well earned sleep. Out to sea, a dull, red sunset faded out into somber clouds, and the soft sound of the waves breaking on the shore was wafted on the evening breeze.

Robert rested his chin on his hand and looked across the vales and hills, where the feathery gray of leafless hardwoods was mingled with the sturdy, unfailing green of the conebearers. He was a tall, bent man, with thin, gray hair, a lined face, and deeply-set, gentle, brown eyes — the eyes of one who, looking through pain, sees rapture beyond.

He felt very happy. He loved his family clannishly, and he was rejoiced that they were all again near to him. He was proud of their success and fame. He was glad that James had prospered so well of late years. There was no canker of envy or discontent in his soul.

He heard absently indistinct voices at the open hall window above the porch, where Aunt Isabel was talking to Kathleen Bell. Presently Aunt Isabel moved nearer to the window, and her words came down to Robert with startling clearness.

" Yes, I can assure you, Miss Bell, that I'm real proud of my nephews and nieces. They're a smart family. They've almost all done well, and they hadn't any of them much to begin with. Ralph had absolutely nothing and to-day he is a millionaire. Their father met with so many losses, what with his ill-health and the bank failing, that he couldn't help them any. But they've all succeeded, except poor Robert — and I must admit that he's a total failure."

" Oh, no, no," said the little teacher deprecatingly.

" A total failure!" Aunt Isabel repeated her words emphatically. She was not going to be contradicted by anybody, least of all a Bell from Avonlea. " He has been a failure since the time he was born. He is the first Monroe to disgrace the old stock that way. I'm sure his brothers and sisters must be dreadfully ashamed of him. He has lived sixty years and he hasn't done a thing worth while. He can't even make his farm pay. If he's kept out of debt it's as much as he's ever managed to do."

" Some men can't even do that," murmured the little school teacher. She was really so much in awe of this imperious, clever old Aunt Isabel that it was positive heroism on her part to venture even this faint protest.

" More is expected of a Monroe," said Aunt Isabel majestically. " Robert Monroe is a failure, and that is the only name for him."

Robert Monroe stood up below the window in a dizzy, uncertain fashion. Aunt Isabel had been speaking of him! He, Robert, was a failure, a disgrace to his blood, of whom his nearest and dearest were ashamed! Yes, it was true; he had never realized it before; he had known that he could never win power or accumulate riches, but he had not thought that mattered much. Now, through Aunt Isabel's scornful eyes, he saw himself as the world saw him — as his brothers and sisters must see him. *There* lay the sting. What the world thought of him did not matter; but that his own should think him a failure and disgrace was agony. He moaned as he started to walk across the yard, only anxious to hide his pain and shame away from all human sight, and in his eyes was the look of a gentle animal which had been stricken by a cruel and unexpected blow.

Edith Monroe, who, unaware of Robert's proximity, had been standing at the other side of the porch, saw that look, as he hurried past her, unseeing. A moment before her dark eyes had been flashing with anger at Aunt Isabel's words; now the anger was drowned in a sudden rush of tears.

She took a quick step after Robert, but checked the impulse. Not then — and not by her alone — could that deadly hurt be healed. Nay, more, Robert must never suspect that she knew of any hurt. She stood and watched him through her tears as he went away across the low-lying shore fields to hide his broken heart under his own humble roof. She yearned to hurry after him and comfort him, but she knew that comfort was not what Robert needed now. Justice, and justice only, could pluck out the sting, which otherwise must rankle to the death.

Ralph and Malcolm were driving into the yard. Edith went over to them.

"Boys," she said resolutely, "I want to have a talk with you."

The Christmas dinner at the old homestead was a merry one. Mrs. James spread a feast that was fit for the halls of Lucullus. Laughter, jest, and repartee flew from lip to lip. Nobody appeared to notice that Robert ate little, said nothing, and sat with his form shrinking in his shabby "best" suit, his gray head bent even lower than usual, as if desirous of avoiding all observation. When the others spoke to him he answered deprecatingly, and shrank still further into himself.

Finally all had eaten all they could, and the remainder of the plum pudding was carried out. Robert gave a low sigh of relief. It was almost over. Soon he would be able to escape and hide himself and his shame away from the mirthful eyes of these men and women who had earned the right to laugh at the world in which their success gave them power and influence. He — he — only — was a failure.

He wondered impatiently why Mrs. James did not

rise. Mrs. James merely leaned comfortably back in her chair, with the righteous expression of one who has done her duty by her fellow creatures' palates, and looked at Malcolm.

Malcolm rose in his place. Silence fell on the company; everybody looked suddenly alert and expectant, except Robert. He still sat with bowed head, wrapped in his own bitterness.

" I have been told that I must lead off," said Malcolm, " because I am supposed to possess the gift of gab. But, if I do, I am not going to use it for any rhetorical effect to-day. Simple, earnest words must express the deepest feelings of the heart in doing justice to its own. Brothers and sisters, we meet to-day under our own roof-tree, surrounded by the benedictions of the past years. Perhaps invisible guests are here — the spirits of those who founded this home and whose work on earth has long been finished. It is not amiss to hope that this is so and our family circle made indeed complete. To each one of us who are here in visible bodily presence some measure of success has fallen; but only one of us has been supremely successful in the only things that really count — the things that count for eternity as well as time — sympathy and unselfishness and self-sacrifice.

" I shall tell you my own story for the benefit of those who have not heard it. When I was a lad of sixteen I started to work out my own education. Some of you will remember that old Mr. Blair of Avonlea offered me a place in his store for the summer, at wages which would go far towards paying my expenses at the county academy the next winter. I went to work, eager and hopeful. All summer I tried to do my faithful best for my employer. In September the blow fell. A sum of money was missing from Mr. Blair's till. I was suspected and discharged in disgrace. All my neighbors believed me guilty; even some of my own family looked upon me with suspicion — nor could I blame them, for the circumstantial evidence was strongly against me."

Ralph and James looked ashamed; Edith and Margaret, who had not been born at the time referred to, lifted their faces innocently. Robert did not move or glance up. He hardly seemed to be listening.

"I was crushed in an agony of shame and despair," continued Malcolm. "I believed my career was ruined. I was bent on casting all my ambitions behind me, and going west to some place where nobody knew me or my disgrace. But there was one person who believed in my innocence, who said to me, 'You shall not give up — you shall not behave as if you were guilty. You are innocent, and in time your innocence will be proved. Meanwhile show yourself a man. You have nearly enough money to pay your way next winter at the Academy. I have a little I

can give to help you out. Don't give in — never
give in when you have done no wrong.'

" I listened and took his advice. I went to the
Academy. My story was there as soon as I was,
and I found myself sneered at and shunned. Many
a time I would have given up in despair, had it not
been for the encouragement of my counselor. He
furnished the backbone for me. I was determined
that his belief in me should be justified. I studied
hard and came out at the head of my class. Then
there seemed to be no chance of my earning any
more money that summer. But a farmer at Newbridge, who cared nothing about the character of his
help, if he could get the work out of them, offered
to hire me. The prospect was distasteful but, urged
by the man who believed in me, I took the place and
endured the hardships. Another winter of lonely
work passed at the Academy. I won the Farrell
Scholarship the last year it was offered, and that
meant an Arts course for me. I went to Redmond
College. My story was not openly known there, but
something of it got abroad, enough to taint my life
there also with its suspicion. But the year I gradu-
ated, Mr. Blair's nephew, who, as you know, was the
real culprit, confessed his guilt, and I was cleared
before the world. Since then my career has been
what is called a brilliant one. But "—Malcolm
turned and laid his hand on Robert's thin shoulder —

" all my success I owe to my brother Robert.   It is his success — not mine — and here to-day, since we have agreed to say what is too often left to be said over a coffin lid, I thank him for all he did for me, and tell him that there is nothing I am more proud of and thankful for than such a brother."

Robert had looked up at last, amazed, bewildered, incredulous.   His face crimsoned as Malcolm sat down.   But now Ralph was getting up.

" I am no orator as Malcolm is," he quoted gayly, " but I've got a story to tell, too, which only one of you knows.   Forty years ago, when I started in life as a business man, money wasn't so plentiful with me as it may be to-day.   And I needed it badly.   A chance came my way to make a pile of it.   It wasn't a clean chance.   It was a dirty chance.   It looked square on the surface; but, underneath, it meant trickery and roguery.   I hadn't enough perception to see that, though — I was fool enough to think it was all right.   I told Robert what I meant to do.   And Robert saw clear through the outward sham to the real, hideous thing underneath.   He showed me what it meant and he gave me a preachment about a few Monroe Traditions of truth and honor.   I saw what I had been about to do as he saw it — as all good men and true must see it.   And I vowed then and there that I'd never go into anything that I wasn't sure was fair and square and clean through and through. I've kept that vow. I am a rich man, and not a dollar of my money is 'tainted' money. But I didn't make it. Robert really made every cent of my money. If it hadn't been for him I'd have been a poor man to-day, or behind prison bars, as are the other men who went into that deal when I backed out. I've got a son here. I hope he'll be as clever as his Uncle Malcolm; but I hope, still more earnestly, that he'll be as good and honorable a man as his Uncle Robert."

By this time Robert's head was bent again, and his face buried in his hands.

" My turn next," said James. " I haven't much to say — only this. After mother died I took typhoid fever. Here I was with no one to wait on me. Robert came and nursed me. He was the most faithful, tender, gentle nurse ever a man had. The doctor said Robert saved my life. I don't suppose any of the rest of us here can say we have saved a life."

Edith wiped away her tears and sprang up impulsively.

" Years ago," she said, " there was a poor, ambitious girl who had a voice. She wanted a musical education and her only apparent chance of obtaining it was to get a teacher's certificate and earn money enough to have her voice trained. She studied hard, but her brains, in mathematics at least, weren't as good as her voice, and the time was short. She failed.   She was lost in disappointment and despair, for that was the last year in which it was possible to obtain a teacher's certificate without attending Queen's Academy, and she could not afford that. Then her oldest brother came to her and told her he could spare enough money to send her to the conservatory of music in Halifax for a year.   He made her take it.   She never knew till long afterwards that he had sold the beautiful horse which he loved like a human creature, to get the money.   She went to the Halifax conservatory.   She won a musical scholarship.   She has had a happy life and a successful career.   And she owes it all to her brother Robert —"

But Edith could go no further.   Her voice failed her and she sat down in tears.   Margaret did not try to stand up.

"I was only five when my mother died," she sobbed.   "Robert was both father and mother to me.   Never had child or girl so wise and loving a guardian as he was to me.   I have never forgotten the lessons he taught me.   Whatever there is of good in my life or character I owe to him.   I was often headstrong and willful, but he never lost patience with me.   I owe everything to Robert."

Suddenly the little teacher rose with wet eyes and crimson cheeks.

"I have something to say, too," she said resolutely.

" You have spoken for yourselves. I speak for the people of White Sands. There is a man in this settlement whom everybody loves. I shall tell you some of the things he has done.

" Last fall, in an October storm, the harbor lighthouse flew a flag of distress. Only one man was brave enough to face the danger of sailing to the lighthouse to find out what the trouble was. That was Robert Monroe. He found the keeper alone with a broken leg; and he sailed back and made — yes, *made* the unwilling and terrified doctor go with him to the lighthouse. I saw him when he told the doctor he must go; and I tell you that no man living could have set his will against Robert Monroe's at that moment.

" Four years ago old Sarah Cooper was to be taken to the poorhouse. She was broken-hearted. One man took the poor, bed-ridden, fretful old creature into his home, paid for medical attendance, and waited on her himself, when his housekeeper couldn't endure her tantrums and temper. Sarah Cooper died two years afterwards, and her latest breath was a benediction on Robert Monroe — the best man God ever made.

" Eight years ago Jack Blewett wanted a place. Nobody would hire him, because his father was in the penitentiary, and some people thought Jack ought to be there, too. Robert Monroe hired him — and helped him, and kept him straight, and got him started right — and Jack Blewett is a hard-working, respected young man to-day, with every prospect of a useful and honorable life. There is hardly a man, woman, or child in White Sands who doesn't owe something to Robert Monroe!"

As Kathleen Bell sat down, Malcolm sprang up and held out his hands.

"Every one of us stand up and sing Auld Lang Syne," he cried.

Everybody stood up and joined hands, but one did not sing. Robert Monroe stood erect, with a great radiance on his face and in his eyes. His reproach had been taken away; for now his own people rose up as one to pay him honor and to call him blessed.

When the singing ceased Malcolm's stern-faced son reached over and shook Robert's hands.

"Uncle Rob," he said heartily, " I hope that when I'm sixty I'll be as successful a man as you."

"I guess," said Aunt Isabel, aside to the little school teacher, as she wiped the tears from her keen old eyes, " that there's a kind of failure that's the best success."

VII

THE RETURN OF HESTER

Just at dusk, that evening, I had gone upstairs and put on my muslin gown. I had been busy all day attending to the strawberry preserving — for Mary Sloane could not be trusted with that — and I was a little tired, and thought it was hardly worth while to change my dress, especially since there was nobody to see or care, since Hester was gone. Mary Sloane did not count.

But I did it because Hester would have cared if she had been here. She always liked to see me neat and dainty. So, although I was tired and sick at heart, I put on my pale blue muslin and dressed my hair.

At first I did my hair up in a way I had always liked; but had seldom worn, because Hester had disapproved of it. It became me; but I suddenly felt as if it were disloyal to her, so I took the puffs down again and arranged my hair in the plain, old-fashioned way she had liked. My hair, though it had a good many gray threads in it, was thick and long and brown still; but that did not matter — nothing mattered since Hester was dead and I had sent Hugh Blair away for the second time.

The Newbridge people all wondered why I had not put on mourning for Hester. I did not tell them it was because Hester had asked me not to. Hester had never approved of mourning; she said that if the heart did not mourn crape would not mend matters; and if it did there was no need of the external trappings of woe. She told me calmly, the night before she died, to go on wearing my pretty dresses just as I had always worn them, and to make no difference in my outward life because of her going.

"I know there will be a difference in your inward life," she said wistfully.

And oh, there was! But sometimes I wondered uneasily, feeling almost conscience-stricken, whether it were *wholly* because Hester had left me — whether it were not partly because, for a second time, I had shut the door of my heart in the face of love at her bidding.

When I had dressed I went downstairs to the front door, and sat on the sandstone steps under the arch of the Virginia creeper. I was all alone, for Mary Sloane had gone to Avonlea.

It was a beautiful night; the full moon was just rising over the wooded hills, and her light fell through the poplars into the garden before me. Through an open corner on the western side I saw the sky all silvery blue in the afterlight. The garden was very beautiful just then, for it was the time of the roses, and ours were all out — so many of them — great pink, and red, and white, and yellow roses.

Hester had loved roses and could never have enough of them. Her favorite bush was growing by the steps, all gloried over with blossoms — white, with pale pink hearts. I gathered a cluster and pinned it loosely on my breast. But my eyes filled as I did so — I felt so very, very desolate.

I was all alone, and it was bitter. The roses, much as I loved them, could not give me sufficient companionship. I wanted the clasp of a human hand, and the love-light in human eyes. And then I fell to thinking of Hugh, although I tried not to.

I had always lived alone with Hester. I did not remember our parents, who had died in my babyhood. Hester was fifteen years older than I, and she had always seemed more like a mother than a sister. She had been very good to me and had never denied me anything I wanted, save the one thing that mattered.

I was twenty-five before I ever had a lover. This was not, I think, because I was more unattractive than other women. The Merediths had always been the "big" family of Newbridge. The rest of the people looked up to us, because we were the granddaughters of old Squire Meredith. The Newbridge young men would have thought it no use to try to woo a Meredith.

I had not a great deal of family pride, as perhaps I should be ashamed to confess. I found our exalted position very lonely, and cared more for the simple joys of friendship and companionship which other girls had. But Hester possessed it in a double measure; she never allowed me to associate on a level of equality with the young people of Newbridge. We must be very nice and kind and affable to them — *noblesse oblige,* as it were — but we must never forget that we were Merediths.

When I was twenty-five, Hugh Blair came to Newbridge, having bought a farm near the village. He was a stranger, from Lower Carmody, and so was not imbued with any preconceptions of Meredith superiority. In his eyes I was just a girl like others — a girl to be wooed and won by any man of clean life and honest heart. I met him at a little Sunday-School picnic over at Avonlea, which I attended because of my class. I thought him very handsome and manly. He talked to me a great deal, and at last he drove me home. The next Sunday evening he walked up from church with me.

Hester was away, or, of course, this would never have happened. She had gone for a month's visit to distant friends.

In that month I lived a lifetime. Hugh Blair

courted me as the other girls in Newbridge were courted. He took me out driving and came to see me in the evenings, which we spent for the most part in the garden. I did not like the stately gloom and formality of our old Meredith parlor, and Hugh never seemed to feel at ease there. His broad shoulders and hearty laughter were oddly out of place among our faded, old-maidish furnishings.

Mary Sloane was very much pleased at Hugh's visit. She had always resented the fact that I had never had a "beau," seeming to think it reflected some slight or disparagement upon me. She did all she could to encourage him.

But when Hester returned and found out about Hugh she was very angry — and grieved, which hurt me far more. She told me that I had forgotten myself and that Hugh's visits must cease.

I had never been afraid of Hester before, but I was afraid of her then. I yielded. Perhaps it was very weak of me, but then I was always weak. I think that was why Hugh's strength had appealed so to me. I needed love and protection. Hester, strong and self-sufficient, had never felt such a need. She could not understand. Oh, how contemptuous she was.

I told Hugh timidly that Hester did not approve of our friendship and that it must end. He took it quietly enough, and went away. I thought he did not care much, and the thought selfishly made my own heartache worse. I was very unhappy for a long time, but I tried not to let Hester see it, and I don't think she did. She was not very discerning in some things.

After a time I got over it; that is, the heartache ceased to ache all the time. But things were never quite the same again. Life always seemed rather dreary and empty, in spite of Hester and my roses and my Sunday-School.

I supposed that Hugh Blair would find him a wife elsewhere, but he did not. The years went by and we never met, although I saw him often at church. At such times Hester always watched me very closely, but there was no need of her to do so. Hugh made no attempt to meet me, or speak with me, and I would not have permitted it if he had. But my heart always yearned after him. I was selfishly glad he had not married, because if he had I could not have thought and dreamed of him — it would have been wrong. Perhaps, as it was, it was foolish; but it seemed to me that I must have something, if only foolish dreams, to fill my life.

At first there was only pain in the thought of him, but afterwards a faint, misty little pleasure crept in, like a mirage from a land of lost delight.

Ten years slipped away thus. And then Hester died. Her illness was sudden and short; but, before she died, she asked me to promise that I would never marry Hugh Blair.

She had not mentioned his name for years. I thought she had forgotten all about him.

"Oh, dear sister, is there any need of such a promise?" I asked, weeping. "Hugh Blair does not want to marry me now. He never will again."

"He has never married — he has not forgotten you," she said fiercely. "I could not rest in my grave if I thought you would disgrace your family by marrying beneath you. Promise me, Margaret."

I promised. I would have promised anything in my power to make her dying pillow easier. Besides, what did it matter? I was sure that Hugh would never think of me again.

She smiled when she heard me, and pressed my hand.

"Good little sister — that is right. You were always a good girl, Margaret — good and obedient, though a little sentimental and foolish in some ways. You are like our mother — she was always weak and loving. I took after the Merediths."

She did, indeed. Even in her coffin her dark, handsome features preserved their expression of pride and determination. Somehow, that last look of her dead face remained in my memory, blotting out the real affection and gentleness which her living face had almost always shown me. This distressed me, but I could not help it. I wished to think of her as kind and loving, but I could remember only the pride and coldness with which she had crushed out my new-born happiness. Yet I felt no anger or resentment towards her for what she had done. I knew she had meant it for the best — my best. It was only that she was mistaken.

And then, a month after she had died, Hugh Blair came to me and asked me to be his wife. He said he had always loved me, and could never love any other woman.

All my old love for him reawakened. I wanted to say yes — to feel his strong arms about me, and the warmth of his love enfolding and guarding me. In my weakness I yearned for his strength.

But there was my promise to Hester — that promise given by her deathbed. I could not break it, and I told him so. It was the hardest thing I had ever done.

He did not go away quietly this time. He pleaded and reasoned and reproached. Every word of his hurt me like a knife-thrust. But I could not break my promise to the dead. If Hester had been living I would have braved her wrath and her estrangement and gone to him. But she was dead and I could not do it.

Finally he went away in grief and anger. That was three weeks ago — and now I sat alone in the moonlit rose-garden and wept for him.   But after a time my tears dried and a very strange feeling came over me.   I felt calm and happy, as if some wonderful love and tenderness were very near me.

And now comes the strange part of my story — the part which will not, I suppose, be believed.   If it were not for one thing I think I should hardly believe it myself.   I should feel tempted to think I had dreamed it.   But because of that one thing I know it was real.   The night was very calm and still.   Not a breath of wind stirred.   The moonshine was the brightest I had ever seen.   In the middle of the garden, where the shadow of the poplars did not fall, it was almost as bright as day.   One could have read fine print.   There was still a little rose glow in the west, and over the airy boughs of the tall poplars one or two large, bright stars were shining.   The air was sweet with a hush of dreams, and the world was so lovely that I held my breath over its beauty.

Then, all at once, down at the far end of the garden, I saw a woman walking.   I thought at first that it must be Mary Sloane; but, as she crossed a moonlit path, I saw it was not our old servant's stout, homely figure.   This woman was tall and erect.

Although no suspicion of the truth came to me, something about her reminded me of Hester.   Even so had Hester liked to wander about the garden in the twilight.   I had seen her thus a thousand times.

I wondered who the woman could be. Some neighbor, of course. But what a strange way for her to come! She walked up the garden slowly in the poplar shade. Now and then she stooped, as if to caress a flower, but she plucked none. Half way up she came out into the moonlight and walked across the plot of grass in the center of the garden. My heart gave a great throb and I stood up. She was quite near to me now — and I saw that it was Hester.

I can hardly say just what my feelings were at this moment. I know that I was not surprised. I was frightened and yet I was not frightened. Something in me shrank back in a sickening terror; but *I*, the real I, was not frightened. I knew that this was my sister, and that there could be no reason why I should be frightened of her, because she loved me still, as she had always done. Further than this I was not conscious of any coherent thought, either of wonder or attempt at reasoning.

Hester paused when she came to within a few steps of me. In the moonlight I saw her face quite plainly. It wore an expression I had never before seen on it — a humble, wistful, tender look. Often in life Hester had looked lovingly, even tenderly, upon me; but always, as it were, through a mask of pride and sternness. This was gone now, and I felt nearer to her than ever before. I knew suddenly that she understood me. And then the half-conscious awe and terror some part of me had felt vanished, and I only realized that Hester was here, and that there was no terrible gulf of change between us.

Hester beckoned to me and said,

" Come."

I stood up and followed her out of the garden. We walked side by side down our lane, under the willows and out to the road, which lay long and still in that bright, calm moonshine. I felt as if I were in a dream, moving at the bidding of a will not my own, which I could not have disputed even if I had wished to do so. But I did not wish it; I had only the feeling of a strange, boundless content.

We went down the road between the growths of young fir that bordered it. I smelled their balsam as we passed, and noticed how clearly and darkly their pointed tops came out against the sky. I heard the tread of my own feet on little twigs and plants in our way, and the trail of my dress over the grass; but Hester moved noiselessly.

Then we went through the Avenue — that stretch of road under the apple trees that Anne Shirley, over at Avonlea, calls " The White Way of Delight." It was almost dark here; and yet I could see Hester's face just as plainly as if the moon were shining on t; and whenever I looked at her she was always look-

ing at me with that strangely gentle smile on her
lips.

Just as we passed out of the Avenue, James Trent
overtook us, driving. It seems to me that our feelings at a given moment are seldom what we would
expect them to be. I simply felt annoyed that
James Trent, the most notorious gossip in Newbridge, should have seen me walking with Hester.
In a flash I anticipated all the annoyance of it; he
would talk of the matter far and wide.

But James Trent merely nodded and called out,
" Howdy, Miss Margaret. Taking a moonlight
stroll by yourself? Lovely night, ain't it?"

Just then his horse suddenly swerved, as if
startled, and broke into a gallop. They whirled
around the curve of the road in an instant. I felt
relieved, but puzzled. *James Trent had not seen
Hester.*

Down over the hill was Hugh Blair's place.
When we came to it, Hester turned in at the gate.
Then, for the first time, I understood why she had
come back, and a blinding flash of joy broke over my
soul. I stopped and looked at her. Her deep eyes
gazed into mine, but she did not speak.

We went on. Hugh's house lay before us in the
moonlight, grown over by a tangle of vines. His
garden was on our right, a quaint spot, full of old-
fashioned flowers growing in a sort of disorderly

sweetness.   I trod on a bed of mint, and the spice of it floated up to me like the incense of some strange, sacred, solemn ceremonial.   I felt unspeakably happy and blessed.

When we came to the door Hester said,

" Knock, Margaret."

I rapped gently.   In a moment Hugh opened it. Then that happened by which, in after days, I was to know that this strange thing was no dream or fancy of mine.   Hugh looked not at me, but past me.

" Hester ! " he exclaimed, with human fear and horror in his voice.

He leaned against the door-post, the big, strong fellow, trembling from head to foot.

" I have learned," said Hester, " that nothing matters in all God's universe, except love.   There is no pride where I have been and no false ideals."

Hugh and I looked into each other's eyes, wondering, and then we knew that we were alone.

VIII

THE LITTLE BROWN BOOK OF MISS EMILY

THE first summer Mr. Irving and Miss Lavendar — Diana and I could never call her anything else, even after she was married — were at Echo Lodge after their marriage, both Diana and I spent a great deal of time with them. We became acquainted with many of the Grafton people whom we had not known before, and, among others, the family of Mr. Mack Leith. We often went up to the Leiths in the evening to play croquet. Millie and Margaret Leith were very nice girls, and the boys were nice, too. Indeed, we liked every one in the family, except poor old Miss Emily Leith. We tried hard enough to like her, because she seemed to like Diana and me very much, and always wanted to sit with us and talk to us, when we would much rather have been somewhere else. We often felt a good deal of impatience at these times, but I am very glad to think now that we never showed it.

In a way, we felt sorry for Miss Emily. She was Mr. Leith's old-maid sister and she was not of much importance in the household. But, though we felt sorry for her, we couldn't like her. She really was fussy and meddlesome; she liked to poke a finger into every one's pie, and she was not at all tactful. Then, too, she had a sarcastic tongue, and seemed to feel bitter towards all the young folks and their love affairs. Diana and I thought this was because she had never had a lover of her own.

Somehow, it seemed impossible to think of lovers in connection with Miss Emily. She was short and stout and pudgy, with a face so round and fat and red that it seemed quite featureless; and her hair was scanty and gray. She walked with a waddle, just like Mrs. Rachel Lynde, and she was always rather short of breath. It was hard to believe Miss Emily had ever been young; yet old Mr. Murray, who lived next door to the Leiths, not only expected us to believe it, but assured us that she had been very pretty.

"*That*, at least, is impossible," said Diana to me.

And then, one day, Miss Emily died. I'm afraid no one was very sorry. It seems to me a most dreadful thing to go out of the world and leave not one person behind to be sorry because you have gone. Miss Emily was dead and buried before Diana and I heard of it at all. The first I knew of it was when I came home from Orchard Slope one day and found a queer, shabby little black horsehair trunk, all studded with brass nails, on the floor of my room at Green Gables. Marilla told me that Jack Leith had brought it over, and said that it had belonged to Miss Emily and that, when she was dying, she asked them to send it to me.

"But what is in it? And what am I to do with it?" I asked in bewilderment.

"There was nothing said about what you were to do with it. Jack said they didn't know what was in it, and hadn't looked into it, seeing that it was your property. It seems a rather queer proceeding — but you're always getting mixed up in queer proceedings, Anne. As for what is in it, the easiest way to find out, I reckon, is to open it and see. The key is tied to it. Jack said Miss Emily said she wanted you to have it because she loved you and saw her lost youth in you. I guess she was a bit delirious at the last and wandered a good deal. She said she wanted you 'to understand her.'"

I ran over to Orchard Slope and asked Diana to come over and examine the trunk with me. I hadn't received any instructions about keeping its contents secret and I knew Miss Emily wouldn't mind Diana knowing about them, whatever they were.

It was a cool, gray afternoon and we got back to Green Gables just as the rain was beginning to fall. When we went up to my room the wind was rising and whistling through the boughs of the big old Snow Queen outside of my window. Diana was excited, and, I really believe, a little bit frightened.

We opened the old trunk.   It was very small, and there was nothing in it but a big cardboard box. The box was tied up and the knots sealed with wax. We lifted it out and untied it.   I touched Diana's fingers as we did it, and both of us exclaimed at once, " How cold your hand is ! "

In the box was a quaint, pretty, old-fashioned gown, not at all faded, made of blue muslin, with a little darker blue flower in it.   Under it we found a sash, a yellowed feather fan, and an envelope full of withered flowers.   At the bottom of the box was a little brown book.

It was small and thin, like a girl's exercise book, with leaves that had once been blue and pink, but were now quite faded, and stained in places.   On the fly leaf was written, in a very delicate hand, " Emily Margaret Leith," and the same writing covered the first few pages of the book.   The rest were not written on at all.   We sat there on the floor, Diana and I, and read the little book together, while the rain thudded against the window panes.

June 19, 18—

I came to-day to spend a while with Aunt Margaret in Charlottetown.   It is so pretty here, where she lives — and ever so much nicer than on the farm at home.   I have no cows to milk here or pigs to feed.   Aunt Margaret has given me such a lovely blue muslin dress, and I am to have it made to wear at a garden party out at Brighton next week.   I never had a muslin dress before — nothing but ugly prints and dark woolens. I wish we were rich, like Aunt Margaret. Aunt Margaret laughed when I said this, and declared she would give all her wealth for my youth and beauty and light-heartedness. I am only eighteen and I know I am very merry but I wonder if I am really pretty. It seems to me that I am when I look in Aunt Margaret's beautiful mirrors. They make me look very different from the old cracked one in my room at home which always twisted my face and turned me green. But Aunt Margaret spoiled her compliment by telling me I look exactly as she did at my age. If I thought I'd ever look as Aunt Margaret does now, I don't know what I'd do. She is so fat and red.

June 29.

Last week I went to the garden party and I met a young man called Paul Osborne. He is a young artist from Montreal who is boarding over at Heppoch. He is the handsomest man I have ever seen — very tall and slender, with dreamy, dark eyes and a pale, clever face. I have not been able to keep from thinking about him ever since, and to-day he came over here and asked if he could paint me. I felt very much flattered and so pleased when Aunt Margaret gave him permission. He says he wants to paint me as " Spring," standing under the poplars where a fine rain of sunshine falls through. I am o wear my blue muslin gown and a wreath of flowers on my hair. He says I have such beautiful hair. He has never seen any of such a real pale gold. Somehow it seems prettier than ever to me since he praised it.

I had a letter from home to-day. Ma says the blue hen stole her nest and came off with fourteen chickens, and that pa has sold the little spotted calf. Somehow those things don't interest me like they once did.

July 9.

The picture is coming on very well, Mr. Osborne says. I know he is making me look far too pretty in it, although he persists in saying he can't do me justice. He is going to send it to some great exhibition when finished, but he says he will make a little water-color copy for me.

He comes over every day to paint and we talk a great deal and he reads me lovely things out of his books. I don't understand them all, but I try to, and he explains them so nicely and is so patient with my stupidity. And he says any one with my eyes and hair and coloring does not need to be clever. He says I have the sweetest, merriest laugh in the world. But I will not write down all the compliments he has paid me. I dare say he does not mean them at all.

In the evening we stroll among the spruces or sit on the bench under the acacia tree. Sometimes we don't talk at all, but I never find the time long. Indeed, the minutes just seem to fly — and then the moon will come up, round and red, over the harbor and Mr. Osborne will sigh and say he supposes it is time for him to go.

July 24.

I am so happy. I am frightened at my happiness. Oh, I didn't think life could ever be so beautiful for me as it is!

Paul loves me! He told me so to-night as we walked by the harbor and watched the sunset, and he asked me to be his wife. I have cared for him ever since I met him, but I am afraid I am not clever and well-educated enough for a wife for Paul. Because, of course, I'm only an ignorant little country girl and have lived all my life on a farm. Why, my hands are quite rough yet from the work I've done. But Paul just laughed when I said so, and took my hands and kissed them. Then he looked into my eyes and laughed again, because I couldn't hide from him how much I loved him.

We are to be married next spring and Paul says he will take me to Europe. That will be very nice, but nothing matters so long as I am with him.

Paul's people are very wealthy and his mother and sisters are very fashionable. I am frightened of them, but I did not tell Paul so because I think it would hurt him and oh, I wouldn't do that for the world.

There is nothing I wouldn't suffer if it would do him any good. I never thought any one could feel so. I used to think if I loved anybody I would want him to do everything for me and wait on me as if I were a princess. But that is not the way at all. Love makes you very humble and you want to do everything yourself for the one you love.

August 10.

Paul went home to-day. Oh, it is so terrible! I don't know how I can bear to live even for a little while without him. But this is silly of me, because I know he has to go and he will write often and come to me often. But, still, it is so lonesome. I didn't cry when he left me because I wanted him to remember me smiling in the way he liked best, but I have been crying ever since and I can't stop, no matter how hard I try. We have had such a beautiful fortnight. Every day seemed dearer and happier than the last, and now it is ended and I feel as if it could never be the same again. Oh, I am very foolish —

but I love him so dearly and if I were to lose his love I know I would die.

August 17.

I think my heart is dead.   But no, it can't be, for it aches too much.

Paul's mother came here to see me to-day.   She was not angry or disagreeable.   I wouldn't have been so frightened of her if she had been.   As it was, I felt that I couldn't say a word.   She is very beautiful and stately and wonderful, with a low, cold voice and proud, dark eyes.   Her face is like Paul's but without the lovableness of his.

She talked to me for a long time and she said terrible things — terrible, because I knew they were all true.   I seemed to see everything through her eyes. She said that Paul was infatuated with my youth and beauty but that it would not last and what else had I to give him?   She said Paul must marry a woman of his own class, who could do honor to his fame and position.   She said that he was very talented and had a great career before him, but that if he married me it would ruin his life.

I saw it all, just as she explained it out, and I told her at last that I would not marry Paul, and she might tell him so.   But she smiled and said I must tell him myself, because he would not believe any one else.   I could have begged her to spare me that, but I knew it would be of no use.   I do not think she has any pity or mercy for any one.   Besides, what she said was quite true.

When she thanked me for being so *reasonable* I told her I was not doing it to please her, but for Paul's sake, because I would not spoil his life, and that I would always hate her.   She smiled again and went away.

Oh, how can I bear it? I did not know any one could suffer like this!

August 18.

I have done it. I wrote to Paul to-day. I knew I must tell him by letter, because I could never make him believe it face to face. I was afraid I could not even do it by letter. I suppose a clever woman easily could, but I am so stupid. I wrote a great many letters and tore them up, because I felt sure they wouldn't convince Paul. At last I got one that I thought would do. I knew I must make it seem as if I were very frivolous and heartless, or he would never believe. I spelled some words wrong and put in some mistakes of grammar on purpose. I told him I had just been flirting with him, and that I had another fellow at home I liked better. I said *fellow* because I knew it would disgust him. I said that it was only because he was rich that I was tempted to marry him.

I thought my heart would break while I was writing those dreadful falsehoods. But it was for his sake, because I must not spoil his life. His mother told me I would be a millstone around his neck. I love Paul so much that I would do anything rather than be that. It would be easy to die for him, but I don't see how I can go on living. I think my letter will convince Paul.

I suppose it convinced Paul, because there was no further entry in the little brown book. When we had finished it the tears were running down both our faces.

"Oh, poor, dear Miss Emily," sobbed Diana.

" I'm so sorry I ever thought her funny and meddlesome."

" She was good and strong and brave," I said. " I could never have been as unselfish as she was."

And I thought of Whittier's lines,

> "The outward, wayward life we see
> The hidden springs we may not know."

At the back of the little brown book we found a faded water-color sketch of a young girl — such a slim, pretty little thing, with big blue eyes and lovely, long, rippling, golden hair.   Paul Osborne's name was written in faded ink across the corner.

We put everything back in the box.   Then we sat for a long time by my window in silence and thought of many things, until the rainy twilight came down and blotted out the world.

IX

SARA'S WAY

THE warm June sunshine was coming down through the trees, white with the virginal bloom of apple-blossoms, and through the shining panes, making a tremulous mosaic upon Mrs. Eben Andrews' spotless kitchen floor. Through the open door, a wind, fragrant from long wanderings over orchards and clover meadows, drifted in, and, from the window, Mrs. Eben and her guest could look down over a long, misty valley sloping to a sparkling sea.

Mrs. Jonas Andrews was spending the afternoon with her sister-in-law. She was a big, sonsy woman, with full-blown peony cheeks and large, dreamy, brown eyes. When she had been a slim, pink-and-white girl those eyes had been very romantic. Now they were so out of keeping with the rest of her appearance as to be ludicrous.

Mrs. Eben, sitting at the other end of the small tea-table that was drawn up against the window, was a thin little woman, with a very sharp nose and light, faded blue eyes. She looked like a woman whose opinions were always very decided and warranted to wear.

146

"How does Sara like teaching at Newbridge?" asked Mrs. Jonas, helping herself a second time to Mrs. Eben's matchless black fruit cake, and thereby bestowing a subtle compliment which Mrs. Eben did not fail to appreciate.

"Well, I guess she likes it pretty well — better than down at White Sands, anyway," answered Mrs. Eben. "Yes, I may say it suits her. Of course it's a long walk there and back. I think it would have been wiser for her to keep on boarding at Morrison's, as she did all winter, but Sara is bound to be home all she can. And I must say the walk seems to agree with her."

"I was down to see Jonas' aunt at Newbridge last night," said Mrs. Jonas, "and she said she'd heard that Sara had made up her mind to take Lige Baxter at last, and that they were to be married in the fall. She asked me if it was true. I said I didn't know, but I hoped to mercy it was. Now, is it, Louisa?"

"Not a word of it," said Mrs. Eben sorrowfully. "Sara hasn't any more notion of taking Lige than ever she had. I'm sure it's not *my* fault. I've talked and argued till I'm tired. I declare to you, Amelia, I am terribly disappointed. I'd set my heart on Sara's marrying Lige — and now to think she won't!"

"She is a very foolish girl," said Mrs. Jonas,

judicially. " If Lige Baxter isn't good enough for her, who is? "

" And he's so well off," said Mrs. Eben, " and does such a good business, and is well spoken of by every one. And that lovely new house of his at Newbridge, with bay windows and hardwood floors! I've dreamed and dreamed of seeing Sara there as mistress."

" Maybe you'll see her there yet," said Mrs. Jonas, who always took a hopeful view of everything, even of Sara's contrariness. But she felt discouraged, too. Well, she had done her best.

If Lige Baxter's broth was spoiled it was not for lack of cooks. Every Andrews in Avonlea had been trying for two years to bring about a match between him and Sara, and Mrs. Jonas had borne her part valiantly.

Mrs. Eben's despondent reply was cut short by the appearance of Sara herself. The girl stood for a moment in the doorway and looked with a faintly amused air at her aunts. She knew quite well that they had been discussing her, for Mrs. Jonas, who carried her conscience in her face, looked guilty, and Mrs. Eben had not been able wholly to banish her aggrieved expression.

Sara put away her books, kissed Mrs. Jonas' rosy cheek, and sat down at the table. Mrs. Eben brought her some fresh tea, some hot rolls, and a little jelly-pot of the apricot preserves Sara liked, and she cut some more fruit cake for her in moist plummy slices. She might be out of patience with Sara's "contrariness," but she spoiled and petted her for all that, for the girl was the very core of her childless heart.

Sara Andrews was not, strictly speaking, pretty; but there was that about her which made people look at her twice. She was very dark, with a rich, dusky sort of darkness, her deep eyes were velvety brown, and her lips and cheeks were crimson.

She ate her rolls and preserves with a healthy appetite, sharpened by her long walk from New-bridge, and told amusing little stories of her day's work that made the two older women shake with laughter, and exchange shy glances of pride over her cleverness.

When tea was over she poured the remaining contents of the cream jug into a saucer.

"I must feed my pussy," she said as she left the room.

"That girl beats me," said Mrs. Eben with a sigh of perplexity. "You know that black cat we've had for two years? Eben and I have always made a lot of him, but Sara seemed to have a dislike to him. Never a peaceful nap under the stove could he have when Sara was home — out he must go. Well, a little spell ago he got his leg broke accidentally and we thought he'd have to be killed. But Sara wouldn't hear of it. She got splints and set his leg just as knacky, and bandaged it up, and she has tended him like a sick baby ever since. He's just about well now, and he lives in clover, that cat does. It's just her way. There's them sick chickens she's been doctoring for a week, giving them pills and things!

"And she thinks more of that wretched-looking calf that got poisoned with paris green than of all the other stock on the place."

As the summer wore away Mrs. Eben tried to reconcile herself to the destruction of her air castles. But she scolded Sara considerably.

"Sara, why don't you like Lige? I'm sure he is a model young man."

"I don't like model young men," answered Sara impatiently. "And I really think I hate Lige Baxter. He has always been held up to me as such a paragon. I'm tired of hearing about all his perfections. I know them all off by heart. He doesn't drink, he doesn't smoke, he doesn't steal, he doesn't tell fibs, he never loses his temper, he doesn't swear, and he goes to church regularly. Such a faultless creature as that would certainly get on my nerves. No, no, you'll have to pick out another mistress for your new house at the Bridge, Aunt Louisa."

When the apple trees, that had been pink and white in June, were russet and bronze in October, Mrs. Eben had a quilting. The quilt was of the " Rising Star " pattern, which was considered in Avonlea to be very handsome. Mrs. Eben had intended it for part of Sara's " setting out," and, while she sewed the red-and-white diamonds together, she had regaled her fancy by imagining she saw it spread out on the spare-room bed of the house at Newbridge, with herself laying her bonnet and shawl on it when she went to see Sara. Those bright visions had faded with the apple blossoms, and Mrs. Eben hardly had the heart to finish the quilt at all.

The quilting came off on Saturday afternoon, when Sara could be home from school. All Mrs. Eben's particular friends were ranged around the quilt, and tongues and fingers flew. Sara flitted about, helping her aunt with the supper preparations. She was in the room, getting the custard dishes out of the cupboard, when Mrs. George Pye arrived.

Mrs. George had a genius for being late. She was later than usual to-day, and she looked excited. Every woman around the " Rising Star " felt that Mrs. George had some news worth listening to, and there was an expectant silence while she pulled out her chair and settled herself at the quilt.

She was a tall, thin woman, with a long pale face and liquid green eyes. As she looked around the circle she had the air of a cat daintily licking its chops over some titbit.

" I suppose," she said, " that you have heard the news? "

She knew perfectly well that they had not. Every other woman at the frame stopped quilting. Mrs. Eben came to the door with a pan of puffy, smoking-hot soda biscuits in her hand. Sara stopped counting her custard dishes, and turned her ripely-colored face over her shoulder. Even the black cat, at her feet, ceased preening his fur. Mrs. George felt that the undivided attention of her audience was hers.

" Baxter Brothers have failed," she said, her green eyes shooting out flashes of light. " Failed *disgracefully!* "

She paused for a moment; but, since her hearers were as yet speechless from surprise, she went on.

" George came home from Newbridge, just before I left, with the news. You could have knocked me down with a feather. I should have thought that firm was as steady as the rock of Gibraltar! But they're ruined — absolutely ruined. Louisa, dear, can you find me a good needle? "

" Louisa, dear," had set her biscuits down with a sharp thud, reckless of results. A sharp, metallic tinkle sounded at the closet where Sara had struck the edge of her tray against a shelf. The sound seemed to loosen the paralyzed tongues, and everybody began talking and exclaiming at once. Clear and shrill above the confusion rose Mrs. George Pye's voice.

"Yes, indeed, you may well say so. It *is* disgraceful. And to think how everybody trusted them! George will lose considerable by the crash, and so will a good many folks. Everything will have to go — Peter Baxter's farm and Lige's grand new house. Mrs. Peter won't carry her head so high after this, I'll be bound. George saw Lige at the Bridge, and he said he looked dreadful cut up and ashamed."

" Who, or what's to blame for the failure? " asked Mrs. Rachel Lynde sharply. She did not like Mrs. George Pye.

" There are a dozen different stories on the go," was the reply. " As far as George could make out, Peter Baxter has been speculating with other folks' money, and this is the result. Everybody always suspected that Peter was crooked; but you'd have thought that Lige would have kept him straight. *He* had always such a reputation for saintliness."

" I don't suppose Lige knew anything about it," said Mrs. Rachel indignantly.

" Well, he'd ought to, then. If he isn't a knave he's a fool," said Mrs. Harmon Andrews, who had formerly been among his warmest partisans. " He should have kept watch on Peter and found out how the business was being run. Well, Sara, you were the level-headest of us all — I'll admit that now. A nice mess it would be if you were married or engaged to Lige, and him left without a cent — even if he can clear his character!"

" There is a good deal of talk about Peter, and swindling, and a lawsuit," said Mrs. George Pye, quilting industriously. " Most of the Newbridge folks think it's all Peter's fault, and that Lige isn't to blame. But you can't tell. I dare say Lige is as deep in the mire as Peter. He was always a little too good to be wholesome, *I* thought."

There was a clink of glass at the cupboard, as Sara set the tray down. She came forward and stood behind Mrs. Rachel Lynde's chair, resting her shapely hands on that lady's broad shoulders. Her face was very pale, but her flashing eyes sought and faced defiantly Mrs. George Pye's cat-like orbs. Her voice quivered with passion and contempt.

" You'll all have a fling at Lige Baxter, now that he's down. You couldn't say enough in his praise, once. I'll not stand by and hear it hinted that Lige Baxter is a swindler. You all know perfectly well that Lige is as honest as the day, if he *is* so unfortunate as to have an unprincipled brother. You, Mrs. Pye, know it better than any one, yet you come here and run him down the minute he's in trouble. If there's another word said here against Lige Baxter I'll leave the room and the house till you're gone, every one of you."

She flashed a glance around the quilt that cowed the gossips. Even Mrs. George Pye's eyes flickered and waned and quailed. Nothing more was said until Sara had picked up her glasses and marched from the room. Even then they dared not speak above a whisper. Mrs. Pye, alone, smarting from her snub, ventured to ejaculate, " Pity save us! " as Sara slammed the door.

For the next fortnight gossip and rumor held high carnival in Avonlea and Newbridge, and Mrs. Eben grew to dread the sight of a visitor.

" They're bound to talk about the Baxter failure and criticize Lige," she deplored to Mrs. Jonas. " And it riles Sara up so terrible. She used to declare that she hated Lige, and now she won't listen to a word against him. Not that I say any, myself. I'm sorry for him, and I believe he's done his best. But I can't stop other people from talking."

One evening Harmon Andrews came in with a fresh budget of news.

" The Baxter business is pretty near wound up at last," he said, as he lighted his pipe. " Peter has got his lawsuits settled and has hushed up the talk about swindling, somehow. Trust him for slipping out of a scrape clean and clever. He don't seem to worry any, but Lige looks like a walking skeleton. Some folks pity him, but I say he should have kept the run of things better and not have trusted everything to Peter. I hear he's going out West in the Spring, to take up land in Alberta and try his hand at farming. Best thing he can do, I guess. Folks hereabouts have had enough of the Baxter breed. Newbridge will be well rid of them."

Sara, who had been sitting in the dark corner by the stove, suddenly stood up, letting the black cat slip from her lap to the floor. Mrs. Eben glanced at her apprehensively, for she was afraid the girl was going to break out into a tirade against the complacent Harmon.

But Sara only walked fiercely out of the kitchen, with a sound as if she were struggling for breath. In the hall she snatched a scarf from the wall, flung open the front door, and rushed down the lane in the chill, pure air of the autumn twilight. Her heart was throbbing with the pity she always felt for bruised and baited creatures.

On and on she went heedlessly, intent only on walking away her pain, over gray, brooding fields and winding slopes, and along the skirts of ruinous, dusky pine woods, shrouded in a haze of bluish purple. Her dress brushed against the brittle grasses and sere ferns, and the moist night wind, loosed from wild places far away, blew her hair about her face.

At last she came to a little rustic gate, leading into a shadowy wood-lane. The gate was bound with willow withes, and, as Sara fumbled vainly at them with her chilled hands, a man's firm step came up behind her, and Lige Baxter's hand closed over her's.

"Oh, Lige!" she said, with something like a sob.

He opened the gate and drew her through. She left her hand in his, as they walked through the lane where lissome boughs of young saplings flicked against their heads, and the air was wildly sweet with the woodsy odors.

"It's a long while since I've seen you, Lige," Sara said at last.

Lige looked wistfully down at her through the gloom.

"Yes, it seems very long to me, Sara. But I didn't think you'd care to see me, after what you said last spring. And you know things have been going against me. People have said hard things. I've been unfortunate, Sara, and may be too easy-going, but I've been honest. Don't believe folks if they tell you I wasn't."

"Indeed, I never did — not for a minute!" fired Sara.

"I'm glad of that. I'm going away, later on. I

felt bad enough when you refused to marry me, Sara; but it's well that you didn't. I'm man enough to be thankful my troubles don't fall on you."

Sara stopped and turned to him. Beyond them the lane opened into a field and a clear lake of crocus sky cast a dim light into the shadow where they stood. Above it was a new moon, like a gleaming silver scimitar. Sara saw it was over her left shoulder, and she saw Lige's face above her, tender and troubled.

"Lige," she said softly, "do you love me still?"

"You know I do," said Lige sadly.

That was all Sara wanted. With a quick movement she nestled into his arms, and laid her warm, tear-wet cheek against his cold one.

When the amazing rumor that Sara was going to marry Lige Baxter, and go out West with him, circulated through the Andrews clan, hands were lifted and heads were shaken. Mrs. Jonas puffed and panted up the hill to learn if it were true. She found Mrs. Eben stitching for dear life on an "Irish Chain" quilt, while Sara was sewing the diamonds on another "Rising Star" with a martyr-like expression on her face. Sara hated patchwork above everything else, but Mrs. Eben was mistress up to a certain point.

"You'll have to make that quilt, Sara Andrews.

If you're going to live out on those prairies, you'll need piles of quilts, and you shall have them if I sew my fingers to the bone. But you'll have to help make them."

And Sara had to.

When Mrs. Jonas came, Mrs. Eben sent Sara off to the post-office to get her out of the way.

" I suppose it's true, this time? " said Mrs. Jonas.

" Yes, indeed," said Mrs. Eben briskly. " Sara is set on it. There is no use trying to move her — you know that — so I've just concluded to make the best of it. I'm no turn-coat. Lige Baxter is Lige Baxter still, neither more nor less. I've always said he was a fine young man, and I say so still. After all, he and Sara won't be any poorer than Eben and I were when we started out."

Mrs. Jonas heaved a sigh of relief.

" I'm real glad you take that view of it, Louisa. I'm not displeased, either, although Mrs. Harmon would take my head off if she heard me say so. I always liked Lige. But I must say I'm amazed, too, after the way Sara used to rail at him."

" Well we might have expected it," said Mrs. Eben sagely. " It was always Sara's way. When any creature got sick or unfortunate she seemed to take it right into her heart. So you may say Lige Baxter's failure was a success after all."

X

THE SON OF HIS MOTHER

THYRA CAREWE was waiting for Chester to come home. She sat by the west window of the kitchen, looking out into the gathering of the shadows with the expectant immovability that characterized her. She never twitched or fidgeted. Into whatever she did she put the whole force of her nature. If it was sitting still, she sat still.

"A stone image would be twitchedly beside Thyra," said Mrs. Cynthia White, her neighbor across the lane. "It gets on my nerves, the way she sits at that window sometimes, with no more motion than a statue and her great eyes burning down the lane. When I read the commandment, ' Thou shalt have no other gods before me,' I declare I always think of Thyra. She worships that son of hers far ahead of her Creator. She'll be punished for it yet."

Mrs. White was watching Thyra now, knitting furiously, as she watched, in order to lose no time. Thyra's hands were folded idly in her lap. She had not moved a muscle since she sat down. Mrs. White complained that it gave her the weeps.

"It doesn't seem natural to see a woman sit so

still," she said. "Sometimes the thought comes to me, ' what if she's had a stroke, like her old Uncle Horatio, and is sitting there stone dead!'"

The evening was cold and autumnal. There was a fiery red spot out at sea, where the sun had set, and, above it, over a chill, clear, saffron sky, were reefs of purple-black clouds. The river, below the Carewe homestead, was livid. Beyond it, the sea was dark and brooding. It was an evening to make most people shiver and forebode an early winter; but Thyra loved it, as she loved all stern, harshly beautiful things. She would not light a lamp because it would blot out the savage grandeur of sea and sky. It was better to wait in the darkness until Chester came home.

He was late to-night. She thought he had been detained over-time at the harbor, but she was not anxious. He would come straight home to her as soon as his business was completed — of that she felt sure. Her thoughts went out along the bleak harbor road to meet him. She could see him plainly, coming with his free stride through the sandy hollows and over the windy hills, in the harsh, cold light of that forbidding sunset, strong and handsome in his comely youth, with her own deeply cleft chin and his father's dark gray, straightforward eyes. No other woman in Avonlea had a son like hers — her only one. In his brief absences she yearned after

him with a maternal passion that had in it something
of physical pain, so intense was it. She thought of
Cynthia White, knitting across the road, with contemptuous pity. That woman had no son — nothing but pale-faced girls. Thyra had never wanted a
daughter, but she pitied and despised all sonless
women.

Chester's dog whined suddenly and piercingly on
the doorstep outside. He was tired of the cold stone
and wanted his warm corner behind the stove.
Thyra smiled grimly when she heard him. She had
no intention of letting him in. She said she had
always disliked dogs, but the truth, although she
would not glance at it, was that she hated the animal because Chester loved him. She could not share
his love with even a dumb brute. She loved no living creature in the world but her son, and fiercely
demanded a like concentrated affection from him.
Hence it pleased her to hear his dog whine.

It was now quite dark; the stars had begun to
shine out over the shorn harvest fields, and Chester
had not come. Across the lane Cynthia White had
pulled down her blind, in despair of out-watching
Thyra, and had lighted a lamp. Lively shadows of
little girl-shapes passed and repassed on the pale ob-
long of light. They made Thyra conscious of her
exceeding loneliness. She had just decided that she
would walk down the lane and wait for Chester on

the bridge, when a thunderous knock came at the east kitchen door.

She recognized August Vorst's knock and lighted a lamp in no great haste, for she did not like him. He was a gossip and Thyra hated gossip, in man or woman. But August was privileged.

She carried the lamp in her hand, when she went to the door, and its upward-striking light gave her face a ghastly appearance. She did not mean to ask August in, but he pushed past her cheerfully, not waiting to be invited. He was a midget of a man, lame of foot and hunched of back, with a white, boyish face, despite his middle age and deep-set, malicious black eyes.

He pulled a crumpled newspaper from his pocket and handed it to Thyra. He was the unofficial mail-carrier of Avonlea. Most of the people gave him a trifle for bringing their letters and papers from the office. He earned small sums in various other ways, and so contrived to keep the life in his stunted body. There was always venom in August's gossip. It was said that he made more mischief in Avonlea in a day than was made otherwise in a year, but people tolerated him by reason of his infirmity. To be sure, it was the tolerance they gave to inferior creatures, and August felt this. Perhaps it accounted for a good deal of his malignity. He hated most those who were kindest to him, and, of these, Thyra

Carewe above all. He hated Chester, too, as he hated strong, shapely creatures. His time had come at last to wound them both, and his exultation shone through his crooked body and pinched features like an illuminating lamp. Thyra perceived it and vaguely felt something antagonistic in it. She pointed to the rocking-chair, as she might have pointed out a mat to a dog.

August crawled into it and smiled. He was going to make her writhe presently, this woman who looked down upon him as some venomous creeping thing she disdained to crush with her foot.

" Did you see anything of Chester on the road? " asked Thyra, giving August the very opening he desired. " He went to the harbor after tea to see Joe Raymond about the loan of his boat, but it's past the time he should be back. I can't think what keeps the boy."

" Just what keeps most men — leaving out creatures like me — at some time or other in their lives. A girl — a pretty girl, Thyra. It pleases me to look at her. Even a hunchback can use his eyes, eh? Oh, she's a rare one! "

" What is the man talking about? " said Thyra wonderingly.

" Damaris Garland, to be sure. Chester's down at Tom Blair's now, talking to her — and looking more than his tongue says, too, of that you may be sure. Well, well, we were all young once, Thyra — all young once, even crooked little August Vorst. Eh, now?"

"What do you mean?" said Thyra.

She had sat down in a chair before him, with her hands folded in her lap. Her face, always pale, had not changed; but her lips were curiously white. August Vorst saw this and it pleased him. Also, her eyes were worth looking at, if you liked to hurt people — and that was the only pleasure August took in life. He would drink this delightful cup of revenge for her long years of disdainful kindness — Ah, he would drink it slowly to prolong its sweetness. Sip by sip — he rubbed his long, thin, white hands together — sip by sip, tasting each mouthful.

"Eh, now? You know well enough, Thyra."

"I know nothing of what you would be at, August Vorst. You speak of my son and Damaris — was that the name? — Damaris Garland as if they were something to each other. I ask you what you mean by it?"

"Tut, tut, Thyra, nothing very terrible. There's no need to look like that about it. Young men will be young men to the end of time, and there's no harm in Chester's liking to look at a lass, eh, now? Or in talking to her either? The little baggage, with the red lips of her! She and Chester will make a pretty pair. He's not so ill-looking for a man, Thyra."

"I am not a very patient woman, August," said Thyra coldly. "I have asked you what you mean, and I want a straight answer. Is Chester down at Tom Blair's while I have been sitting here, alone, waiting for him?"

August nodded. He saw that it would not be wise to trifle longer with Thyra.

"That he is. I was there before I came here. He and Damaris were sitting in a corner by themselves, and very well-satisfied they seemed to be with each other. Tut, tut, Thyra, don't take the news so. I thought you knew. It's no secret that Chester has been going after Damaris ever since she came here. But what then? You can't tie him to your apron strings forever, woman. He'll be finding a mate for himself, as he should. Seeing that he's straight and well-shaped, no doubt Damaris will look with favor on him. Old Martha Blair declares the girl loves him better than her eyes."

Thyra made a sound like a strangled moan in the middle of August's speech. She heard the rest of it inmovably. When it came to an end she stood up and looked down upon him in a way that silenced him.

"You've told the news you came to tell, and

gloated over it, and now get you gone," she said slowly.

"Now, Thyra," he began, but she interrupted him threateningly.

"Get you gone, I say! And you need not bring my mail here any longer. I want no more of your misshapen body and lying tongue!"

August went, but at the door he turned for a parting stab.

"My tongue is not a lying one, Mrs. Carewe. I've told you the truth, as all Avonlea knows it. Chester is mad about Damaris Garland. It's no wonder I thought you knew what all the settlement can see. But you're such a jealous, odd body, I suppose the boy hid it from you for fear you'd go into a tantrum. As for me, I'll not forget that you've turned me from your door because I chanced to bring you news you'd no fancy for."

Thyra did not answer him. When the door closed behind him she locked it and blew out the light. Then she threw herself face downward on the sofa and burst into wild tears. Her very soul ached. She wept as tempestuously and unreasoningly as youth weeps, although she was not young. It seemed as if she was afraid to stop weeping lest she should go mad thinking. But, after a time, tears failed her, and she began bitterly to go over, word by word, what August Vorst had said.

That her son should ever cast eyes of love on any girl was something Thyra had never thought about. She would not believe it possible that he should love any one but herself, who loved him so much. And now the possibility invaded her mind as subtly and coldly and remorselessly as a stealthy sea-fog creeping towards the land.

Chester had been born to her at an age when most women are letting their children slip from them into the world, with some natural tears and heartaches, but content to let them go, after enjoying their sweetest years. Thyra's late-come motherhood was all the more intense and passionate because of its very lateness. She had been very ill when her son was born, and had lain helpless for long weeks, during which other women had tended her baby for her. She had never been able to forgive them for this.

Her husband had died before Chester was a year old. She had laid their son in his dying arms and received him back again with a last benediction. To Thyra that moment had something of a sacrament in it. It was as if the child had been doubly given to her, with a right to him solely that nothing could take away or transcend.

Marrying! She had never thought of it in connection with him. He did not come of a marrying race. His father had been sixty when he had married her, Thyra Lincoln, likewise well on in life.

Few of the Lincolns or Carewes had married young, many not at all. And, to her, Chester was her baby still. He belonged solely to her.

And now another woman had dared to look upon him with eyes of love. Damaris Garland! Thyra now remembered seeing her. She was a new-comer in Avonlea, having come to live with her uncle and aunt after the death of her mother. Thyra had met her on the bridge one day a month previously. Yes, a man might think she was pretty — a low-browed girl, with a wave of reddish-gold hair, and crimson lips blossoming out against the strange, milk-whiteness of her skin. Her eyes, too — Thyra recalled them — hazel in tint, deep, and laughter-brimmed.

The girl had gone past her with a smile that brought out many dimples. Her bearing was that of self-pleased youth and she flaunted her beauty for all to see. But she was lovely to look at, conceded Thyra, as she measured the charms of this dazzling creature.

And to-night, while she, his mother, waited for him in darkness and loneliness, he was down at Blairs', talking to this girl! He loved her; and it was past doubt that she loved him. The thought was more bitter than death to Thyra. That she should dare! Her anger was all against the girl. She had laid a snare to get Chester and he, like a fool, was entangled in it, thinking, man-fashion, only of her great eyes and red lips.   Thyra thought savagely of Damaris' beauty.

" She shall not have him," she said, with slow emphasis.   " I will never give him up to any other woman, and, least of all, to her.   She would leave me no place in his heart at all — me, his mother, who almost died to give him life.   He belongs to me! Let her look for the son of some other woman — some woman who has many sons.   She shall not have my only one! "

She got up, wrapped a shawl about her head, and went out into the darkly golden evening.   The clouds had cleared away, and the moon was shining.   The air was chill, with a bell-like clearness.   The alders by the river rustled eerily as she walked by them and out upon the bridge.   Here she paced up and down, peering with troubled eyes along the road beyond, or leaning over the rail, looking at the silvery light of the moon flecking the dark waters below.   Late travelers passed her, and wondered at her presence on the bridge and strange mien.   Carl White saw her, and told his wife about her when he got home.

" Striding to and fro over the bridge like mad! At first I thought it was old, crazy May Blair.   What do you suppose she was doing down there at this hour of the night? "

" Watching for Ches, no doubt," said Cynthia.

"He ain't home yet. Likely he's snug at Blairs'. I do wonder if Thyra suspicions that he goes after Damaris. I've never dared to hint it to her. She'd be as liable to fly at me, tooth and claw, as not."

"Well, she picks out a precious queer night for moon-gazing," said Carl, who was a jolly soul and took life as he found it. "It's bitter cold — there'll be a hard frost. It's a pity she can't get it grained into her that the boy is grown up and must have his fling like other lads. She'll go out of her mind yet, like her old grandmother Lincoln, if she doesn't ease up. I've a notion to go down to the bridge and reason a bit with her."

"Indeed, and you'll do no such thing!" cried Cynthia. "Thyra Carewe is best left alone, if she is in a tantrum. She's like no other woman in Avonlea — or out of it. I'd as soon meddle with a tiger as her, if she's rampaging about Chester. I don't envy Damaris Garland her life if she goes in there. Thyra'd sooner strangle her than not, I guess."

"You women are all terrible hard on Thyra," said Carl, good-naturedly. He had been in love with Thyra, himself, long ago, and he still liked her in a friendly fashion. He always stood up for her when the Avonlea women ran her down. He felt troubled about her all night, recalling her as she paced the

bridge. He wished he had gone back, in spite of
Cynthia.

When Chester came home he met his mother on
the bridge. In the faint, yet penetrating, moonlight
they looked curiously alike, but Chester had the
milder face. He was very handsome. Even in the
seething of her pain and jealousy Thyra yearned
over his beauty. She would have liked to put up
her hands and caress his face, but her voice was very
hard when she asked him where he had been so
late.

" I called in at Tom Blair's on my way home from
the harbor," he answered, trying to walk on. But
she held him back by his arm.

" Did you go there to see Damaris? " she demanded fiercely.

Chester was uncomfortable. Much as he loved
his mother, he felt, and always had felt, an awe of
her and an impatient dislike of her dramatic ways
of speaking and acting. He reflected, resentfully,
that no other young man in Avonlea, who had been
paying a friendly call, would be met by his mother
at midnight and held up in such tragic fashion to
account for himself. He tried vainly to loosen her
hold upon his arm, but he understood quite well that
he must give her an answer. Being strictly straightforward by nature and upbringing, he told the truth,

albeit with more anger in his tone than he had ever shown to his mother before.

"Yes," he said shortly.

Thyra released his arm, and struck her hands together with a sharp cry. There was a savage note in it. She could have slain Damaris Garland at that moment.

"Don't go on so, mother," said Chester, impatiently. "Come in out of the cold. It isn't fit for you to be here. Who has been tampering with you? What if I did go to see Damaris?"

"Oh — oh — oh!" cried Thyra. "I was waiting for you — alone — and you were thinking only of her! Chester, answer me — do you love her?"

The blood rolled rapidly over the boy's face. He muttered something and tried to pass on, but she caught him again. He forced himself to speak gently.

"What if I do, mother? It wouldn't be such a dreadful thing, would it?"

"And me? And me?" cried Thyra. "What am I to you, then?"

"You are my mother. I wouldn't love you any the less because I cared for another, too."

"I won't have you love another," she cried. "I want all your love — all! What's that baby-face to you, compared to your mother? I have the best right to you. I won't give you up."

Chester realized that there was no arguing with such a mood. He walked on, resolved to set the matter aside until she might be more reasonable. But Thyra would not have it so. She followed on after him, under the alders that crowded over the lane.

" Promise me that you'll not go there again," she entreated. " Promise me that you'll give her up."

" I can't promise such a thing," he cried angrily.

His anger hurt her worse than a blow, but she did not flinch.

" You're not engaged to her? " she cried out.

" Now, mother, be quiet. All the settlement will hear you. Why do you object to Damaris? You don't know how sweet she is. When you do know her —"

" I will never know her! " cried Thyra furiously. " And she shall not have you! She shall not, Chester! "

He made no answer. She suddenly broke into tears and loud sobs. Touched with remorse, he stopped and put his arms about her.

" Mother, mother, don't! I can't bear to see you cry so. But, indeed, you are unreasonable. Didn't you ever think the time would come when I would want to marry, like other men? "

" No, no! And I will not have it — I cannot bear

it, Chester. You must promise not to go to see her again. I won't go into the house this night until you do. I'll stay out here in the bitter cold until you promise to put her out of your thoughts."

" That's beyond my power, mother. Oh, mother, you're making it hard for me. Come in, come in! You're shivering with cold now. You'll be sick."

" Not a step will I stir till you promise. Say you won't go to see that girl any more, and there's nothing I won't do for you. But, if you put her before me, I'll not go in — I never will go in."

With most women this would have been an empty threat; but it was not so with Thyra, and Chester knew it. He knew she would keep her word. And he feared more than that. In this frenzy of hers what might she not do? She came of a strange breed, as had been said disapprovingly when Luke Carewe married her. There was a strain of insanity in the Lincolns. A Lincoln woman had drowned herself once. Chester thought of the river, and grew sick with fright. For a moment even his passion for Damaris weakened before the older tie.

" Mother, calm yourself. Oh, surely there's no need of all this! Let us wait until to-morrow, and talk it over then. I'll hear all you have to say. Come in, dear."

Thyra loosened her arms from about him, and

stepped back into a moon-lit space.   Looking at him tragically, she extended her arms and spoke slowly and solemnly.

" Chester, choose between us.   If you choose her, I shall go from you to-night, and you will never see me again ! "

" Mother ! "

" Choose ! " she reiterated, fiercely.

He felt her long ascendancy.   Its influence was not to be shaken off in a moment.   In all his life he had never disobeyed her.   Besides, with it all, he loved her more deeply and understandingly than most sons love their mothers.   He realized that, since she would have it so, his choice was already made — or, rather that he had no choice.

" Have your way," he said sullenly.

She ran to him and caught him to her heart.   In the reaction of her feeling she was half laughing, half crying.   All was well again — all would be well; she never doubted this, for she knew he would keep his ungracious promise sacredly.

" Oh, my son, my son," she murmured, " you'd have sent me to my death if you had chosen otherwise.   But now you are mine again ! "

She did not heed that he was sullen — that he resented her unjustice with all her own intensity.   She did not heed his silence as they went into the house together.   Strangely enough, she slept well and soundly that night.   Not until many days had passed did she understand that, though Chester might keep his promise in the letter, it was beyond his power to keep it in the spirit.   She had taken him from Damaris Garland; but she had not won him back to herself.   He could never be wholly her son again. There was a barrier between them which not all her passionate love could break down.   Chester was gravely kind to her, for it was not in his nature to remain sullen long, or visit his own unhappiness upon another's head; besides, he understood her exacting affection, even in its injustice, and it has been well-said that to understand is to forgive.   But he avoided her, and she knew it.   The flame of her anger burned bitterly towards Damaris.

"He thinks of her all the time," she moaned to herself.   "He'll come to hate me yet, I fear, because it's I who made him give her up.   But I'd rather even that than share him with another woman.   Oh, my son, my son!"

She knew that Damaris was suffering, too.   The girl's wan face told that when she met her.   But this pleased Thyra.   It eased the ache in her bitter heart to know that pain was gnawing at Damaris' also.

Chester was absent from home very often now. He spent much of his spare time at the harbor, consorting with Joe Raymond and others of that ilk who were but sorry associates for him, Avonlea people thought.

In late November he and Joe started for a trip down the coast in the latter's boat. Thyra protested against it, but Chester laughed at her alarm.

Thyra saw him go with a heart sick from fear. She hated the sea, and was afraid of it at any time; but, most of all, in this treacherous month, with its sudden, wild gales.

Chester had been fond of the sea from boyhood. She had always tried to stifle this fondness and break off his associations with the harbor fishermen, who liked to lure the high-spirited boy out with them on fishing expeditions. But her power over him was gone now.

After Chester's departure she was restless and miserable, wandering from window to window to scan the dour, unsmiling sky. Carl White, dropping in to pay a call, was alarmed when he heard that Chester had gone with Joe, and had not tact enough to conceal his alarm from Thyra.

" 'T isn't safe this time of year," he said.   " Folks expect no better from that reckless, harum-scarum Joe Raymond. He'll drown himself some day, there's nothing surer. This mad freak of starting off down the shore in November is just of a piece with his usual performances. But you shouldn't have let Chester go, Thyra."

"I couldn't prevent him. Say what I could, he would go. He laughed when I spoke of danger. Oh, he's changed from what he was! I know who has wrought the change, and I hate her for it!"

Carl shrugged his fat shoulders. He knew quite well that Thyra was at the bottom of the sudden coldness between Chester Carewe and Damaris Garland, about which Avonlea gossip was busying itself. He pitied Thyra, too. She had aged rapidly the past month.

"You're too hard on Chester, Thyra. He's out of leading-strings now, or should be. You must just let me take an old friend's privilege, and tell you that you're taking the wrong way with him. You're too jealous and exacting, Thyra."

"You don't know anything about it. You have never had a son," said Thyra, cruelly enough, for she knew that Carl's sonlessness was a rankling thorn in his mind. "You don't know what it is to pour out your love on one human being, and have it flung back in your face!"

Carl could not cope with Thyra's moods. He had never understood her, even in youth. Now he went home, still shrugging his shoulders, and thinking that it was a good thing Thyra had not looked on him with favor in the old days. Cynthia was much easier to get along with.

More than Thyra looked anxiously to sea and

sky that night in Avonlea. Damaris Garland listened to the smothered roar of the Atlantic in the murky northeast with a prescience of coming disaster. Friendly longshoremen shook their heads and said that Ches and Joe would better have kept to good, dry land.

"It's sorry work joking with a November gale," said Abel Blair. He was an old man and, in his life, had seen some sad things along the shore.

Thyra could not sleep that night. When the gale came shrieking up the river, and struck the house, she got out of bed and dressed herself. The wind screamed like a ravening beast at her window. All night she wandered to and fro in the house, going from room to room, now wringing her hands with loud outcries, now praying below her breath with white lips, now listening in dumb misery to the fury of the storm.

The wind raged all the next day; but spent itself in the following night, and the second morning was calm and fair. In the east, clouds tinged with gold and crimson announced the early rising sun. Thyra, looking from her kitchen window, saw a group of men on the bridge. They were talking to Carl White, with looks and gestures directed towards the Carewe house.

She went out and down to them. None of these

who saw her white, rigid face that day ever forgot the sight.

"You have news for me," she said.

They looked at each other, each man mutely imploring his neighbor to speak.

"You need not fear to tell me," said Thyra calmly. "I know what you have come to say. My son is drowned."

"We don't know *that,* Mrs. Carewe," said Abel Blair quickly. "We haven't got the worst to tell you — there's hope yet. But Joe Raymond's boat was found last night, stranded, bottom up, on the Blue Point sand shore, forty miles down the coast."

"Don't look like that, Thyra," said Carl White pityingly. "They may have escaped — they may have been picked up."

Thyra looked at him with dull eyes.

"You know they have not. Not one of you has any hope. I have no son. The sea has taken him from me — my bonny baby!"

She turned and went back to her desolate home. None dared to follow her. Carl White went home and sent his wife over to her.

Cynthia found Thyra sitting in her accustomed chair. Her hands lay, palms upward, on her lap. Her eyes were dry and burning. She met Cynthia's compassionate look with a fearful smile.

"Long ago, Cynthia White," she said slowly,

"you were vexed with me one day, and you told me that God would punish me yet, because I made an idol of my son, and set it up in His place. Do you remember? Your word was a true one. God saw that I loved Chester too much, and He meant to take him from me. I thwarted one way when I made him give up Damaris. But one can't fight against the Almighty. It was decreed that I must lose him — if not in one way, then in another. He has been taken from me utterly. I shall not even have his grave to tend, Cynthia."

"As near to a mad woman as anything you ever saw, with her awful eyes," Cynthia told Carl, afterwards. But she did not say so there. Although she was a shallow, commonplace soul, she had her share of womanly sympathy, and her own life had not been free from suffering. It taught her the right thing to do now. She sat down by the stricken creature and put her arms about her, while she gathered the cold hands in her own warm clasp. The tears filled her big blue eyes and her voice trembled as she said:

"Thyra, I'm sorry for you. I — I — lost a child once — my little first-born. And Chester was a dear, good lad."

For a moment Thyra strained her small, tense body away from Cynthia's embrace. Then she shuddered and cried out. The tears came, and she wept her agony out on the other woman's breast.

As the ill news spread, other Avonlea women kept dropping in all through the day to condole with Thyra. Many of them came in real sympathy, but some out of mere curiosity to see how she took it. Thyra knew this, but she did not resent it, as she would once have done. She listened very quietly to all the halting efforts at consolation, the forced words, the words that were proper, the words that tried in vain to ease her grief.

When darkness came Cynthia said she must go home, but would send one of her girls over for the night.

"You won't feel like staying alone," she said.

Thyra looked up steadily.

"No. But I want you to send for Damaris Garland."

"Damaris Garland!" Cynthia repeated the name as if disbelieving her own ears. There was never any knowing what whim Thyra might take, but Cynthia had not expected this.

"Yes. Tell her I want her — tell her she must come. She must hate me bitterly; but I am punished enough to satisfy even her hate. Tell her to come to me for Chester's sake."

Cynthia did as she was bid, she sent her daughter, Jeanette, for Damaris. Then she waited. No matter what duties were calling for her at home she must see the interview between Thyra and Damaris.

Her curiosity would be the last thing to fail Cynthia White. She had done very well all day; but it would be asking too much of her to expect that she would consider the meeting of these two women sacred from her eyes.

She half believed that Damaris would refuse to come. But Damaris came. Jeanette brought her in amid the fiery glow of a November sunset. Thyra stood up, and for a moment they looked at each other.

The insolence of Damaris' beauty was gone. Her eyes were dull and heavy with weeping, her lips were pale, and her face had lost its laughter and dimples. Only her hair, escaping from the shawl she had cast around it, gushed forth in warm splendor in the sunset light, and framed her wan face like the aureole of a Madonna. Thyra looked upon her with a shock of remorse. This was not the radiant creature she had met on the bridge that summer afternoon. This — this — was *her* work. She held out her arms.

"Oh, Damaris, forgive me. We both loved him — that must be a bond between us for life."

Damaris came forward and threw her arms about the older woman, lifting her face. As their lips met even Cynthia White realized that she had no business there. She vented the irritation of her embarrassment on the innocent Jeanette.

"Come away," she whispered crossly. "Can't you see we're not wanted here?"

She drew Jeanette out, leaving Thyra rocking Damaris in her arms, and crooning over her like a mother over her child.

When December had grown old Damaris was still with Thyra. It was understood that she was to remain there for the winter, at least. Thyra could not bear her to be out of her sight. They talked constantly about Chester; Thyra confessed all her anger and hatred. Damaris had forgiven her; but Thyra could never forgive herself. She was greatly changed, and had grown very gentle and tender. She even sent for August Vorst and begged him to pardon her for the way she had spoken to him.

Winter came late that year, and the season was a very open one. There was no snow on the ground and, a month after Joe Raymond's boat had been cast up on the Blue Point sand shore, Thyra, wandering about in her garden, found some pansies blooming under their tangled leaves. She was picking them for Damaris when she heard a buggy rumble over the bridge and drive up the White lane, hidden from her sight by the alders and firs. A few minutes later Carl and Cynthia came hastily across their yard under the huge balm-of-gileads. Carl's face was flushed, and his big body quivered with excitement. Cynthia ran behind him, with tears rolling down her face.

Thyra felt herself growing sick with fear. Had

anything happened to Damaris? A glimpse of the girl, sewing by an upper window of the house, reassured her.

"Oh, Thyra, Thyra!" gasped Cynthia.

"Can you stand some good news, Thyra?" asked Carl, in a trembling voice. "Very, very good news!"

Thyra looked wildly from one to the other.

"There's but one thing you would dare to call good news to me," she cried. "Is it about — about —"

"Chester! Yes, it's about Chester! Thyra, he is alive — he's safe — he and Joe, both of them, thank God! Cynthia, catch her!"

"No, I am not going to faint," said Thyra, steadying herself by Cynthia's shoulder. "My son alive! How did you hear? How did it happen? Where has he been?"

"I heard it down at the harbor, Thyra. Mike McCready's vessel, the *Nora Lee,* was just in from the Magdalens. Ches and Joe got capsized the night of the storm, but they hung on to their boat somehow, and at daybreak they were picked up by the *Nora Lee,* bound for Quebec. But she was damaged by the storm and blown clear out of her course. Had to put into the Magdalens for repairs, and has been there ever since. The cable to the islands was out of order, and no vessels call there this time of

year for mails.   If it hadn't been an extra open season the *Nora Lee* wouldn't have got away, but would
have had to stay there till spring.   You never saw
such rejoicing as there was this morning at the
harbor, when the *Nora Lee* came in, flying flags at
the mast head."

"And Chester — where is he?" demanded Thyra.

Carl and Cynthia looked at each other.

"Well, Thyra," said the latter, "the fact is, he's
over there in our yard this blessed minute.   Carl
brought him home from the harbor, but I wouldn't
let him come over until we had prepared you for it.
He's waiting for you there."

Thyra made a quick step in the direction of the
gate.   Then she turned, with a little of the glow
dying out of her face.

"No, there's one has a better right to go to him
first.   I can atone to him — thank God, I can atone
to him!"

She went into the house and called Damaris.   As
the girl came down the stairs Thyra held out her
hands with a wonderful light of joy and renuncia-
tion on her face.

"Damaris," she said, "Chester has come back to
us — the sea has given him back to us.   He is over
at Carl White's house.   Go to him, my daughter,
and bring him to me!"

XI

THE EDUCATION OF BETTY

WHEN Sara Currie married Jack Churchill I was broken-hearted . . . or believed myself to be so, which, in a boy of twenty-two, amounts to pretty much the same thing. Not that I took the world into my confidence; that was never the Douglas way, and I held myself in honor bound to live up to the family traditions. I thought, then, that nobody but Sara knew; but I dare say, now, that Jack knew it also, for I don't think Sara could have helped telling him. If he did know, however, he did not let me see that he did, and never insulted me by any implied sympathy; on the contrary, he asked me to be his best man. Jack was always a thoroughbred.

I was best man. Jack and I had always been bosom friends, and, although I had lost my sweetheart, I did not intend to lose my friend into the bargain. Sara had made a wise choice, for Jack was twice the man I was; he had had to work for his living, which perhaps accounts for it.

So I danced at Sara's wedding as if my heart were as light as my heels; but, after she and Jack had settled down at Glenby I closed The Maples and went abroad . . . being, as I have hinted, one of those unfortunate mortals who need consult nothing but their own whims in the matter of time and money.   I stayed away for ten years, during which The Maples was given over to moth and rust, while I enjoyed life elsewhere.   I did enjoy it hugely, but always under protest, for I felt that a broken-hearted man ought not to enjoy himself as I did.   It jarred on my sense of fitness, and I tried to moderate my zest, and think more of the past than I did.   It was no use; the present insisted on being intrusive and pleasant; as for the future . . . well, there was no future.

Then Jack Churchill, poor fellow, died.   A year after his death, I went home and again asked Sara to marry me, as in duty bound.   Sara again declined, alleging that her heart was buried in Jack's grave, or words to that effect.   I found that it did not much matter . . . of course, at thirty-two one does not take these things to heart as at twenty-two. I had enough to occupy me in getting The Maples into working order, and beginning to educate Betty.

Betty was Sara's ten-year-old daughter, and she had been thoroughly spoiled.   That is to say, she had been allowed her own way in everything and, having inherited her father's outdoor tastes, had simply run wild.   She was a thorough tomboy, a thin, scrawny little thing without a trace of Sara's beauty. Betty took after her father's dark, tall race and, on the occasion of my first introduction to her, seemed to be all legs and neck. There were points about her, though, which I considered promising. She had fine, almond-shaped, hazel eyes, the smallest and most shapely hands and feet I ever saw, and two enormous braids of thick, nut-brown hair.

For Jack's sake I decided to bring his daughter up properly. Sara couldn't do it, and didn't try. I saw that, if somebody didn't take Betty in hand, wisely and firmly, she would certainly be ruined. There seemed to be nobody except myself at all interested in the matter, so I determined to see what an old bachelor could do as regards bringing up a girl in the way she should go. I might have been her father; as it was, her father had been my best friend. Who had a better right to watch over his daughter? I determined to be a father to Betty, and do all for her that the most devoted parent could do. It was, self-evidently, my duty.

I told Sara I was going to take Betty in hand. Sara sighed one of the plaintive little sighs which I had once thought so charming, but now, to my surprise, found faintly irritating, and said that she would be very much obliged if I would.

" I feel that I am not able to cope with the problem of Betty's education, Stephen," she admitted. " Betty is a strange child . . . all Churchill. Her poor father indulged her in everything, and she has a will of her own, I assure you. I have really no control over her, whatever. She does as she pleases, and is ruining her complexion by running and galloping out of doors the whole time. Not that she had much complexion to start with. The Churchills never had, you know." . . . Sara cast a complacent glance at her delicately tinted reflection in the mirror. . . . " I tried to make Betty wear a sunbonnet this summer, but I might as well have talked to the wind."

A vision of Betty in a sunbonnet presented itself to my mind, and afforded me so much amusement that I was grateful to Sara for having furnished it. I rewarded her with a compliment.

" It is to be regretted that Betty has not inherited her mother's charming color," I said, " but we must do the best we can for her under her limitations. She may have improved vastly by the time she has grown up. And, at least, we must make a lady of her; she is a most alarming tomboy at present, but there is good material to work upon . . . there must be, in the Churchill and Currie blend. But even the best material may be spoiled by unwise handling. I think I can promise you that I will not spoil it. I feel that Betty is my vocation; and I shall set myself up as a rival of Wordsworth's ' nature,' of whose methods I have always had a de cided distrust, in spite of his insidious verses."

Sara did not understand me in the least; but, then, she did not pretend to.

"I confide Betty's education entirely to you, Stephen," she said, with another plaintive sigh. "I feel sure I could not put it into better hands. You have always been a person who could be thoroughly depended on."

Well, that was something by way of reward for a life-long devotion. I felt that I was satisfied with my position as unofficial adviser-in-chief to Sara and self-appointed guardian of Betty. I also felt that, for the furtherance of the cause I had taken to heart, it was a good thing that Sara had again refused to marry me. I had a sixth sense which informed me that a staid old family friend might succeed with Betty where a stepfather would have signally failed. Betty's loyalty to her father's memory was passionate and vehement; she would view his supplanter with resentment and distrust; but his old familiar comrade was a person to be taken to her heart.

Fortunately for the success of my enterprise, Betty liked me. She told me this with the same engaging candor she would have used in informing me that she hated me, if she had happened to take a bias in that direction, saying frankly:

"You are one of the very nicest old folks I know,

Stephen. Yes, you are a ripping good fellow!"

This made my task a comparatively easy one; I sometimes shudder to think what it might have been if Betty had not thought I was a "ripping good fellow." I should have stuck to it, because that is my way; but Betty would have made my life a misery to me. She had startling capacities for tormenting people when she chose to exert them; I certainly should not have liked to be numbered among Betty's foes.

I rode over to Glenby the next morning after my paternal interview with Sara, intending to have a frank talk with Betty and lay the foundations of a good understanding on both sides. Betty was a sharp child, with a disconcerting knack of seeing straight through grindstones; she would certainly perceive and probably resent any underhand management. I thought it best to tell her plainly that I was going to look after her.

When, however, I had encountered Betty, tearing madly down the beech avenue with a couple of dogs, her loosened hair streaming behind her like a banner of independence, and had lifted her, hatless and breathless, up before me on my mare, I found that Sara had saved me the trouble of an explanation.

"Mother says you are going to take charge of my education, Stephen," said Betty, as soon as she could speak. "I'm glad, because I think that, for an old person, you have a good deal of sense. I suppose my education has to be seen to, some time or other, and I'd rather you'd do it than anybody else I know."

"Thank you, Betty," I said gravely. "I hope I shall deserve your good opinion of my sense. I shall expect you to do as I tell you, and be guided by my advice in everything."

"Yes, I will," said Betty, "because I'm sure you won't tell me to do anything I'd really hate to do. You won't shut me up in a room and make me sew, will you? Because I won't do it."

I assured her I would not.

"Nor send me to a boarding-school," pursued Betty. "Mother's always threatening to send me to one. I suppose she would have done it before this, only she knew I'd run away. You won't send me to a boarding-school, will you, Stephen? Because I won't go."

"No," I said obligingly, "I won't. I should never dream of cooping a wild little thing, like you, up in a boarding-school. You'd fret your heart out like a caged skylark."

"I know you and I are going to get along together splendidly, Stephen," said Betty, rubbing her brown cheek chummily against my shoulder. "You are so good at understanding. Very few people are.

Even dad darling didn't understand. He let me do just as I wanted to, just because I wanted to, not because he really understood that I couldn't be tame and play with dolls. I hate dolls! Real live babies are jolly; but dogs and horses are ever so much nicer than dolls."

" But you must have lessons, Betty. I shall select your teachers and superintend your studies, and I shall expect you to do me credit along that line, as well as along all others."

" I'll try, honest and true, Stephen," declared Betty. And she kept her word.

At first I looked upon Betty's education as a duty; in a very short time it had become a pleasure . . . the deepest and most abiding interest of my life. As I had premised, Betty was good material, and responded to my training with gratifying plasticity. Day by day, week by week, month by month, her character and temperament unfolded naturally under my watchful eye. It was like beholding the gradual development of some rare flower in one's garden. A little checking and pruning here, a careful training of shoot and tendril there, and, lo, the reward of grace and symmetry!

Betty grew up as I would have wished Jack Churchill's girl to grow — spirited and proud, with the fine spirit and gracious pride of pure womanhood, loyal and loving, with the loyalty and love of a frank unspoiled nature; true to her heart's core, hating falsehood and sham — as crystal-clear a mirror of maidenhood as ever man looked into and saw himself reflected back in such a halo as made him ashamed of not being more worthy of it. Betty was kind enough to say that I had taught her everything she knew. But what had she not taught me? If there were a debt between us, it was on my side.

Sara was fairly well satisfied. It was not my fault that Betty was not better looking, she said. I had certainly done everything for her mind and character that could be done. Sara's manner implied that these unimportant details did not count for much, balanced against the lack of a pink-and-white skin and dimpled elbows; but she was generous enough not to blame me.

" When Betty is twenty-five," I said patiently — I had grown used to speaking patiently to Sara — " she will be a magnificent woman — far handsomer than you ever were, Sara, in your pinkest and whitest prime. Where are your eyes, my dear lady, that you can't see the promise of loveliness in Betty? "

" Betty is seventeen, and she is as lanky and brown as ever she was," sighed Sara. " When I was seventeen I was the belle of the county and had had five proposals. I don't believe the thought of a lover has ever entered Betty's head."

" I hope not," I said shortly. Somehow, I did not

like the suggestion. "Betty is a child yet. For pity's sake, Sara, don't go putting nonsensical ideas into her head."

"I'm afraid I can't," mourned Sara, as if it were something to be regretted. "You have filled it too full of books and things like that. I've every confidence in your judgment, Stephen — and really you've done wonders with Betty. But don't you think you've made her rather too clever? Men don't like women who are too clever. Her poor father, now — he always said that a woman who liked books better than beaux was an unnatural creature."

I didn't believe Jack had ever said anything so foolish. Sara imagined things. But I resented the aspersion of blue-stockingness cast on Betty.

"When the time comes for Betty to be interested in beaux," I said severely, "she will probably give them all due attention. Just at present her head is a great deal better filled with books than with silly premature fancies and sentimentalities. I'm a critical old fellow — but I'm satisfied with Betty, Sara — perfectly satisfied."

Sara sighed.

"Oh, I dare say she is all right, Stephen. And I'm really grateful to you. I'm sure I could have done nothing at all with her. It's not your fault, of course,— but I can't help wishing she were a little more like other girls."

I galloped away from Glenby in a rage. What a blessing Sara had not married me in my absurd youth! She would have driven me wild with her sighs and her obtuseness and her everlasting pink-and-whiteness. But there — there — there — gently! She was a sweet, good-hearted little woman; she had made Jack happy; and she had contrived, heaven only knew how, to bring a rare creature like Betty into the world. For that, much might be forgiven her. By the time I reached The Maples and had flung myself down in an old, kinky, comfortable chair in my library I had forgiven her and was even paying her the compliment of thinking seriously over what she had said.

Was Betty really unlike other girls? That is to say, unlike them in any respect wherein she should resemble them? I did not wish this; although I was a crusty old bachelor I approved of girls, holding them the sweetest things the good God has made. I wanted Betty to have her full complement of girlhood in all its best and highest manifestation. Was there anything lacking?

I observed Betty very closely during the next week or so, riding over to Glenby every day and riding back at night, meditating upon my observations. Eventually I concluded to do what I had never thought myself in the least likely to do. I would send Betty to a boarding-school for a year. It was necessary that she should learn how to live with other girls.

I went over to Glenby the next day and found Betty under the beeches on the lawn, just back from a canter. She was sitting on the dappled mare I had given her on her last birthday, and was laughing at the antics of her rejoicing dogs around her. I looked at her with pleasure; it gladdened me to see how much, nay, how totally a child she still was, despite her Churchill height. Her hair, under her velvet cap, still hung over her shoulders in the same thick plaits; her face had the firm leanness of early youth, but its curves were very fine and delicate. The brown skin, that worried Sara so, was flushed through with dusky color from her gallop; her long, dark eyes were filled with the beautiful unconsciousness of childhood. More than all, the soul in her was still the soul of a child. I found myself wishing that it could always remain so. But I knew it could not; the woman must blossom out some day; it was my duty to see that the flower fulfilled the promise of the bud.

When I told Betty that she must go away to a school for a year, she shrugged, frowned and consented. Betty had learned that she must consent to what I decreed, even when my decrees were opposed to her likings, as she had once fondly believed they never would be. But Betty had acquired confidence in me to the beautiful extent of acquiescing in everything I commanded.

"I'll go, of course, since you wish it, Stephen," she said. "But why do you want me to go? You must have a reason — you always have a reason for anything you do. What is it?"

"That is for you to find out, Betty," I said. "By the time you come back you will have discovered it, I think. If not, it will not have proved itself a good reason and shall be forgotten."

When Betty went away I bade her good-by without burdening her with any useless words of advice.

"Write to me every week, and remember that you are Betty Churchill," I said.

Betty was standing on the steps above, among her dogs. She came down a step and put her arms about my neck.

"I'll remember that you are my friend and that I must live up to you," she said. "Good-by, Stephen."

She kissed me two or three times — good, hearty smacks! did I not say she was still a child? — and stood waving her hand to me as I rode away. I looked back at the end of the avenue and saw her standing there, short-skirted and hatless, fronting the lowering sun with those fearless eyes of hers. So I looked my last on the child Betty.

That was a lonely year. My occupation was gone

and I began to fear that I had outlived my usefulness. Life seemed flat, stale and unprofitable. Betty's weekly letters were all that lent it any savor. They were spicy and piquant enough. Betty was discovered to have unsuspected talents in the epistolary line. At first she was dolefully homesick, and begged me to let her come home. When I refused — it was amazingly hard to refuse — she sulked through three letters, then cheered up and began to enjoy herself. But it was nearly the end of the year when she wrote:

"I've found out why you sent me here, Stephen — and I'm glad you did."

I had to be away from home on unavoidable business the day Betty returned to Glenby. But the next afternoon I went over. I found Betty out and Sara in. The latter was beaming. Betty was so much improved, she declared delightedly. I would hardly know "the dear child."

This alarmed me terribly. What on earth had they done to Betty? I found that she had gone up to the pineland for a walk, and thither I betook myself speedily. When I saw her coming down a long, golden-brown alley I stepped behind a tree to watch her — I wished to see her, myself unseen. As she drew near I gazed at her with pride, and admiration and amazement — and, under it all, a strange, dreadful, heart-sinking, which I could not understand and which I had never in all my life experienced before — no, not even when Sara had refused me.

Betty was a woman! Not by virtue of the simple white dress that clung to her tall, slender figure, revealing lines of exquisite grace and litheness; not by virtue of the glossy masses of dark brown hair heaped high on her head and held there in wonderful shining coils; not by virtue of added softness of curve and daintiness of outline; not because of all these, but because of the dream and wonder and seeking in her eyes. She was a woman, looking, all unconscious of her quest, for love.

The understanding of the change in her came home to me with a shock that must have left me, I think, something white about the lips. I was glad. She was what I had wished her to become. But I wanted the child Betty back; this womanly Betty seemed far away from me.

I stepped out into the path and she saw me, with a brightening of her whole face. She did not rush forward and fling herself into my arms as she would have done a year ago; but she came towards me swiftly, holding out her hand. I had thought her slightly pale when I had first seen her; but now I concluded I had been mistaken, for there was a wonderful sunrise of color in her face. I took her hand — there were no kisses this time.

" Welcome home, Betty," I said.

"Oh, Stephen, it is so good to be back," she breathed, her eyes shining.

She did not say it was good to see me again, as I had hoped she would do. Indeed, after the first minute of greeting, she seemed a trifle cool and distant. We walked for an hour in the pine wood and talked. Betty was brilliant, witty, self-possessed, altogether charming. I thought her perfect and yet my heart ached. What a glorious young thing she was, in that splendid youth of hers! What a prize for some lucky man — confound the obtrusive thought! No doubt we should soon be overrun at Glenby with lovers. I should stumble over some forlorn youth at every step! Well, what of it? Betty would marry, of course. It would be my duty to see that she got a good husband, worthy of her as men go. I thought I preferred the old duty of superintending her studies. But there, it was all the same thing — merely a post-graduate course in applied knowledge. When she began to learn life's greatest lesson of love, I, the tried and true old family friend and mentor, must be on hand to see that the teacher was what I would have him be, even as I had formerly selected her instructor in French and botany. Then, and not until then, would Betty's education be complete.

I rode home very soberly. When I reached The

Maples I did what I had not done for years . . . looked critically at myself in the mirror. The realization that I had grown older came home to me with a new and unpleasant force. There were marked lines on my lean face, and silver glints in the dark hair over my temples. When Betty was ten she had thought me " an old person." Now, at eighteen, she probably thought me a veritable ancient of days. Pshaw, what did it matter? And yet . . . I thought of her as I had seen her, standing under the pines, and something cold and painful laid its hand on my heart.

My premonitions as to lovers proved correct. Glenby was soon infested with them. Heaven knows where they all came from. I had not supposed there was a quarter as many young men in the whole county; but there they were. Sara was in the seventh heaven of delight. Was not Betty at last a belle? As for the proposals . . . well, Betty never counted her scalps in public; but every once in a while a visiting youth dropped out and was seen no more at Glenby. One could guess what that meant.

Betty apparently enjoyed all this. I grieve to say that she was a bit of a coquette. I tried to cure her of this serious defect, but for once I found that I had undertaken something I could not accomplish. In vain I lectured, Betty only laughed; in vain I gravely rebuked, Betty only flirted more vivaciously than before. Men might come and men might go, but Betty went on forever. I endured this sort of thing for a year and then I decided that it was time to interfere seriously. I must find a husband for Betty . . . my fatherly duty would not be fulfilled until I had . . . nor, indeed, my duty to society. She was not a safe person to have running at large.

None of the men who haunted Glenby was good enough for her. I decided that my nephew, Frank, would do very well. He was a capital young fellow, handsome, clean-souled, and whole-hearted. From a worldly point of view he was what Sara would have termed an excellent match; he had money, social standing and a rising reputation as a clever young lawyer. Yes, he should have Betty, confound him!

They had never met. I set the wheels going at once. The sooner all the fuss was over the better. I hated fuss and there was bound to be a good deal of it. But I went about the business like an accomplished matchmaker. I invited Frank to visit The Maples and, before he came, I talked much . . . but not too much . . . of him to Betty, mingling judicious praise and still more judicious blame together. Women never like a paragon. Betty heard me with more gravity than she usually accorded to my dissertations on young men. She even condescended to ask several questions about him. This I thought a good sign.

To Frank I had not said a word about Betty; when he came to The Maples I took him over to Glenby and, coming upon Betty wandering about among the beeches in the sunset, I introduced him without any warning.

He would have been more than mortal if he had not fallen in love with her upon the spot. It was not in the heart of man to resist her . . . that dainty, alluring bit of womanhood. She was all in white, with flowers in her hair, and, for a moment, I could have murdered Frank or any other man who dared to commit the sacrilege of loving her.

Then I pulled myself together and left them alone. I might have gone in and talked to Sara . . . two old folks gently reviewing their youth while the young folks courted outside . . . but I did not. I prowled about the pine wood, and tried to forget how blithe and handsome that curly-headed boy, Frank, was, and what a flash had sprung into his eyes when he had seen Betty. Well, what of it? Was not that what I had brought him there for? And was I not pleased at the success of my scheme? Certainly I was! Delighted!

Next day Frank went to Glenby without even making the poor pretense of asking me to accompany him.   I spent the time of his absence overseeing the construction of a new greenhouse I was having built.   I was conscientious in my supervision; but I felt no interest in it.   The place was intended for roses, and roses made me think of the pale yellow ones Betty had worn at her breast one evening the week before, when, all lovers being unaccountably absent, we had wandered together under the pines and talked as in the old days before her young womanhood and my gray hairs had risen up to divide us.   She had dropped a rose on the brown floor, and I had sneaked back, after I had left her in the house, to get it, before I went home.   I had it now in my pocket-book.   Confound it, mightn't a future uncle cherish a family affection for his prospective niece?

Frank's wooing seemed to prosper.   The other young sparks, who had haunted Glenby, faded away after his advent.   Betty treated him with most encouraging sweetness; Sara smiled on him; I stood in the background, like a benevolent god of the machine, and flattered myself that I pulled the strings.

At the end of a month something went wrong. Frank came home from Glenby one day in the dumps, and moped for two whole days.   I rode down myself on the third.   I had not gone much to Glenby that month; but, if there were trouble

Bettyward, it was my duty to make smooth the rough places.

As usual, I found Betty in the pineland. I thought she looked rather pale and dull . . . fretting about Frank no doubt. She brightened up when she saw me, evidently expecting that I had come to straighten matters out; but she pretended to be haughty and indifferent.

"I am glad you haven't forgotten us altogether, Stephen," she said coolly. "You haven't been down for a week."

"I'm flattered that you noticed it," I said, sitting down on a fallen tree and looking up at her as she stood, tall and lithe, against an old pine, with her eyes averted. "I shouldn't have supposed you'd want an old fogy like myself poking about and spoiling the idyllic moments of love's young dream."

"Why do you always speak of yourself as old?" said Betty, crossly, ignoring my reference to Frank.

"Because I am old, my dear. Witness these gray hairs."

I pushed up my hat to show them the more recklessly.

Betty barely glanced at them.

"You have just enough to give you a distinguished look," she said, "and you are only forty. A man is in his prime at forty. He never has any sense until he is forty — and sometimes he doesn't seem to have any even then," she concluded impertinently.

My heart beat. Did Betty suspect? Was that last sentence meant to inform me that she was aware of my secret folly, and laughed at it?

" I came over to see what has gone wrong between you and Frank," I said gravely.

Betty bit her lips.

" Nothing," she said.

" Betty," I said reproachfully, " I brought you up . . . or endeavored to bring you up . . . to speak the truth, the whole truth, and nothing but the truth. Don't tell me I have failed. I'll give you another chance. Have you quarreled with Frank? "

" No," said that maddening Betty, " *he* quarreled with me. He went away in a temper and I do not care if he never comes back! "

I shook my head.

" This won't do, Betty. As your old family friend I still claim the right to scold you until you have a husband to do the scolding. You mustn't torment Frank. He is too fine a fellow. You must marry him, Betty."

" Must I? " said Betty, a dusky red flaming out on her cheek. She turned her eyes on me in a most disconcerting fashion. " Do *you* wish me to marry Frank, Stephen? "

Betty had a wretched habit of emphasizing pronouns in a fashion calculated to rattle anybody.

"Yes, I do wish it, because I think it will be best for you," I replied, without looking at her. "You must marry some time, Betty, and Frank is the only man I know to whom I could trust you. As your guardian, I have an interest in seeing you well and wisely settled for life. You have always taken my advice and obeyed my wishes; and you've always found my way the best, in the long run, haven't you, Betty? You won't prove rebellious now, I'm sure. You know quite well that I am advising you for your own good. Frank is a splendid young fellow, who loves you with all his heart. Marry him, Betty. Mind, I don't *command*. I have no right to do that, and you are too old to be ordered about, if I had. But I wish and advise. Isn't that enough, Betty?"

I had been looking away from her all the time I was talking, gazing determinedly down a sunlit vista of pines. Every word I said seemed to tear my heart, and come from my lips stained with lifeblood. Yes, Betty should marry Frank! But, good God, what would become of me!

Betty left her station under the pine tree, and walked around me until she got right in front of my face. I couldn't help looking at her, for if I moved my eyes she moved, too. There was nothing meek or submissive about her; her head was held high, her eyes were blazing, and her cheeks were crimson. But her words were meek enough.

"I will marry Frank if you wish it, Stephen," she said. "You are my friend. I have never crossed your wishes, and, as you say, I have never regretted being always guided by them. I will do exactly as you wish in this case also, I promise you that. But, in so solemn a question, I must be very certain what you *do* wish. There must be no doubt in my mind or heart. Look me squarely in the eyes, Stephen — as you haven't done once to-day, no, nor once since I came home from school — and, so looking, tell me that you wish me to marry Frank Douglas and I will do it! *Do* you, Stephen?"

I had to look her in the eyes, since nothing else would do her; and, as I did so, all the might of manhood in me rose up in hot revolt against the lie I would have told her. That unfaltering, impelling gaze of hers drew the truth from my lips in spite of myself.

"No, I don't wish you to marry Frank Douglas, a thousand times no!" I said passionately. "I don't wish you to marry any man on earth but myself. I love you — I love you, Betty. You are dearer to me than life — dearer to me than my own happiness. It was your happiness I thought of — and so I asked you to marry Frank because I believed he would make you a happy woman. That is all!"

Betty's defiance went from her like a flame blown out. She turned away and drooped her proud head.

"It could not have made me a happy woman to marry one man, loving another," she said, in a whisper.

I got up and went over to her.

"Betty, whom do you love?" I asked, also in a whisper.

"You," she murmured meekly — oh, so meekly, my proud little girl!

"Betty," I said brokenly, "I'm old — too old for you — I'm more than twenty years your senior — I'm —"

"Oh!" Betty wheeled around on me and stamped her foot. "Don't mention your age to me again. I don't care if you're as old as Methusaleh. But I'm not going to coax you to marry me, sir! If you won't, I'll never marry anybody — I'll live and die an old maid. You can please yourself, of course!"

She turned away, half-laughing, half-crying; but I caught her in my arms and crushed her sweet lips against mine.

"Betty, I'm the happiest man in the world — and I was the most miserable when I came here."

"You deserved to be," said Betty cruelly. "I'm glad you were. Any man as stupid as you deserves to be unhappy. What do you think I felt like, loving you with all my heart, and seeing you simply throwing me at another man's head. Why, I've always loved you, Stephen; but I didn't know it until I went to that detestable school. Then I found out — and I thought that was why you had sent me. But, when I came home, you almost broke my heart. That was why I flirted so with all those poor, nice boys — I wanted to hurt you but I never thought I succeeded. You just went on being *fatherly*. Then, when you brought Frank here, I almost gave up hope; and I tried to make up my mind to marry him; I should have done it if you had insisted. But I had to have one more try for happiness first. I had just one little hope to inspire me with sufficient boldness. I saw you, that night, when you came back here and picked up my rose! I had come back, myself, to be alone and unhappy."

"It is the most wonderful thing that ever happened — that you should love me," I said.

"It's not — I couldn't help it," said Betty, nestling her brown head on my shoulder. "You taught me everything else, Stephen, so nobody but you could teach me how to love. You've made a thorough thing of educating me."

"When will you marry me, Betty?" I asked.

"As soon as I can fully forgive you for trying to make me marry somebody else," said Betty.

It was rather hard lines on Frank, when you come to think of it. But, such is the selfishness of human nature that we didn't think much about Frank. The young fellow behaved like the Douglas he was. Went a little white about the lips when I told him, wished me all happiness, and went quietly away, " gentleman unafraid."

He has since married and is, I understand, very happy. Not as happy as I am, of course; that is impossible, because there is only one Betty in the world, and she is my wife.

XII

IN HER SELFLESS MOOD

The raw wind of an early May evening was puffing in and out the curtains of the room where Naomi Holland lay dying. The air was moist and chill, but the sick woman would not have the window closed.

"I can't get my breath if you shut everything up so tight," she said. "Whatever comes, I ain't going to be smothered to death, Car'line Holland."

Outside of the window grew a cherry tree, powdered with moist buds with the promise of blossoms she would not live to see. Between its boughs she saw a crystal cup of sky over hills that were growing dim and purple. The outside air was full of sweet, wholesome springtime sounds that drifted in fitfully. There were voices and whistles in the barnyard, and now and then faint laughter. A bird alighted for a moment on a cherry bough, and twittered restlessly. Sounds and silence told Naomi of the familiar things she could not see — the red maple near the gate-post, the gray mists upon the lowlands, and the silver stars in the soft spring skies.

The room was a small, plain one. The floor was

bare, save for a couple of braided rugs, the plaster discolored, the walls dingy and glaring. There had never been much beauty in Naomi Holland's environment, and, now that she was dying, there was even less.

At the open window a boy of about ten years was leaning out over the sill and whistling. He was tall for his age, and beautiful — the hair a rich auburn with a glistening curl in it, skin very white and warm-tinted, eyes small and of a greenish blue, with dilated pupils and long lashes. He had a weak chin, and a full, sullen mouth.

The bed was in the corner farthest from the window; on it the sick woman, in spite of the pain that was her portion continually, was lying as quiet and motionless as she had done ever since she had lain down upon it for the last time. Naomi Holland never complained; when the agony was at its worst, she shut her teeth more firmly over her bloodless lip, and her great black eyes glared at the blank wall before her in a way that gave her attendants what they called " the creeps," but no word or moan escaped her.

Between the paroxysms she kept up her keen interest in the life that went on about her. Nothing escaped her sharp, alert eyes and ears. This evening she lay spent on the crumpled pillows; she had had a bad spell in the afternoon and it had left

her very weak.   In the dim light her extremely long
face looked corpse-like already.   Her black hair lay
in a heavy braid over the pillow and down the coun-
terpane.   It was all that was left of her beauty, and
she took a fierce joy in it.   Those long, glistening,
sinuous tresses must be combed and braided every
day, no matter what came.

A girl of fourteen was curled up on a chair at the
head of the bed, with her head resting on the pillow.
The boy at the window was her half-brother; but,
between Christopher Holland and Eunice Carr, not
the slightest resemblance existed.

Presently the sibilant silence was broken by a
low, half-strangled sob.   The sick woman, who had
been watching a white evening star through the
cherry boughs, turned impatiently at the sound.

" I wish you'd get over that, Eunice," she said
sharply.   " I don't want any one crying over me
until I'm dead; and then you'll have plenty else to
do, most likely.   If it wasn't for Christopher I
wouldn't be anyways unwilling to die.   When one
has had such a life as I've had, there isn't much in
death to be afraid of.   Only, a body would like
to go right off, and not die by inches, like this.
'Tain't fair! "

She snapped out the last sentence as if addressing
some unseen, tyrannical presence; her voice, at least,
had not weakened, but was as clear and incisive as

ever. The boy at the window stopped whistling, and the girl silently wiped her eyes on her faded gingham apron.

Naomi drew her own hair over her lips, and kissed it.

" You'll never have hair like that, Eunice," she said. " It does seem most too pretty to bury, doesn't it? Mind you see that it is fixed nice when I'm laid out. Comb it right up on my head and braid it there."

A sound, such as might be wrung from a suffering animal, came from the girl, but at the same moment the door opened and a woman entered.

" Chris," she said sharply, " you get right off for the cows, you lazy little scamp! You knew right well you had to go for them, and here you've been idling, and me looking high and low for you. Make haste now; it's ridiculous late."

The boy pulled in his head and scowled at his aunt, but he dared not disobey, and went out slowly with a sulky mutter.

His aunt subdued a movement, that might have developed into a sound box on his ears, with a rather frightened glance at the bed. Naomi Holland was spent and dying, but her temper was still a thing to hold in dread, and her sister-in-law did not choose to rouse it by slapping Christopher. To her and her co-nurse the spasms of rage, which the sick woman sometimes had, seemed to partake of the nature of devil possession. The last one, only three days before, had been provoked by Christopher's complaint of some real or fancied ill-treatment from his aunt, and the latter had no mind to bring on another. She went over to the bed, and straightened the clothes.

"Sarah and I are going out to milk, Naomi. Eunice will stay with you. She can run for us if you feel another spell coming on."

Naomi Holland looked up at her sister-in-law with something like malicious enjoyment.

"I ain't going to have any more spells, Car'line Anne. I'm going to die to-night. But you needn't hurry milking for that, at all. I'll take my time."

She liked to see the alarm that came over the other woman's face. It was richly worth while to scare Caroline Holland like that.

"Are you feeling any worse, Naomi?" asked the latter shakily. "If you are I'll send for Charles to go for the doctor."

"No, you won't. What good can the doctor do me? I don't want either his or Charles' permission to die. You can go and milk at your ease. I won't die till you're done — I won't deprive you of the pleasure of seeing me."

Mrs. Holland shut her lips and went out of the room with a martyr-like expression. In some ways

Naomi Holland was not an exacting patient, but she took her satisfaction out in the biting, malicious speeches she never failed to make. Even on her death-bed her hostility to her sister-in-law had to find vent.

Outside, at the steps, Sarah Spencer was waiting, with the milk pails over her arm. Sarah Spencer had no fixed abiding place, but was always to be found where there was illness. Her experience, and an utter lack of nerves, made her a good nurse. She was a tall, homely woman with iron gray hair and a lined face. Beside her, the trim little Caroline Anne, with her light step and round, apple-red face, looked almost girlish.

The two women walked to the barnyard, discussing Naomi in undertones as they went. The house they had left behind grew very still.

In Naomi Holland's room the shadows were gathering. Eunice timidly bent over her mother.

" Ma, do you want the light lit? "

" No, I'm watching that star just below the big cherry bough. I'll see it set behind the hill. I've seen it there, off and on, for twelve years, and now I'm taking a good-by look at it. I want you to keep still, too. I've got a few things to think over, and I don't want to be disturbed."

The girl lifted herself about noiselessly and locked her hands over the bed-post. Then she laid her face down on them, biting at them silently until the marks of her teeth showed white against their red roughness.

Naomi Holland did not notice her. She was looking steadfastly at the great, pearl-like sparkle in the faint-hued sky. When it finally disappeared from her vision she struck her long, thin hands together twice, and a terrible expression came over her face for a moment. But, when she spoke, her voice was quite calm.

"You can light the candle now, Eunice. Put it up on the shelf here, where it won't shine in my eyes. And then sit down on the foot of the bed where I can see you. I've got something to say to you."

Eunice obeyed her noiselessly. As the pallid light shot up, it revealed the child plainly. She was thin and ill-formed — one shoulder being slightly higher than the other. She was dark, like her mother, but her features were irregular, and her hair fell in straggling, dim locks about her face. Her eyes were a dark brown, and over one was the slanting red scar of a birth mark.

Naomi Holland looked at her with the contempt she had never made any pretense of concealing. The girl was bone of her bone and flesh of her flesh, but she had never loved her; all the mother love in her had been lavished on her son.

When Eunice had placed the candle on the shelf and drawn down the ugly blue paper blinds, shutting out the strips of violet sky where a score of glimmering points were now visible, she sat down on the foot of the bed, facing her mother.

" The door is shut, is it, Eunice? "

Eunice nodded.

" Because I don't want Car'line or any one else peeking and harking to what I've got to say. She's out milking now, and I must make the most of the chance. Eunice, I'm going to die, and . . ."

" Ma! "

" There now, no taking on! You knew it had to come sometime soon. I haven't the strength to talk much, so I want you just to be quiet and listen. I ain't feeling any pain now, so I can think and talk pretty clear. Are you listening, Eunice? "

" Yes, ma."

" Mind you are. It's about Christopher. It hasn't been out of my mind since I laid down here. I've fought for a year to live, on his account, and it ain't any use. I must just die and leave him, and I don't know what he'll do. It's dreadful to think of."

She paused, and struck her shrunken hand sharply against the table.

" If he was bigger and could look out for himself it wouldn't be so bad. But he is only a little fellow, and Car'line hates him. You'll both have to live with her until you're grown up. She'll put on him and abuse him. He's like his father in some ways; he's got a temper and he is stubborn. He'll never get on with Car'line. Now, Eunice, I'm going to get you to promise to take my place with Christopher when I'm dead, as far as you can. You've got to; it's your duty. But I want you to promise."

" I will, ma," whispered the girl solemnly.

" You haven't much force — you never had. If you was smart, you could do a lot for him. But you'll have to do your best. I want you to promise me faithfully that you'll stand by him and protect him — that you won't let people impose on him; that you'll never desert him as long as he needs you, no matter what comes. Eunice, promise me this! "

In her excitement the sick woman raised herself up in the bed, and clutched the girl's thin arm. Her eyes were blazing and two scarlet spots glowed in her thin cheeks.

Eunice's face was white and tense. She clasped her hands as one in prayer.

" Mother, I promise it! "

Naomi relaxed her grip on the girl's arm and sank back exhausted on the pillow. A death-like look came over her face as the excitement faded.

" My mind is easier now. But if I could only have lived another year or two! And I hate Car'-

line — hate her! Eunice, don't you ever let her abuse my boy! If she did, or if you neglected him, I'd come back from my grave to you! As for the property, things will be pretty straight. I've seen to that. There'll be no squabbling and doing Christopher out of his rights. He's to have the farm as soon as he's old enough to work it, and he's to provide for you. And, Eunice, remember what you've promised!"

Outside, in the thickly gathering dusk, Caroline Holland and Sarah Spencer were at the dairy, straining the milk into creamers, for which Christopher was sullenly pumping water. The house was far from the road, up to which a long red lane led; across the field was the old Holland homestead where Caroline lived; her unmarried sister-in-law, Electa Holland, kept house for her while she waited on Naomi.

It was her night to go home and sleep, but Naomi's words haunted her, although she believed they were born of pure " cantankerousness."

" You'd better go in and look at her, Sarah," she said, as she rinsed out the pails. " If you think I'd better stay here to-night, I will. If the woman was like anybody else a body would know what to do; but, if she thought she could scare us by saying she was going to die, she'd say it."

When Sarah went in, the sick room was very quiet. In her opinion Naomi was no worse than usual, and she told Caroline so; but the latter felt vaguely uneasy and concluded to stay.

Naomi was as cool and defiant as customary. She made them bring Christopher in to say goodnight and had him lifted up on the bed to kiss her. Then she held him back and looked at him admiringly — at the bright curls and rosy cheeks and round, firm limbs. The boy was uncomfortable under her gaze and squirmed hastily down. Her eyes followed him greedily, as he went out. When the door closed behind him she groaned. Sarah Spencer was startled. She had never heard Naomi Holland groan since she had come to wait on her.

"Are you feeling any worse, Naomi? Is the pain coming back?"

"No. Go and tell Car'line to give Christopher some of that grape jelly on his bread before he goes to bed. She'll find it in the cupboard under the stairs."

Presently the house grew very still. Caroline had dropped asleep on the sitting-room lounge, across the hall. Sarah Spencer nodded over her knitting by the table in the sick room. She had told Eunice to go to bed, but the child refused. She still sat huddled up on the foot of the bed, watching her mother's face intently. Naomi appeared to sleep. The candle by her bedside burned slowly. To Eunice the elfin flame, which flickered gaily, seemed like an impish eye upon her. The wavering light cast grotesque shadows of Sarah Spencer's head on the wall. The thin curtains at the window wavered to and fro, as if shaken by ghostly hands.

At midnight Naomi Holland opened her eyes. The child she had never loved was the only one to go with her to the brink of the Unseen.

" Eunice — remember ! "

It was the faintest whisper. The soul, passing over the threshold of another life, strained back to its only earthly tie. A quiver passed over the long, pallid face.

A horrible scream rang through the silent house. Sarah Spencer sprang out of her doze in consternation, and gazed blankly at the shrieking child. Caroline came hurrying in with distended eyes. On the bed Naomi Holland lay dead.

In the room where she had died Naomi Holland lay in her coffin. It was dim and hushed; but, in the rest of the house, the preparations for the funeral were being hurried on. Through it all Eunice moved, calm and silent. Since her one wild spasm of screaming by her mother's death-bed she had shed no tear, given no sign of grief. Perhaps, as her mother had said, she had no time. There was Christopher to be looked after. The boy's grief was stormy and uncontrolled. He had cried until he was utterly exhausted. It was Eunice who soothed him, coaxed him to eat, kept him constantly by her. At night she took him to her own room and watched over him while he slept.

When the funeral was over the household furniture was packed away or sold. The house was locked up and the farm rented. There was nowhere for the children to go, save to their uncle's. Caroline Holland did not want them, but, having to take them, she grimly made up her mind to do what she considered her duty by them. She had five children of her own and between them and Christopher a standing feud had existed from the time he could walk.

She had never liked Naomi. Few people did. Benjamin Holland had not married until late in life, and his wife had declared war on his family at sight. She was a stranger in Avonlea,— a widow, with a three-year-old child. She made few friends, as some people always asserted that she was not in her right mind.

Within a year of her second marriage Christopher was born, and from the hour of his birth his mother had worshiped him blindly. He was her only solace. For him she toiled and pinched and saved. Benjamin Holland had not been " fore-handed " when she married him; but, when he died, six years after his marriage, he was a well-to-do man.

Naomi made no pretense of mourning for him. It was an open secret that they had quarreled like the proverbial cat and dog. Charles Holland and his wife had naturally sided with Benjamin, and Naomi fought her battles single-handed. After her husband's death, she managed to farm alone, and made it pay. When the mysterious malady which was to end her life first seized on her she fought against it with all the strength and stubbornness of her strong and stubborn nature. Her will won for her an added year of life, and then she had to yield. She tasted all the bitterness of death the day on which she lay down on her bed, and saw her enemy come in to rule her house.

But Caroline Holland was not a bad or unkind woman. True, she did not love Naomi or her children; but the woman was dying and must be looked after for the sake of common humanity. Caroline thought she had done well by her sister-in-law.

When the red clay was heaped over Naomi's grave in the Avonlea burying ground, Caroline took Eunice and Christopher home with her. Christopher did not want to go; it was Eunice who reconciled him. He clung to her with an exacting affection born of loneliness and grief.

In the days that followed Caroline Holland was

obliged to confess to herself that there would have been no doing anything with Christopher had it not been for Eunice. The boy was sullen and obstinate, but his sister had an unfailing influence over him.

In Charles Holland's household no one was allowed to eat the bread of idleness. His own children were all girls, and Christopher came in handy as a chore boy. He was made to work — perhaps too hard. But Eunice helped him, and did half his work for him when nobody knew. When he quarreled with his cousins, she took his part; whenever possible she took on herself the blame and punishment of his misdeeds.

Electa Holland was Charles' unmarried sister. She had kept house for Benjamin until he married; then Naomi had bundled her out. Electa had never forgiven her for it. Her hatred passed on to Naomi's children. In a hundred petty ways she revenged herself on them. For herself, Eunice bore it patiently; but it was a different matter when it touched Christopher.

Once Electa boxed Christopher's ears. Eunice, who was knitting by the table, stood up. A resemblance to her mother, never before visible, came out in her face like a brand. She lifted her hand and slapped Electa's cheek deliberately twice, leaving a dull red mark where she struck.

" If you ever strike my brother again," she said, slowly and vindictively, " I will slap your face every time you do. You have no right to touch him."

" My patience, what a fury!" said Electa. " Naomi Holland'll never be dead as long as you're alive!"

She told Charles of the affair and Eunice was severely punished. But Electa never interfered with Christopher again.

All the discordant elements in the Holland household could not prevent the children from growing up. It was a consummation which the harassed Caroline devoutly wished. When Christopher Holland was seventeen he was a man grown — a big, strapping fellow. His childish beauty had coarsened, but he was thought handsome by many.

He took charge of his mother's farm then, and the brother and sister began their new life together in the long-unoccupied house. There were few regrets on either side when they left Charles Holland's roof. In her secret heart Eunice felt an unspeakable relief.

Christopher had been " hard to manage," as his uncle said, in the last year. He was getting into the habit of keeping late hours and doubtful company. This always provoked an explosion of wrath from

Charles Holland, and the conflicts between him and his nephew were frequent and bitter.

For four years after their return home Eunice had a hard and anxious life. Christopher was idle and dissipated. Most people regarded him as a worthless fellow, and his uncle washed his hands of him utterly. Only Eunice never failed him; she never reproached or railed; she worked like a slave to keep things together. Eventually her patience prevailed. Christopher, to a great extent, reformed and worked harder. He was never unkind to Eunice, even in his rages. It was not in him to appreciate or return her devotion; but his tolerant acceptance of it was her solace.

When Eunice was twenty-eight, Edward Bell wanted to marry her. He was a plain, middle-aged widower with four children; but, as Caroline did not fail to remind her, Eunice herself was not for every market, and the former did her best to make the match. She might have succeeded had it not been for Christopher. When he, in spite of Caroline's skillful management, got an inkling of what was going on, he flew into a true Holland rage. If Eunice married and left him — he would sell the farm and go to the Devil by way of the Klondike. He could not, and would not, do without her. No arrangement suggested by Caroline availed to pacify him, and, in the end, Eunice refused to marry Edward

Bell. She could not leave Christopher, she said simply, and in this she stood rock-firm. Caroline could not budge her an inch.

" You're a fool, Eunice," she said, when she was obliged to give up in despair. " It's not likely you'll ever have another chance. As for Chris, in a year or two he'll be marrying himself, and where will you be then? You'll find your nose nicely out of joint when he brings a wife in here."

The shaft went home. Eunice's lips turned white. But she said, faintly, " The house is big enough for us both, if he does."

Caroline sniffed.

" Maybe so. You'll find out. However, there's no use talking. You're as set as your mother was, and nothing would ever budge her an inch. I only hope you won't be sorry for it."

When three more years had passed Christopher began to court Victoria Pye. The affair went on for some time before either Eunice or the Hollands got wind of it. When they did there was an explosion. Between the Hollands and the Pyes, root and branch, existed a feud that dated back for three generations. That the original cause of the quarrel was totally forgotten did not matter; it was a matter of family pride that a Holland should have no dealings with a Pye.

When Christopher flew so openly in the face of

this cherished hatred, there could be nothing less than consternation. Charles Holland broke through his determination to have nothing to do with Christopher, to remonstrate. Caroline went to Eunice in as much of a splutter as if Christopher had been her own brother.

Eunice did not care a row of pins for the Holland-Pye feud. Victoria was to her what any other girl, upon whom Christopher cast eyes of love, would have been — a supplanter. For the first time in her life she was torn with passionate jealousy; existence became a nightmare to her. Urged on by Caroline, and her own pain, she ventured to remonstrate with Christopher, also. She had expected a burst of rage, but he was surprisingly good-natured. He seemed even amused.

" What have you got against Victoria? " he asked, tolerantly.

Eunice had no answer ready. It was true that nothing could be said against the girl. She felt helpless and baffled. Christopher laughed at her silence.

" I guess you're a little jealous," he said. " You must have expected I would get married some time. This house is big enough for us all. You'd better look at the matter sensibly, Eunice. Don't let Charles and Caroline put nonsense into your head. A man must marry to please himself."

Christopher was out late that night. Eunice

waited up for him, as she always did. It was a chilly spring evening, reminding her of the night her mother had died. The kitchen was in spotless order, and she sat down on a stiff-backed chair by the window to wait for her brother.

She did not want a light. The moonlight fell in with faint illumination. Outside, the wind was blowing over a bed of new-sprung mint in the garden, and was suggestively fragrant. It was a very old-fashioned garden, full of perennials Naomi Holland had planted long ago. Eunice always kept it primly neat. She had been working in it that day, and felt tired.

She was all alone in the house and the loneliness filled her with a faint dread. She had tried all that day to reconcile herself to Christopher's marriage, and had partially succeeded. She told herself that she could still watch over him and care for his comfort. She would even try to love Victoria; after all, it might be pleasant to have another woman in the house. So, sitting there, she fed her hungry soul with these husks of comfort.

When she heard Christopher's step she moved about quickly to get a light. He frowned when he saw her; he had always resented her sitting up for him. He sat down by the stove and took off his boots, while Eunice got a lunch for him. After he had eaten it in silence he made no move to go to bed.   A chill, premonitory fear crept over Eunice. It did not surprise her at all when Christopher finally said, abruptly, " Eunice, I've a notion to get married this spring."

Eunice clasped her hands together under the table. It was what she had been expecting.   She said so, in a monotonous voice.

" We must make some arrangement for — for you, Eunice," Christopher went on, in a hurried, hesitant way, keeping his eyes riveted doggedly on his plate.   " Victoria doesn't exactly like — well, she thinks it's better for young married folks to begin life by themselves, and I guess she's about right.   You wouldn't find it comfortable, anyhow, having to step back to second place after being mistress here so long."

Eunice tried to speak, but only an indistinct murmur came from her bloodless lips.   The sound made Christopher look up.   Something in her face irritated him.   He pushed back his chair impatiently.

" Now, Eunice, don't go to taking on.   It won't be any use.   Look at this business in a sensible way. I'm fond of you, and all that, but a man is bound to consider his wife first.   I'll provide for you comfortably."

" Do you mean to say that your wife is going to turn me out?"   Eunice gasped, rather than spoke, the words.

Christopher drew his reddish brows together.

" I just mean that Victoria says she won't marry
me if she has to live with you.   She's afraid of
you.   I told her you wouldn't interfere with her,
but she wasn't satisfied.   It's your own fault, Eunice.
You've always been so queer and close that people
think you're an awful crank.   Victoria's young and
lively, and you and she wouldn't get on at all.   There
isn't any question of turning you out.   I'll build a
little house for you somewhere, and you'll be a great
deal better off there than you would be here.   So
don't make a fuss."

Eunice did not look as if she were going to make
a fuss.   She sat as if turned to stone, her hands lying
palm upward in her lap.   Christopher got up,
hugely relieved that the dreaded explanation was
over.

" Guess I'll go to bed.   You'd better have gone
long ago.   It's all nonsense, this waiting up for
me."

When he had gone Eunice drew a long, sobbing
breath and looked about her lilke a dazed soul.   All
the sorrow of her life was as nothing to the desola-
tion that assailed her now.

She rose and, with uncertain footsteps, passed out
through the hall and into the room where her mother
died.   She had always kept it locked and undisturbed; it was arranged just as Naomi Holland had

left it.   Eunice tottered to the bed and sat down on it.

She recalled the promise she had made to her mother in that very room.   Was the power to keep it to be wrested from her?   Was she to be driven from her home and parted from the only creature she had on earth to love?   And would Christopher allow it, after all her sacrifices for him?   Aye, that he would!   He cared more for that black-eyed, waxen-faced girl at the old Pye place than for his own kin. Eunice put her hands over her dry, burning eyes and groaned aloud.

Caroline Holland had her hour of triumph over Eunice when she heard it all.   To one of her nature there was no pleasure so sweet as that of saying, " I told you so."   Having said it, however, she offered Eunice a home.   Electa Holland was dead, and Eunice might fill her place very acceptably, if she would.

" You can't go off and live by yourself," Caroline told her.   " It's all nonsense to talk of such a thing. We will give you a home, if Christopher is going to turn you out.   You were always a fool, Eunice, to pet and pamper him as you've done.   This is the thanks you get for it — turned out like a dog for his fine wife's whim!   I only wish your mother was alive! "

It was probably the first time Caroline had ever wished this. She had flown at Christopher like a fury about the matter, and had been rudely insulted for her pains. Christopher had told her to mind her own business.

When Caroline cooled down she made some arrangements with him, to all of which Eunice listlessly assented. She did not care what became of her. When Christopher Holland brought Victoria as mistress to the house where his mother had toiled, and suffered, and ruled with her rod of iron, Eunice was gone. In Charles Holland's household she took Electa's place — an unpaid upper servant.

Charles and Caroline were kind enough to her, and there was plenty to do. For five years her dull, colorless life went on, during which time she never crossed the threshold of the house where Victoria Holland ruled with a sway as absolute as Naomi's had been. Caroline's curiosity led her, after her first anger had cooled, to make occasional calls, the observations of which she faithfully reported to Eunice. The latter never betrayed any interest in them, save once. This was when Caroline came home full of the news that Victoria had had the room where Naomi died opened up, and showily furnished as a parlor. Then Eunice's sallow face crimsoned, and her eyes flashed, over the desecration. But no word of comment or complaint ever crossed her lips.

She knew, as every one else knew, that the glamor soon went from Christopher Holland's married life. The marriage proved an unhappy one. Not unnaturally, although unjustly, Eunice blamed Victoria for this, and hated her more than ever for it.

Christopher seldom came to Charles' house. Possibly he felt ashamed. He had grown into a morose, silent man, at home and abroad. It was said he had gone back to his old drinking habits.

One fall Victoria Holland went to town to visit her married sister. She took their only child with her. In her absence Christopher kept house for himself.

It was a fall long remembered in Avonlea. With the dropping of the leaves, and the shortening of the dreary days, the shadow of a fear fell over the land. Charles Holland brought the fateful news home one night.

"There's smallpox in Charlottetown — five or six cases. Came in one of the vessels. There was a concert, and a sailor from one of the ships was there, and took sick the next day."

This was alarming enough. Charlottetown was not so very far away and considerable traffic went on between it and the north shore districts.

When Caroline recounted the concert story to Christopher the next morning his ruddy face turned quite pale. He opened his lips as if to speak, then closed them again. They were sitting in the kitchen; Caroline had run over to return some tea she had borrowed, and, incidentally, to see what she could of Victoria's housekeeping in her absence. Her eyes had been busy while her tongue ran on, so she did not notice the man's pallor and silence.

"How long does it take for smallpox to develop after one has been exposed to it?" he asked abruptly, when Caroline rose to go.

"Ten to fourteen days, I calc'late," was her answer. "I must see about having the girls vaccinated right off. It'll likely spread. When do you expect Victoria home?"

"When she's ready to come, whenever that will be," was the gruff response.

A week later Caroline said to Eunice, "Whatever's got Christopher? He hasn't been out anywhere for ages — just hangs round home the whole time. It's something new for him. I s'pose the place is so quiet, now Madam Victoria's away, that he can find some rest for his soul. I believe I'll run over after milking and see how he's getting on. You might as well come, too, Eunice."

Eunice shook her head. She had all her mother's obstinacy, and darken Victoria's door she would not. She went on patiently darning socks, sitting at the west window, which was her favorite position — perhaps because she could look from it across the sloping field and past the crescent curve of the maple grove to her lost home.

After milking, Caroline threw a shawl over her head and ran across the field. The house looked lonely and deserted. As she fumbled at the latch of the gate the kitchen door opened, and Christopher Holland appeared on the threshold.

" Don't come any farther," he called.

Caroline fell back in blank astonishment. Was this some more of Victoria's work?

" I ain't an agent for the smallpox," she called back viciously.

Christopher did not heed her.

" Will you go home and ask uncle if he'll go, or send for Dr. Spencer? He's the smallpox doctor. I'm sick."

Caroline felt a thrill of dismay and fear. She faltered a few steps backward.

" Sick? What's the matter with you? "

" I was in Charlottetown that night, and went to the concert. That sailor sat right beside me. I thought at the time he looked sick. It was just twelve days ago. I've felt bad all day yesterday and to-day. Send for the doctor. Don't come near the house, or let any one else come near."

He went in and shut the door. Caroline stood for a few moments in an almost ludicrous panic. Then she turned and ran, as if for her life, across the field. Eunice saw her coming and met her at the door.

"Mercy on us!" gasped Caroline. "Christopher's sick and he thinks he's got the smallpox. Where's Charles?"

Eunice tottered back against the door. Her hand went up to her side in a way that had been getting very common with her of late. Even in the midst of her excitement Caroline noticed it.

"Eunice, what makes you do that every time anything startles you?" she asked sharply. "Is it anything about your heart?"

"I don't — know. A little pain — it's gone now. Did you say that Christopher has — the smallpox?"

"Well, he says so himself, and it's more than likely, considering the circumstances. I declare, I never got such a turn in my life. It's a dreadful thing. I must find Charles at once — there'll be a hundred things to do."

Eunice hardly heard her. Her mind was centered upon one idea. Christopher was ill — alone — she must go to him. It did not matter what his disease was. When Caroline came in from her breathless expedition to the barn, she found Eunice standing by the table, with her hat and shawl on, tying up a parcel.

"Eunice! Where on earth are you going?"

"Over home," said Eunice. "If Christopher is

going to be ill he must be nursed, and I'm the one to do it. He ought to be seen to right away."

" Eunice Carr! Have you gone clean out of your senses? It's the smallpox — the smallpox! If he's got it he'll have to be taken to the smallpox hospital in town. You shan't stir a step to go to that house!"

" I will." Eunice faced her excited aunt quietly. The odd resemblance to her mother, which only came out in moments of great tension, was plainly visible. " He shan't go to that hospital — they never get proper attention there. You needn't try to stop me. It won't put you or your family in any danger."

Caroline fell helplessly into a chair. She felt that it would be of no use to argue with a woman so determined. She wished Charles was there. But Charles had already gone, post-haste, for the doctor.

With a firm step, Eunice went across the field foot-path she had not trodden for so long. She felt no fear — rather a sort of elation. Christopher needed her once more; the interloper who had come between them was not there. As she walked through the frosty twilight she thought of the promise made to Naomi Holland, years ago.

Christopher saw her coming and waved her back. " Don't come any nearer, Eunice. Didn't Caroline tell you? I'm taking smallpox."

Eunice did not pause. She went boldly through the yard and up the porch steps. He retreated before her and held the door.

"Eunice, you're crazy, girl! Go home, before it's too late."

Eunice pushed open the door resolutely and went in.

"It's too late now. I'm here, and I mean to stay and nurse you, if it's the smallpox you've got. Maybe it's not. Just now, when a person has a finger-ache, he thinks it's smallpox. Anyhow, whatever it is, you ought to be in bed and looked after. You'll catch cold. Let me get a light and have a look at you."

Christopher had sunk into a chair. His natural selfishness reasserted itself, and he made no further effort to dissuade Eunice. She got a lamp and set it on the table by him, while she scrutinized his face closely.

"You look feverish. What do you feel like? When did you take sick?"

"Yesterday afternoon. I have chills and hot spells and pains in my back. Eunice, do you think it's really smallpox? And will I die?"

He caught her hands, and looked imploringly up at her, as a child might have done. Eunice felt a wave of love and tenderness sweep warmly over her starved heart.

"Don't worry. Lots of people recover from smallpox if they're properly nursed, and you'll be that, for I'll see to it. Charles has gone for the doctor, and we'll know when he comes. You must go straight to bed."

She took off her hat and shawl, and hung them up. She felt as much at home as if she had never been away. She had got back to her kingdom, and there was none to dispute it with her. When Dr. Spencer and old Giles Blewett, who had had smallpox in his youth, came, two hours later, they found Eunice in serene charge. The house was in order and reeking with disinfectants. Victoria's fine furniture and fixings were being bundled out of the parlor. There was no bedroom downstairs, and, if Christopher was going to be ill, he must be installed there.

The doctor looked grave.

"I don't like it," he said, "but I'm not quite sure yet. If it is smallpox the eruption will probably be out by the morning. I must admit he has most of the symptoms. Will you have him taken to the hospital?"

"No," said Eunice, decisively, "I'll nurse him myself. I'm not afraid and I'm well and strong."

The doctor nodded.

"Very well. You've been vaccinated lately?"

"Yes."

" Well, nothing more can be done at present. You may as well lie down for a while and save your strength."

But Eunice could not do that. There was too much to attend to. She went out to the hall and threw up the window. Down below, at a safe distance, Charles Holland was waiting. The cold wind blew up to Eunice the odor of the disinfectants with which he had steeped himself.

" What does the doctor say? " he shouted.

" He thinks it's the smallpox. Have you sent word to Victoria? "

" Yes, Jim Blewett drove into town and told her. She'll stay with her sister till it is over. Of course it's the best thing for her to do. She's terribly frightened."

Eunice's lip curled contemptuously. To her, a wife who could desert her husband, no matter what disease he had, was an incomprehensible creature. But it was better so; she would have Christopher all to herself.

The night was long and wearisome, but the morning came all too soon for the dread certainty it brought. The doctor pronounced the case smallpox. Eunice had hoped against hope, but now, knowing the worst, she was very calm and resolute.

By noon the fateful yellow flag was flying over the house, and all arrangements had been made. Caroline was to do the necessary cooking, and Charles was to bring the food and leave it in the yard. Old Giles Blewett was to come every day and attend to the stock, as well as help Eunice with the sick man; and the long, hard fight with death began.

It was a hard fight, indeed. Christopher Holland, in the clutches of the loathsome disease, was an object from which his nearest and dearest might have been pardoned for shrinking. But Eunice never faltered; she never left her post. Sometimes she dozed in a chair by the bed, but she never lay down. Her endurance was something wonderful, her patience and tenderness almost superhuman. To and fro she went, in noiseless ministry, as the long, dreadful days wore away, with a quiet smile on her lips, and in her dark, sorrowful eyes the rapt look of a pictured saint in some dim cathedral niche. For her there was no world outside the bare room where lay the repulsive object she loved.

One day the doctor looked very grave. He had grown well-hardened to pitiful scenes in his lifetime; but he shrank from telling Eunice that her brother could not live. He had never seen such devotion as hers. It seemed brutal to tell her that it had been in vain.

But Eunice had seen it for herself. She took it very calmly, the doctor thought. And she had her reward at last — such as it was. She thought it amply sufficient.

One night Christopher Holland opened his swollen eyes as she bent over him. They were alone in the old house. It was raining outside, and the drops rattled noisily on the panes.

Christopher smiled at his sister with parched lips, and put out a feeble hand towards her.

"Eunice," he said faintly, "you've been the best sister ever a man had. I haven't treated you right; but you've stood by me to the last. Tell Victoria — tell her — to be good to you —"

His voice died away into an inarticulate murmur. Eunice Carr was alone with her dead.

They buried Christopher Holland in haste and privacy the next day. The doctor disinfected the house, and Eunice was to stay there alone until it might be safe to make other arrangements. She had not shed a tear; the doctor thought she was a rather odd person, but he had a great admiration for her. He told her she was the best nurse he had ever seen. To Eunice, praise or blame mattered nothing. Something in her life had snapped — some vital interest had departed. She wondered how she could live through the dreary, coming years.

Late that night she went into the room where her mother and brother had died. The window was open and the cold, pure air was grateful to her after the drug-laden atmosphere she had breathed so long. She knelt down by the stripped bed.

"Mother," she said aloud, "I have kept my promise."

When she tried to rise, long after, she staggered and fell across the bed, with her hand pressed on her heart. Old Giles Blewett found her there in the morning. There was a smile on her face.

XIII

THE CONSCIENCE CASE OF DAVID BELL

EBEN BELL came in with an armful of wood and banged it cheerfully down in the box behind the glowing Waterloo stove, which was pouring warmth and ruddy color into the dismal little kitchen, making of it a homey, pleasant place.

" There, sis, that's the last chore on my list. Bob's milking. Nothing more for me to do but put on my white collar for meeting. Avonlea is more than lively since the evangelist came, ain't it, though! "

Mollie Bell nodded. She was curling her hair before the tiny mirror that hung on the whitewashed wall and distorted her round, pink-and-white face into a grotesque caricature.

" Wonder who'll stand up to-night," said Eben reflectively, sitting down on the edge of the wood-box. " There ain't many sinners left in Avonlea — only a few hardened chaps like myself."

" You shouldn't talk like that," said Mollie rebukingly. " What if father heard you ? "

" Father wouldn't hear me if I shouted it in his ear," returned Eben. " He goes around, these days, like a man in a dream and a mighty bad dream at that. Father has always been a good man. What's the matter with him?"

"I don't know," said Mollie, dropping her voice. "Mother is dreadfully worried over him. And everybody is talking, Eb. It just makes me squirm. Flora Jane Fletcher asked me last night why father never testified, and him one of the elders. She said the minister was perplexed about it. I felt my face getting red."

"Why didn't you tell her it was no business of hers?" said Eben angrily. "Old Flora Jane had better mind her own business."

"But all the folks are talking about it, Eb. And mother is fretting her heart out over it. Father has never acted like himself since these meetings began. He just goes there night after night, and sits like a mummy, with his head down. And almost everybody else in Avonlea has testified."

"Oh, no, there's lots haven't," said Eben. "Matthew Cuthbert never has, nor Uncle Elisha, nor any of the Whites."

"But everybody knows they don't believe in getting up and testifying, so nobody wonders when they don't. Besides," Mollie laughed —"Matthew could never get a word out in public, if he did believe in it. He'd be too shy. But," she added with a sigh, "it isn't that way with father. He believes in testimony, so people wonder why he doesn't get up. Why, even old Josiah Sloane gets up every night."

"With his whiskers sticking out every which way, and his hair ditto," interjected the graceless Eben.

"When the minister calls for testimonials and all the folks look at our pew, I feel ready to sink through the floor for shame," sighed Mollie. "If father would get up just once!"

Miriam Bell now entered the kitchen. She was ready for the meeting, to which Major Spencer was to take her. She was a tall, pale girl, with a serious face, and dark, thoughtful eyes, totally unlike Mollie. She had "come under conviction" during the meetings, and had stood up for prayer and testimony several times. The evangelist thought her very spiritual. She heard Mollie's concluding sentence and spoke reprovingly.

"You shouldn't criticize your father, Mollie. It isn't for you to judge him."

Eben had hastily slipped out. He was afraid Miriam would begin talking religion to him if he stayed. He had with difficulty escaped from an exhortation by Robert in the cow-stable. There was no peace in Avonlea for the unregenerate, he reflected. Robert and Miriam had both "come out," and Mollie was hovering on the brink.

"Dad and I are the black sheep of the family," he said, with a laugh, for which he at once felt guilty.

Eben had been brought up with a strict reverence for all religious matters. On the surface he might sometimes laugh at them, but the deeps troubled him whenever he did so.

Indoors, Miriam touched her younger sister's shoulder and looked at her affectionately.

" Won't you decide to-night, Mollie? " she asked, in a voice tremulous with emotion.

Mollie crimsoned and turned her face away uncomfortably. She did not know what answer to make, and was glad that a jingle of bells outside saved her the necessity of replying.

" There's your beau, Miriam," she said, as she darted into the sitting room.

Soon after, Eben brought the family pung and his chubby red mare to the door for Mollie. He had not as yet attained to the dignity of a cutter of his own. That was for his elder brother, Robert, who presently came out in his new fur coat and drove dashingly away with bells and glitter.

" Thinks he's the people," remarked Eben, with a fraternal grin.

The rich winter twilight was purpling over the white world as they drove down the lane under the over-arching wild cherry trees that glittered with gemmy hoar-frost. The snow creaked and crisped under the runners. A shrill wind was keening in the leafless dogwoods. Over the trees the sky was a dome of silver, with a lucent star or two on the slope of the west. Earth-stars gleamed warmly out here and there, where homesteads were tucked snugly away in their orchards or groves of birch.

"The church will be jammed to-night," said Eben. "It's so fine that folks will come from near and far. Guess it'll be exciting."

"If only father would testify!" sighed Mollie, from the bottom of the pung, where she was snuggled amid furs and straw. "Miriam can say what she likes, but I do feel as if we were all disgraced. It sends a creep all over me to hear Mr. Bentley say, 'Now, isn't there one more to say a word for Jesus?' and look right over at father."

Eben flicked his mare with his whip, and she broke into a trot. The silence was filled with a faint, fairy-like melody from afar down the road where a pungful of young folks from White Sands were singing hymns on their way to meeting.

"Look here, Mollie," said Eben awkwardly at last, "are you going to stand up for prayers to-night?"

"I — I can't as long as father acts this way," answered Mollie, in a choked voice. "I — I want to, Eb, and Mirry and Bob want me to, but I can't. I do hope that the evangelist won't come and talk to me special to-night. I always feel as if I was being pulled two different ways, when he does."

Back in the kitchen at home Mrs. Bell was waiting for her husband to bring the horse to the door.   She was a slight, dark-eyed little woman, with thin, vivid-red cheeks.   From out of the swathings in which she had wrapped her bonnet, her face gleamed sad and troubled.   Now and then she sighed heavily.

The cat came to her from under the stove, languidly stretching himself, and yawning until all the red cavern of his mouth and throat was revealed. At the moment he had an uncanny resemblance to Elder Joseph Blewett of White Sands — Roaring Joe, the irreverent boys called him — when he grew excited and shouted.   Mrs. Bell saw it — and then reproached herself for the sacrilege.

" But it's no wonder I've wicked thoughts," she said, wearily.   " I'm that worried I ain't rightly myself.   If he would only tell me what the trouble is, maybe I could help him.   At any rate, I'd *know*.   It hurts me so to see him going about, day after day, with his head hanging and that look on his face, as if he had something fearful on his conscience — him that never harmed a living soul.   And then the way he groans and mutters in his sleep!   He has always lived a just, upright life.   He hasn't no right to go on like this, disgracing his family."

Mrs. Bell's angry sob was cut short by the sleigh at the door.   Her husband poked in his bushy, iron-gray head and said, " Now, mother."   He helped her into the sleigh, tucked the rugs warmly around her, and put a hot brick at her feet. His solicitude hurt her. It was all for her material comfort. It did not matter to him what mental agony she might suffer over his strange attitude. For the first time in their married life Mary Bell felt resentment against her husband.

They drove along in silence, past the snow-powdered hedges of spruce, and under the arches of the forest roadways. They were late, and a great stillness was over all the land. David Bell never spoke. All his usual cheerful talkativeness had disappeared since the revival meetings had begun in Avonlea. From the first he had gone about as a man over whom some strange doom is impending, seemingly oblivious to all that might be said or thought of him in his own family or in the church. Mary Bell thought she would go out of her mind if her husband continued to act in this way. Her reflections were bitter and rebellious as they sped along through the glittering night of the winter's prime.

"I don't get one bit of good out of the meetings," she thought resentfully. "There ain't any peace or joy for me, not even in testifying myself, when David sits there like a stick or stone. If he'd been opposed to the revivalist coming here, like old Uncle Jerry, or if he didn't believe in public testimony, I wouldn't mind. I'd understand. But, as it is, I feel dreadful humiliated."

Revival meetings had never been held in Avonlea before. "Uncle" Jerry MacPherson, who was the supreme local authority in church matters, taking precedence of even the minister, had been uncompromisingly opposed to them. He was a stern, deeply religious Scotchman, with a horror of the emotional form of religion. As long as Uncle Jerry's spare, ascetic form and deeply-graved square-jawed face filled his accustomed corner by the northwest window of Avonlea church no revivalist might venture therein, although the majority of the congregation, including the minister, would have welcomed one warmly.

But now Uncle Jerry was sleeping peacefully under the tangled grasses and white snows of the burying ground, and, if dead people ever do turn in their graves, Uncle Jerry might well have turned in his when the revivalist came to Avonlea church, and there followed the emotional services, public testimonies, and religious excitement which the old man's sturdy soul had always abhorred.

Avonlea was a good field for an evangelist. The Rev. Geoffrey Mountain, who came to assist the Avonlea minister in revivifying the dry bones thereof, knew this and reveled in the knowledge. It was not often that such a virgin parish could be found nowadays, with scores of impressionable, unspoiled souls on which fervid oratory could play skillfully, as a master on a mighty organ, until every note in them thrilled to life and utterance.   The Rev. Geoffrey Mountain was a good man; of the earth, earthy, to be sure, but with an unquestionable sincerity of belief and purpose which went far to counterbalance the sensationalism of some of his methods.

He was large and handsome, with a marvelously sweet and winning voice — a voice that could melt into irresistible tenderness, or swell into sonorous appeal and condemnation, or ring like a trumpet calling to battle.

His frequent grammatical errors, and lapses into vulgarity, counted for nothing against its charm, and the most commonplace words in the world would have borrowed much of the power of real oratory from its magic.   He knew its value and used it effectively — perhaps even ostentatiously.

Geoffrey Mountain's religion and methods, like the man himself, were showy, but, of their kind, sincere, and, though the good he accomplished might not be unmixed, it was a quantity to be reckoned with.

So the Rev. Geoffrey Mountain came to Avonlea, conquering and to conquer.   Night after night the church was crowded with eager listeners, who hung breathlessly on his words and wept and thrilled and exulted as he willed. Into many young souls his appeals and warnings burned their way, and each night they rose for prayer in response to his invitation. Older Christians, too, took on a new lease of intensity, and even the unregenerate and the scoffers found a certain fascination in the meetings. Threading through it all, for old and young, converted and unconverted, was an unacknowledged feeling for religious dissipation. Avonlea was a quiet place,— and the revival meetings were lively.

When David and Mary Bell reached the church the services had begun, and they heard the refrain of a hallelujah hymn as they were crossing Harmon Andrews' field. David Bell left his wife at the platform and drove to the horse-shed.

Mrs. Bell unwound the scarf from her bonnet and shook the frost crystals from it. In the porch Flora Jane Fletcher and her sister, Mrs. Harmon Andrews, were talking in low whispers. Presently Flora Jane put out her lank, cashmere-gloved hand and plucked Mrs. Bell's shawl.

"Mary, is the elder going to testify to-night?" she asked, in a shrill whisper.

Mrs. Bell winced. She would have given much to be able to answer "Yes," but she had to say stiffly,

"I don't know."

Flora Jane lifted her chin.

" Well, Mrs. Bell, I only asked because every one thinks it is strange he doesn't — and an elder, of all people. It looks as if he didn't think himself a Christian, you know. Of course, we all know better, but it *looks* that way. If I was you, I'd tell him folks was talking about it. Mr. Bentley says it is hindering the full success of the meetings."

Mrs. Bell turned on her tormentor in swift anger. She might resent her husband's strange behavior herself, but nobody else should dare to criticize him to her.

" I don't think you need worry yourself about the elder, Flora Jane," she said bitingly. " Maybe 'tisn't the best Christians that do the most talking about it always. I guess, as far as living up to his profession goes, the elder will compare pretty favorably with Levi Boulter, who gets up and testifies every night, and cheats the very eye-teeth out of people in the daytime."

Levi Boulter was a middle-aged widower, with a large family, who was supposed to have cast a matrimonial eye Flora Janeward. The use of his name was an effective thrust on Mrs. Bell's part, and silenced Flora Jane. Too angry for speech she seized her sister's arm and hurried her into church.

But her victory could not remove from Mary Bell's soul the sting implanted there by Flora Jane's words. When her husband came up to the platform she put her hand on his snowy arm appealingly.

"Oh, David, won't you get up to-night? I do feel so dreadful bad — folks are talking so — I just feel humiliated."

David Bell hung his head like a shamed school-boy.

"I can't, Mary," he said huskily. "'Tain't no use to pester me."

"You don't care for my feelings," said his wife bitterly. "And Mollie won't come out because you're acting so. You're keeping her back from salvation. And you're hindering the success of the revival — Mr. Bentley says so."

David Bell groaned. This sign of suffering wrung his wife's heart. With quick contrition she whispered,

"There, never mind, David. I oughtn't to have spoken to you so. You know your duty best. Let's go in."

"Wait." His voice was imploring.

"Mary, is it true that Mollie won't come out because of me? Am I standing in my child's light?"

"I — don't — know. I guess not. Mollie's just a foolish young girl yet. Never mind — come in."

He followed her dejectedly in, and up the aisle to their pew in the center of the church. The building was warm and crowded. The pastor was reading

the Bible lesson for the evening. In the choir, behind him, David Bell saw Mollie's girlish face, tinged
with a troubled seriousness. His own wind-ruddy
face and bushy gray eyebrows worked convulsively
with his inward throes. A sigh that was almost a
groan burst from him.

" I'll have to do it," he said to himself in agony.

When several more hymns had been sung, and
late arrivals began to pack the aisles, the evangelist
arose. His style for the evening was the tender, the
pleading, the solemn. He modulated his tones to
marvelous sweetness, and sent them thrillingly over
the breathless pews, entangling the hearts and souls
of his listeners in a mesh of subtle emotion. Many
of the women began to cry softly. Fervent amens
broke from some of the members. When the evangelist sat down, after a closing appeal which, in its
way, was a masterpiece, an audible sigh of relieved
tension passed like a wave over the audience.

After prayer the pastor made the usual request
that, if any of those present wished to come out on
the side of Christ, they would signify the wish by
rising for a moment in their places. After a brief
interval, a pale boy under the gallery rose, followed
by an old man at the top of the church. A frightened, sweet-faced child of twelve got tremblingly
upon her feet, and a dramatic thrill passed over the
congregation when her mother suddenly stood up

beside her. The evangelist's " Thank God " was hearty and insistent.

David Bell looked almost imploringly at Mollie; but she kept her seat, with downcast eyes. Over in the big square " stone pew " he saw Eben bending forward, with his elbows on his knees, gazing frowningly at the floor.

" I'm a stumbling block to them both," he thought bitterly.

A hymn was sung and prayer offered for those under conviction. Then testimonies were called for. The evangelist asked for them in tones which made it seem a personal request to every one in that building.

Many testimonies followed, each infused with the personality of the giver. Most of them were brief and stereotyped. Finally a pause ensued. The evangelist swept the pews with his kindling eyes and exclaimed, appealingly,

" Has *every* Christian in this church to-night spoken a word for his Master? "

There were many who had not testified, but every eye in the building followed the pastor's accusing glance to the Bell pew. Mollie crimsoned with shame. Mrs. Bell cowered visibly.

Although everybody looked thus at David Bell, nobody now expected him to testify. When he rose to his feet, a murmur of surprise passed over the audience, followed by a silence so complete as to be terrible. To David Bell it seemed to possess the awe of final judgment.

Twice he opened his lips, and tried vainly to speak. The third time he succeeded; but his voice sounded strangely in his own ears. He gripped the back of the pew before him with his knotty hands, and fixed his eyes unseeingly on the Christian Endeavor pledge that hung over the heads of the choir.

"Brethren and sisters," he said hoarsely, "before I can say a word of Christian testimony here tonight I've got something to confess. It's been lying hard and heavy on my conscience ever since these meetings begun. As long as I kept silence about it I couldn't get up and bear witness for Christ. Many of you have expected me to do it. Maybe I've been a stumbling block to some of you. This season of revival has brought no blessing to me because of my sin, which I repented of, but tried to conceal. There has been a spiritual darkness over me.

"Friends and neighbors, I have always been held by you as an honest man. It was the shame of having you know I was not which has kept me back from open confession and testimony. Just afore these meetings commenced I come home from town one night and found that somebody had passed a counterfeit ten-dollar bill on me. Then Satan entered into

me and possessed me. When Mrs. Rachel Lynde
come next day, collecting for foreign missions, I
give her that ten dollar bill. She never knowed the
difference, and sent it away with the rest. But I
knew I'd done a mean and sinful thing. I couldn't
drive it out of my thoughts. A few days afterwards
I went down to Mrs. Rachel's and give her ten good
dollars for the fund. I told her I had come to the
conclusion I ought to give more than ten dollars,
out of my abundance, to the Lord. That was a lie.
Mrs. Lynde thought I was a generous man, and I
felt ashamed to look her in the face. But I'd done
what I could to right the wrong, and I thought it
would be all right. But it wasn't. I've never
known a minute's peace of mind or conscience since.
I tried to cheat the Lord, and then tried to patch it
up by doing something that redounded to my worldly
credit. When these meetings begun, and everybody
expected me to testify, I couldn't do it. It would
have seemed like blasphemy. And I couldn't endure
the thought of telling what I'd done, either. I
argued it all out a thousand times that I hadn't done
any real harm after all, but it was no use. I've been
so wrapped up in my own brooding and misery that
I didn't realize I was inflicting suffering on those
dear to me by my conduct, and, maybe, holding some
of them back from the paths of salvation. But my
eyes have been opened to this to-night, and the Lord

has given me strength to confess my sin and glorify His holy name."

The broken tones ceased, and David Bell sat down, wiping the great drops of perspiration from his brow. To a man of his training, and cast of thought, no ordeal could be more terrible than that through which he had just passed. But underneath the turmoil of his emotion he felt a great calm and peace, threaded with the exultation of a hard-won spiritual victory.

Over the whole church was a solemn hush. The evangelist's "amen" was not spoken with his usual unctuous fervor, but very gently and reverently. In spite of his coarse fiber, he could appreciate the nobility behind such a confession as this, and the deeps of stern suffering it sounded.

Before the last prayer the pastor paused and looked around.

"Is there yet one," he asked gently, "who wishes to be especially remembered in our concluding prayer?"

For a moment nobody moved. Then Mollie Bell stood up in the choir seat, and, down by the stove, Eben, his flushed, boyish face held high, rose sturdily to his feet in the midst of his companions.

"Thank God," whispered Mary Bell.

"Amen," said her husband, huskily.

"Let us pray," said Mr. Bentley.

XIV

ONLY A COMMON FELLOW

ON my dearie's wedding morning I wakened early and went to her room. Long and long ago she had made me promise that I would be the one to wake her on the morning of her wedding day.

" You were the first to take me in your arms when I came into the world, Aunt Rachel," she had said, " and I want you to be the first to greet me on that wonderful day."

But that was long ago, and now my heart foreboded that there would be no need of wakening her. And there was not. She was lying there awake, very quiet, with her hand under her cheek, and her big blue eyes fixed on the window, through which a pale, dull light was creeping in — a joyless light it was, and enough to make a body shiver. I felt more like weeping than rejoicing, and my heart took to aching when I saw her there so white and patient, more like a girl who was waiting for a winding-sheet than for a bridal veil. But she smiled brave-like, when I sat down on her bed and took her hand.

" You look as if you haven't slept all night, dearie," I said.

" I didn't — not a great deal," she answered me.
" But the night didn't seem long; no, it seemed too
short. I was thinking of a great many things.
What time is it, Aunt Rachel? "

" Five o'clock."

" Then in six hours more —"

She suddenly sat up in her bed, her great, thick
rope of brown hair falling over her white shoulders,
and flung her arms about me, and burst into tears on
my old breast. I petted and soothed her, and said
not a word; and, after a while, she stopped crying;
but she still sat with her head so that I couldn't see
her face.

" We didn't think it would be like this once, did
we, Aunt Rachel? " she said, very softly.

" It shouldn't be like this, now," I said. I had to
say it. I never could hide the thought of that marriage, and I couldn't pretend to. It was all her step-
mother's doings — right well I knew that. My
dearie would never have taken Mark Foster else.

" Don't let us talk of that," she said, soft and be-
seeching, just the same way she used to speak when
she was a baby-child and wanted to coax me into
something. " Let us talk about the old days — and
him."

" I don't see much use in talking of *him,* when
you're going to marry Mark Foster to-day," I said.

But she put her hand on my mouth.

" It's for the last time, Aunt Rachel. After to-day I can never talk of him, or even think of him. It's four years since he went away. Do you remember how he looked, Aunt Rachel? "

" I mind well enough, I reckon," I said, kind of curt-like. And I did. Owen Blair hadn't a face a body could forget — that long face of his with its clean color and its eyes made to look love into a woman's. When I thought of Mark Foster's sallow skin and lank jaws I felt sick-like. Not that Mark was ugly — he was just a common-looking fellow.

" He was so handsome, wasn't he, Aunt Rachel? " my dearie went on, in that patient voice of hers. " So tall and strong and handsome. I wish we hadn't parted in anger. It was so foolish of us to quarrel. But it would have been all right if he had lived to come back. I know it would have been all right. I know he didn't carry any bitterness against me to his death. I thought once, Aunt Rachel, that I would go through life true to him, and then, over on the other side, I'd meet him just as before, all his and his only. But it isn't to be."

" Thanks to your stepma's wheedling and Mark Foster's scheming," said I.

" No, Mark didn't scheme," she said patiently. " Don't be unjust to Mark, Aunt Rachel. He has been very good and kind."

" He's as stupid as an owlet and as stubborn as

Solomon's mule," I said, for I *would* say it. "He's just a common fellow, and yet he thinks he's good enough for my beauty."

"Don't talk about Mark," she pleaded again. "I mean to be a good, faithful wife to him. But I'm my own woman yet — *yet* — for just a few more sweet hours, and I want to give them to *him*. The last hours of my maidenhood — they must belong to *him*."

So she talked of him, me sitting there and holding her, with her lovely hair hanging down over my arm, and my heart aching so for her that it hurt bitter. She didn't feel as bad as I did, because she'd made up her mind what to do and was resigned. She was going to marry Mark Foster, but her heart was in France, in that grave nobody knew of, where the Huns had buried Owen Blair — if they had buried him at all. And she went over all they had been to each other, since they were mites of babies, going to school together and meaning, even then, to be married when they grew up; and the first words of love he'd said to her, and what she'd dreamed and hoped for. The only thing she didn't bring up was the time he thrashed Mark Foster for bringing her apples. She never mentioned Mark's name; it was all Owen — Owen — and how he looked, and what might have been, if he hadn't gone off to the awful war and got shot. And there was me, holding her and listening to it all, and her stepma sleeping sound and triumphant in the next room.

When she had talked it all out she lay down on her pillow again. I got up and went downstairs to light the fire. I felt terrible old and tired. My feet seemed to drag, and the tears kept coming to my eyes, though I tried to keep them away, for well I knew it was a bad omen to be weeping on a wedding day.

Before long Isabella Clark came down; bright and pleased-looking enough, *she* was. I'd never liked Isabella, from the day Phillippa's father brought her here; and I liked her less than ever this morning. She was one of your sly, deep women, always smiling smooth, and scheming underneath it. I'll say it for her, though, she had been good to Phillippa; but it was her doings that my dearie was to marry Mark Foster that day.

"Up betimes, Rachel," she said, smiling and speaking me fair, as she always did, and hating me in her heart, as I well knew. "That is right, for we'll have plenty to do to-day. A wedding makes lots of work."

"Not this sort of a wedding," I said, sour-like. "I don't call it a wedding when two people get married and sneak off as if they were ashamed of it — as well they might be in this case."

"It was Phillippa's own wish that all should be very quiet," said Isabella, as smooth as cream.

" You know I'd have given her a big wedding, if she'd wanted it."

" Oh, it's better quiet," I said. " The fewer to see Phillippa marry a man like Mark Foster the better."

" Mark Foster is a good man, Rachel."

" No good man would be content to buy a girl as he's bought Phillippa," I said, determined to give it in to her. " He's a common fellow, not fit for my dearie to wipe her feet on. It's well that her mother didn't live to see this day; but this day would never have come, if she'd lived."

" I dare say Phillippa's mother would have remembered that Mark Foster is very well off, quite as readily as worse people," said Isabella, a little spitefully.

I liked her better when she was spiteful than when she was smooth. I didn't feel so scared of her then.

The marriage was to be at eleven o'clock, and, at nine, I went up to help Phillippa dress. She was no fussy bride, caring much what she looked like. If Owen had been the bridegroom it would have been different. Nothing would have pleased her then; but now it was only just " That will do very well, Aunt Rachel," without even glancing at it.

Still, nothing could prevent her from looking lovely when she was dressed. My dearie would have been a beauty in a beggarmaid's rags. In her white dress and veil she was as fair as a queen. And she was as good as she was pretty. It was a down-to-earth kind of goodness, with a sprinkling of gaiety and lightheartedness, which served to heighten her natural irresistible charm.

Then she sent me out.

"I want to be alone my last hour," she said. "Kiss me, Aunt Rachel — *Mother* Rachel."

When I'd gone down, crying like the old fool I was, I heard a rap at the door. My first thought was to go out and send Isabella to it, for I supposed it was Mark Foster, come ahead of time, and small stomach I had for seeing him. I fall trembling, even yet, when I think, "What if I had sent Isabella to that door?"

But go I did, and opened it, defiant-like, kind of hoping it was Mark Foster to see the tears on my face. I opened it — and staggered back like I'd got a blow.

"Owen! Lord ha' mercy on us! Owen!" I said, just like that, going cold all over, for it's the truth that I thought it was his spirit come back to forbid that unholy marriage.

But he sprang right in, and caught my wrinkled old hands in a grasp that was of flesh and blood.

"Aunt Rachel, I'm not too late?" he said, savage-like. "Tell me I'm in time."

I looked up at him, standing over me there, tall and handsome, no change in him except he was so brown and had a little white scar on his forehead; and, though I couldn't understand at all, being all bewildered-like, I felt a great deep thankfulness.

"No, you're not too late," I said.

"Thank God," said he, under his breath. And then he pulled me into the parlor and shut the door.

"They told me at the station that Phillippa was to be married to Mark Foster to-day. I couldn't believe it, but I came here as fast as horse-flesh could bring me. Aunt Rachel, it can't be true! She can't care for Mark Foster, even if she had forgotten me!"

"It's true enough that she is to marry Mark," I said, half-laughing, half-crying, "but she doesn't care for him. Every beat of her heart is for you. It's all her stepma's doings. Mark has got a mortgage on the place, and he told Isabella Clark that, if Phillippa would marry him, he'd burn the mortgage, and, if she wouldn't, he'd foreclose. Phillippa is sacrificing herself to save her stepma for her dead father's sake. It's all your fault," I cried, getting over my bewilderment. "We thought you were dead. Why didn't you come home when you were alive? Why didn't you write?"

"I *did* write, after I got out of the hospital, several times," he said, "and never a word in answer,

Aunt Rachel.   What was I to think when Phillippa
wouldn't answer my letters?"

"She never got one," I cried.   "She wept her
sweet eyes out over you.   *Somebody* must have got
those letters."

And I knew then, and I know now, though never a
shadow of proof have I, that Isabella Clark had got
them — and kept them.   That woman would stick at
nothing.

"Well, we'll sift that matter some other time,"
said Owen impatiently.   "There are other things to
think of now.   I must see Phillippa."

"I'll manage it for you," I said eagerly; but, just
as I spoke, the door opened and Isabella and Mark
came in.   Never shall I forget the look on Isabella's
face.   I almost felt sorry for her.   She turned
sickly yellow and her eyes went wild; they were looking at the downfall of all her schemes and hopes.   I
didn't look at Mark Foster, at first, and, when I did,
there wasn't anything to see.   His face was just as
sallow and wooden as ever; he looked undersized and
common beside Owen.   Nobody'd ever have picked
him out for a bridegroom.

Owen spoke first.

"I want to see Phillippa," he said, as if it were
but yesterday that he had gone away.

All Isabella's smoothness and policy had dropped
away from her, and the real woman stood there, plot-

ting and unscrupulous, as I'd always known her.

"You can't see her," she said desperate-like. "She doesn't want to see you. You went and left her and never wrote, and she knew you weren't worth fretting over, and she has learned to care for a better man."

"I *did* write and I think you know that better than most folks," said Owen, trying hard to speak quiet. "As for the rest, I'm not going to discuss it with you. When I hear from Phillippa's own lips that she cares for another man I'll believe it — and not before."

"You'll never hear it from her lips," said I.

Isabella gave me a venomous look.

"You'll not see Phillippa until she is a better man's wife," she said stubbornly, "and I order you to leave my house, Owen Blair."

"No!"

It was Mark Foster who spoke. He hadn't said a word; but he came forward now, and stood before Owen. Such a difference as there was between them! But he looked Owen right in the face, quiet-like, and Owen glared back in fury.

"Will it satisfy you, Owen, if Phillippa comes down here and chooses between us?"

"Yes, it will," said Owen.

Mark Foster turned to me.

"Go and bring her down," said he.

Isabella, judging Phillippa by herself, gave a little moan of despair, and Owen, blinded by love and hope, thought his cause was won. But I knew my dearie too well to be glad, and Mark Foster did, too, and I hated him for it.

I went up to my dearie's room, all pale and shaking. When I went in she came to meet me, like a girl going to meet death.

"Is — it — time?" she said, with her hands locked tight together.

I said not a word, hoping that the unlooked-for sight of Owen would break down her resolution. I just held out my hand to her, and led her downstairs. She clung to me and her hands were as cold as snow. When I opened the parlor door I stood back, and pushed her in before me.

She just cried, "Owen!" and shook so that I put my arms about her to steady her.

Owen made a step towards her, his face and eyes all aflame with his love and longing, but Mark barred his way.

"Wait till she has made her choice," he said, and then he turned to Phillippa. I couldn't see my dearie's face, but I could see Mark's, and there wasn't a spark of feeling in it. Behind it was Isabella's, all pinched and gray.

"Phillippa," said Mark, "Owen Blair has come back. He says he has never forgotten you, and that he wrote to you several times. I have told him that you have promised me, but I leave you freedom of choice. Which of us will you marry, Phillippa?"

My dearie stood straight up and the trembling left her. She stepped back, and I could see her face, white as the dead, but calm and resolved.

"I have promised to marry you, Mark, and I will keep my word," she said.

The color came back to Isabella Clark's face; but Mark's did not change.

"Phillippa," said Owen, and the pain in his voice made my old heart ache bitterer than ever, "have you ceased to love me?"

My dearie would have been more than human, if she could have resisted the pleading in his tone. She said no word, but just looked at him for a moment. We all saw the look; her whole soul, full of love for Owen, showed out in it. Then she turned and stood by Mark.

Owen said never a word. He went as white as death, and started for the door. But again Mark Foster put himself in the way.

"Wait," he said. "She has made her choice, as I knew she would; but I have yet to make mine. And I choose to marry no woman whose love belongs to another living man. Phillippa, I thought Owen Blair was dead, and I believed that, when you were my wife, I could win your love. But I love you too well to make you miserable. Go to the man you love — you are free!"

"And what is to become of me?" wailed Isabella.

"Oh, you! — I had forgotten about you," said Mark, kind of weary-like. He took a paper from his pocket, and dropped it in the grate. "There is the mortgage. That is all you care about, I think. Good-morning."

He went out. He was only a common fellow, but, somehow, just then he looked every inch the gentleman. I would have gone after him and said something but — the look on his face — no, it was no time for my foolish old words!

Phillippa was crying, with her head on Owen's shoulder. Isabella Clark waited to see the mortgage burned up, and then she came to me in the hall, all smooth and smiling again.

"Really, it's all very romantic, isn't it? I suppose it's better as it is, all things considered. Mark behaved splendidly, didn't he? Not many men would have done as he did."

For once in my life I agreed with Isabella. But I felt like having a good cry over it all — and I had it. I was glad for my dearie's sake and Owen's; but Mark Foster had paid the price of their joy, and I knew it had beggared him of happiness for life.

XV

TANNIS OF THE FLATS

Few people in Avonlea could understand why Elinor Blair had never married. She had been one of the most beautiful girls in our part of the Island and, as a woman of fifty, she was still very attractive. In her youth she had had ever so many beaux, as we of our generation well remembered; but, after her return from visiting her brother Tom in the Canadian Northwest, more than twenty-five years ago, she had seemed to withdraw within herself, keeping all men at a safe, though friendly, distance. She had been a gay, laughing girl when she went West; she came back quiet and serious, with a shadowed look in her eyes which time could not quite succeed in blotting out.

Elinor had never talked much about her visit, except to describe the scenery and the life, which in that day was rough indeed. Not even to me, who had grown up next door to her and who had always seemed more a sister than a friend, did she speak of other than the merest commonplaces. But when Tom Blair made a flying trip back home, some ten years later, there were one or two of us to whom he

related the story of Jerome Carey,— a story revealing only too well the reason for Elinor's sad eyes
and utter indifference to masculine attentions. I
can recall almost his exact words and the inflections
of his voice, and I remember, too, that it seemed to
me a far cry from the tranquil, pleasant scene before us, on that lovely summer day, to the elemental
life of the Flats.

The Flats was a forlorn little trading station fifteen miles up the river from Prince Albert, with a
scanty population of half-breeds and three white
men. When Jerome Carey was sent to take charge
of the telegraph office there, he cursed his fate in
the picturesque language permissible in the far
Northwest.

Not that Carey was a profane man, even as men
go in the West. He was an English gentleman, and
he kept both his life and his vocabulary pretty clean.
But — the Flats!

Outside of the ragged cluster of log shacks, which
comprised the settlement, there was always a shifting
fringe of teepees where the Indians, who drifted
down from the Reservation, camped with their dogs
and squaws and papooses. There are standpoints
from which Indians are interesting, but they cannot
be said to offer congenial social attractions. For
three weeks after Carey went to the Flats he was
lonelier than he had ever imagined it possible to be,

even in the Great Lone Land. If it had not been for teaching Paul Dumont the telegraphic code, Carey believed that he would have been driven to suicide in self-defense.

The telegraphic importance of the Flats consisted in the fact that it was the starting point of three telegraph lines to remote trading posts up North. Not many messages came therefrom, but the few that did come generally amounted to something worth while. Days and even weeks would pass without a single one being clicked to the Flats. Carey was debarred from talking over the wires to the Prince Albert man for the reason that they were on officially bad terms. He blamed the latter for his transfer to the Flats.

Carey slept in a loft over the office, and got his meals at Joe Esquint's, across the "street." Joe Esquint's wife was a good cook, as cooks go among the breeds, and Cary soon became a great pet of hers. Carey had a habit of becoming a pet with women. He had the "way" that has to be born in a man and can never be acquired. Besides, he was as hand-some as clean-cut features, deep-set, dark-blue eyes, fair curls and six feet of muscle could make him. Mrs. Joe Esquint thought that his mustache was the most wonderfully beautiful thing, in its line, that she had ever seen.

Fortunately, Mrs. Joe was so old and fat and ugly

that even the malicious and inveterate gossip of skulking breeds and Indians, squatting over teepee fires, could not hint at anything questionable in the relations between her and Carey. But it was a different matter with Tannis Dumont.

Tannis came home from the academy at Prince Albert early in July, when Carey had been at the Flats a month and had exhausted all the few novelties of his position. Paul Dumont had already become so expert at the code that his mistakes no longer afforded Carey any fun, and the latter was getting desperate. He had serious intentions of throwing up the business altogether, and betaking himself to an Alberta ranch, where at least one would have the excitement of roping horses. When he saw Tannis Dumont he thought he would hang on a while longer, anyway.

Tannis was the daughter of old Auguste Dumont, who kept the one small store at the Flats, lived in the one frame house that the place boasted, and was reputed to be worth an amount of money which, in half-breed eyes, was a colossal fortune. Old Auguste was black and ugly and notoriously bad-tempered. But Tannis was a beauty.

Tannis' great-grandmother had been a Cree squaw who married a French trapper. The son of this union became in due time the father of Auguste Dumont. Auguste married a woman whose mother

was a French half-breed and whose father was a
pure-bred Highland Scotchman. The result of this
atrocious mixture was its justification — Tannis of
the Flats — who looked as if all the blood of all the
Howards might be running in her veins.

But, after all, the dominant current in those same
veins was from the race of plain and prairie. The
practiced eye detected it in the slender stateliness of
carriage, in the graceful, yet voluptuous, curves of
the lithe body, in the smallness and delicacy of hand
and foot, in the purple sheen on straight-falling
masses of blue-black hair, and, more than all else, in
the long, dark eye, full and soft, yet alight with a
slumbering fire. France, too, was responsible for
somewhat in Tannis. It gave her a light step in
place of the stealthy half-breed shuffle, it arched her
red upper lip into a more tremulous bow, it lent a
note of laughter to her voice and a sprightlier wit to
her tongue. As for her red-headed Scotch grand-
father, he had bequeathed her a somewhat whiter
skin and ruddier bloom than is usually found in the
breeds.

Old Auguste was mightily proud of Tannis. He
sent her to school for four years in Prince Albert,
bound that his girl should have the best. A High
School course and considerable mingling in the
social life of the town — for old Auguste was a
man to be conciliated by astute politicians, since he

controlled some two or three hundred half-breed votes — sent Tannis home to the Flats with a very thin, but very deceptive, veneer of culture and civilization overlying the primitive passions and ideas of her nature.

Carey saw only the beauty and the veneer. He made the mistake of thinking that Tannis was what she seemed to be — a fairly well-educated, up-to-date young woman with whom a friendly flirtation was just what it was with white womankind — the pleasant amusement of an hour or season. It was a mistake — a very big mistake. Tannis understood something of piano playing, something less of grammar and Latin, and something less still of social prevarications. But she understood absolutely nothing of flirtation. You can never get an Indian to see the sense of Platonics.

Carey found the Flats quite tolerable after the homecoming of Tannis. He soon fell into the habit of dropping into the Dumont house to spend the evening, talking with Tannis in the parlor — which apartment was amazingly well done for a place like the Flats — Tannis had not studied Prince Albert parlors four years for nothing — or playing violin and piano duets with her. When music and conversation palled, they went for long gallops over the prairies together. Tannis rode to perfection, and managed her bad-tempered brute of a pony with a skill and grace that made Carey applaud her. She was glorious on horseback.

Sometimes he grew tired of the prairies and then he and Tannis paddled themselves over the river in Nitchie Joe's dug-out, and landed on the old trail that struck straight into the wooded belt of the Saskatchewan valley, leading north to trading posts on the frontier of civilization. There they rambled under huge pines, hoary with the age of centuries, and Carey talked to Tannis about England and quoted poetry to her. Tannis liked poetry; she had studied it at school, and understood it fairly well. But once she told Carey that she thought it a long, round-about way of saying what you could say just as well in about a dozen plain words. Carey laughed. He liked to evoke those little speeches of hers. They sounded very clever, dropping from such arched, ripely-tinted lips.

If you had told Carey that he was playing with fire he would have laughed at you. In the first place he was not in the slightest degree in love with Tannis — he merely admired and liked her. In the second place, it never occurred to him that Tannis might be in love with him. Why, he had never attempted any love-making with her! And, above all, he was obsessed with that aforesaid fatal idea that Tannis was like the women he had associated with all his life, in reality as well as in appearance. He did not know enough of the racial characteristics to understand.

But, if Carey thought that his relationship with Tannis was that of friendship merely, he was the only one at the Flats who did think so. All the half-breeds and quarter-breeds and any-fractional breeds there believed that he meant to marry Tannis. There would have been nothing surprising to them in that. They did not know that Carey's second cousin was a baronet, and they would not have understood that it need make any difference, if they had. They thought that rich old Auguste's heiress, who had been to school for four years in Prince Albert, was a catch for anybody.

Old Auguste himself shrugged his shoulders over it and was well-pleased enough. An Englishman was a prize by way of a husband for a half-breed girl, even if he were only a telegraph operator. Young Paul Dumont worshiped Carey, and the half-Scotch mother, who might have understood, was dead. In all the Flats there were but two people who disapproved of the match they thought an assured thing. One of these was the little priest, Father Gabriel. He liked Tannis, and he liked Carey; but he shook his head dubiously when he heard the gossip of the shacks and teepees. Religions might mingle, but the different bloods — ah, it was not the right thing! Tannis was a good girl, and a beautiful one; but she was no fit mate for the fair, thorough-bred Englishman. Father Gabriel wished fervently that Jerome Carey might soon be transferred elsewhere. He even went to Prince Albert and did a little wire-pulling on his own account, but nothing came of it. He was on the wrong side of politics.

The other malcontent was Lazarre Mérimée, a lazy, besotted French half-breed, who was, after his fashion, in love with Tannis. He could never have got her, and he knew it — old Auguste and young Paul would have incontinently riddled him with bullets had he ventured near the house as a suitor,— but he hated Carey none the less, and watched for a chance to do him an ill-turn. There is no worse enemy in all the world than a half-breed. Your true Indian is bad enough, but his diluted descendant is ten times worse.

As for Tannis, she loved Carey with all her heart, and that was all there was about it.

If Elinor Blair had never gone to Prince Albert there is no knowing what might have happened, after all. Carey, so powerful in propinquity, might even have ended by learning to love Tannis and marrying her, to his own worldly undoing. But Elinor did go to Prince Albert, and her going ended all things for Tannis of the Flats.

Carey met her one evening in September, when he had ridden into town to attend a dance, leaving Paul

Dumont in charge of the telegraph office. Elinor had just arrived in Prince Albert on a visit to Tom, to which she had been looking forward during the five years since he had married and moved out West from Avonlea. As I have already said, she was very beautiful at that time, and Carey fell in love with her at the first moment of their meeting.

During the next three weeks he went to town nine times and called at Dumonts' only once. There were no more rides and walks with Tannis. This was not intentional neglect on his part. He had simply forgotten all about her. The breeds surmised a lover's quarrel, but Tannis understood. There was another woman back there in town.

It would be quite impossible to put on paper any adequate idea of her emotions at this stage. One night, she followed Carey when he went to Prince Albert, riding out of earshot, behind him on her plains pony, but keeping him in sight. Lazarre, in a fit of jealousy, had followed Tannis, spying on her until she started back to the Flats. After that he watched both Carey and Tannis incessantly, and months later had told Tom all he had learned through his low sneaking.

Tannis trailed Carey to the Blair house, on the bluffs above the town, and saw him tie his horse at the gate and enter. She, too, tied her pony to a poplar, lower down, and then crept stealthily through the willows at the side of the house until she was close to the windows. Through one of them she could see Carey and Elinor. The half-breed girl crouched down in the shadow and glared at her rival. She saw the pretty, fair-tinted face, the fluffy coronal of golden hair, the blue, laughing eyes of the woman whom Jerome Carey loved, and she realized very plainly that there was nothing left to hope for. She, Tannis of the Flats, could never compete with that other. It was well to know so much, at least.

After a time, she crept softly away, loosed her pony, and lashed him mercilessly with her whip through the streets of the town and out the long, dusty river trail. A man turned and looked after her as she tore past a brightly lighted store on Water Street.

" That was Tannis of the Flats," he said to a companion. " She was in town last winter, going to school — a beauty and a bit of a devil, like all those breed girls. What in thunder is she riding like that for ? "

One day, a fortnight later, Carey went over the river alone for a ramble up the northern trail, and an undisturbed dream of Elinor. When he came back Tannis was standing at the canoe landing, under a pine tree, in a rain of finely sifted sunlight. She was waiting for him and she said, without any preface:

" Mr. Carey, why do you never come to see me, now ? "

Carey flushed like any girl. Her tone and look made him feel very uncomfortable. He remembered, self-reproachfully, that he must have seemed very neglectful, and he stammered something about having been busy.

" Not very busy," said Tannis, with her terrible directness. " It is not that. It is because you are going to Prince Albert to see a white woman ! "

Even in his embarrassment Carey noted that this was the first time he had ever heard Tannis use the expression, " a white woman," or any other that would indicate her sense of a difference between herself and the dominant race. He understood, at the same moment, that this girl was not to be trifled with — that she would have the truth out of him, first or last. But he felt indescribably foolish.

" I suppose so," he answered lamely.

" And what about me ? " asked Tannis.

When you come to think of it, this was an embarrassing question, especially for Carey, who had believed that Tannis understood the game, and played it for its own sake, as he did.

" I don't understand you, Tannis," he said hurriedly.

" You have made me love you," said Tannis.

The words sound flat enough on paper. They did

not sound flat to Tom, as repeated by Lazarre, and they sounded anything but flat to Carey, hurled at him as they were by a woman trembling with all the passions of her savage ancestry. Tannis had justified her criticism of poetry. She had said her half-dozen words, instinct with all the despair and pain and wild appeal that all the poetry in the world had ever expressed.

They made Carey feel like a scoundrel. All at once he realized how impossible it would be to explain matters to Tannis, and that he would make a still bigger fool of himself, if he tried.

" I am very sorry," he stammered, like a whipped schoolboy.

" It is no matter," interrupted Tannis violently. " What difference does it make about me — a half-breed girl? We breed girls are only born to amuse the white men. That is so — is it not? Then, when they are tired of us, they push us aside and go back to their own kind. Oh, it is very well. But I will not forget — my father and brother will not forget. They will make you sorry to some purpose ! "

She turned, and stalked away to her canoe. He waited under the pines until she crossed the river; then he, too, went miserably home. What a mess he had contrived to make of things! Poor Tannis! How handsome she had looked in her fury — and how much like a squaw! The racial marks always come out plainly under the stress of emotion, as Tom noted later.

Her threat did not disturb him. If young Paul and old Auguste made things unpleasant for him, he thought himself more than a match for them. It was the thought of the suffering he had brought upon Tannis that worried him. He had not, to be sure, been a villain; but he had been a fool, and that is almost as bad, under some circumstances.

The Dumonts, however, did not trouble him. After all, Tannis' four years in Prince Albert had not been altogether wasted. She knew that white girls did not mix their male relatives up in a vendetta when a man ceased calling on them — and she had nothing else to complain of that could be put in words. After some reflection she concluded to hold her tongue. She even laughed when old Auguste asked her what was up between her and her fellow, and said she had grown tired of him. Old Auguste shrugged his shoulders resignedly. It was just as well, maybe. Those English sons-in-law sometimes gave themselves too many airs.

So Carey rode often to town and Tannis bided her time, and plotted futile schemes of revenge, and Lazarre Mérimée scowled and got drunk — and life went on at the Flats as usual, until the last week in

October, when a big wind and rainstorm swept over the northland.

It was a bad night. The wires were down between the Flats and Prince Albert and all communication with the outside world was cut off. Over at Joe Esquint's the breeds were having a carouse in honor of Joe's birthday. Paul Dumont had gone over, and Carey was alone in the office, smoking lazily and dreaming of Elinor.

Suddenly, above the plash of rain and whistle of wind, he heard outcries in the street. Running to the door he was met by Mrs. Joe Esquint, who grasped him breathlessly.

"Meestair Carey — come quick! Lazarre, he kill Paul — they fight!"

Carey, with a smothered oath, rushed across the street. He had been afraid of something of the sort, and had advised Paul not to go, for those half-breed carouses almost always ended in a free fight. He burst into the kitchen at Joe Esquint's, to find a circle of mute spectators ranged around the room and Paul and Lazarre in a clinch in the center. Carey was relieved to find it was only an affair of fists. He promptly hurled himself at the combatants and dragged Paul away, while Mrs. Joe Esquint — Joe himself being dead-drunk in a corner — flung her fat arms about Lazarre and held him back.

"Stop this," said Carey sternly.

"Let me get at him," foamed Paul. "He insulted my sister. He said that you — let me get at him!"

He could not writhe free from Carey's iron grip. Lazarre, with a snarl like a wolf, sent Mrs. Joe spinning, and rushed at Paul. Carey struck out as best he could, and Lazarre went reeling back against the table. It went over with a crash and the light went out!

Mrs. Joe's shrieks might have brought the roof down. In the confusion that ensued two pistol shots rang out sharply. There was a cry, a groan, a fall — then a rush for the door. When Mrs. Joe Esquint's sister-in-law, Marie, dashed in with another lamp, Mrs. Joe was still shrieking, Paul Dumont was leaning sickly against the wall with a dangling arm, and Carey lay face downward on the floor, with blood trickling from under him.

Marie Esquint was a woman of nerve. She told Mrs. Joe to shut up, and she turned Carey over. He was conscious, but seemed dazed and could not help himself. Marie put a coat under his head, told Paul to lie down on the bench, ordered Mrs. Joe to get a bed ready, and went for the doctor. It happened that there was a doctor at the Flats that night — a Prince Albert man who had been up at the Reservation, fixing up some sick Indians, and had been stormstaid at old Auguste's on his way back.

Marie soon returned with the doctor, old Auguste, and Tannis. Carey was carried in and laid on Mrs. Esquint's bed. The doctor made a brief examination, while Mrs. Joe sat on the floor and howled at the top of her lungs. Then he shook his head.

"Shot in the back," he said briefly.

"How long?" asked Carey, understanding.

"Perhaps till morning," answered the doctor. Mrs. Joe gave a louder howl than ever at this, and Tannis came and stood by the bed. The doctor, knowing that he could do nothing for Carey, hurried into the kitchen to attend to Paul, who had a badly shattered arm, and Marie went with him.

Carey looked stupidly at Tannis.

"Send for her," he said.

Tannis smiled cruelly.

"There is no way. The wires are down, and there is no man at the Flats who will go to town tonight," she answered.

"My God, I *must* see her before I die," burst out Carey pleadingly. "Where is Father Gabriel? *He* will go."

"The priest went to town last night and has not come back," said Tannis.

Carey groaned and shut his eyes. If Father Gabrial was away, there was indeed no one to go.

Old Auguste and the doctor could not leave Paul and he knew well that no breed of them all at the Flats would turn out on such a night, even if they were not, one and all, mortally scared of being mixed up in the law and justice that would be sure to follow the affair. He must die without seeing Elinor.

Tannis looked inscrutably down on the pale face on Mrs. Joe Esquint's dirty pillows. Her immobile features gave no sign of the conflict raging within her. After a short space she turned and went out, shutting the door softly on the wounded man and Mrs. Joe, whose howls had now simmered down to whines. In the next room Paul was crying out with pain as the doctor worked on his arm, but Tannis did not go to him. Instead, she slipped out and hurried down the stormy street to old Auguste's stable. Five minutes later she was galloping down the black, wind-lashed river trail, on her way to town, to bring Elinor Blair to her lover's deathbed.

I hold that no woman ever did anything more unselfish than this deed of Tannis! For the sake of love she put under her feet the jealousy and hatred that had clamored at her heart. She held, not only revenge, but the dearer joy of watching by Carey to the last, in the hollow of her hand, and she cast both away that the man she loved might draw his dying breath somewhat easier. In a white woman the deed would have been merely commendable. In Tannis of the Flats, with her ancestry and tradition, it was lofty self-sacrifice.

It was eight o'clock when Tannis left the Flats; it was ten when she drew bridle before the house on the bluff. Elinor was regaling Tom and his wife with Avonlea gossip when the maid came to the door.

" Pleas'm, there's a breed girl out on the verandah and she's asking for Miss Blair."

Elinor went out wonderingly, followed by Tom. Tannis, whip in hand, stood by the open door, with the stormy night behind her, and the warm ruby light of the hall lamp showering over her white face and the long rope of drenched hair that fell from her bare head. She looked wild enough.

" Jerome Carey was shot in a quarrel at Joe Esquint's to-night," she said. " He is dying — he wants you — I have come for you."

Elinor gave a little cry, and steadied herself on Tom's shoulder. Tom said he knew he made some exclamation of horror. He had never approved of Carey's attentions to Elinor, but such news was enough to shock anybody. He was determined, however, that Elinor should not go out in such a night and to such a scene, and told Tannis so in no uncertain terms.

" I came through the storm," said Tannis contemptuously. " Cannot she do as much for him as
I can? "

The good, old Island blood in Elinor's veins
showed to some purpose. " Yes," she answered
firmly. " No, Tom, don't object — I must go. Get
my horse — and your own."

Ten minutes later three riders galloped down the
bluff road and took the river trail. Fortunately the
wind was at their backs and the worst of the storm
was over. Still, it was a wild, black ride enough.
Tom rode, cursing softly under his breath. He did
not like the whole thing — Carey done to death in
some low half-breed shack, this handsome, sullen
girl coming as his messenger, this nightmare ride
through wind and rain. It all savored too much of
melodrama, even for the Northland, where people
still did things in a primitive way. He heartily
wished Elinor had never left Avonlea.

It was past twelve when they reached the Flats.
Tannis was the only one who seemed to be able to
think coherently. It was she who told Tom where
to take the horses and who then led Elinor to the
room where Carey was dying. The doctor was sitting by the bedside and Mrs. Joe was curled up in
a corner, sniffling to herself. Tannis took her by
the shoulder and turned her, none too gently, out
of the room. The doctor, understanding, left at

once. As Tannis shut the door she saw Elinor sink on her knees by the bed, and Carey's trembling hand go out to her head.

Tannis sat down on the floor outside of the door and wrapped herself up in a shawl Marie Esquint had dropped. In that attitude she looked exactly like a squaw, and all comers and goers, even old Auguste, who was hunting for her, thought she was one, and left her undisturbed. She watched there until dawn came whitely up over the prairies and Jerome Carey died. She knew when it happened by Elinor's cry.

Tannis sprang up and rushed in. She was too late for even a parting look.

The girl took Carey's hand in hers, and turned to the weeping Elinor with a cold dignity.

"Now go," she said. "You had him in life to the very last. He is mine now."

"There must be some arrangements made," faltered Elinor.

"My father and brother will make all arrangements, as you call them," said Tannis steadily. "He had no near relatives in the world — none at all in Canada — he told me so. You may send out a Protestant minister from town, if you like; but he will be buried here at the Flats and his grave will be mine — all mine! Go!"

And Elinor, reluctant, sorrowful, yet swayed by

a will and an emotion stronger than her own, went slowly out, leaving Tannis of the Flats alone with her dead.

THE END